GW00363843

SWING HIGH, SWEET BIRD

Dea Langmead began life as a professional ballet dancer and actress and has been a published writer since an early age, with special interest in the past and antiques. Later, after training as a nurse, she eventually became a ward sister in a psychiatric hospital. Since retiring, she is now writing full-time. This is her second novel for Book Guild Publishing – her first being *The Lady of Lyonesse*, a blending of fact, legend and fantasy about a lost island near the Isles of Scilly. Dea herself lives near Redruth in Cornwall, her own ancestry being traced back to the Isles of Scilly.

By the same author

The Lady of Lyonesse, Book Guild Publishing 2003

SWING HIGH, SWEET BIRD

Sincere Wishes ~

Dea Hicks Langmead

Dea Hicks Langmead

Book Guild Publishing

Sussex, England

First published in Great Britain in 2007 by
The Book Guild Ltd
Pavilion View
19 New Road
Brighton, BN1 1UF

Typesetting in Baskerville by
SetSystems Ltd, Saffron Walden, Essex

Printed in Great Britain by
Athenaeum Press Ltd, Gateshead

A catalogue record for this book is
available from the British Library

ISBN 978 1 84624 165 9

*This book is for Ray (1916–1955),
Chaz, and Joe Addison.*

*With thanks to Colin Merritt,
who gave me a sycamore whistle.*

Wings in the Sky

Swing high, sweet bird. I see you gently sway
Beneath the peaceful skies, while seeking out your prey.
You are unknowing and uncaring of a future day,
When you might fall to earth in mortal disarray,
At once becoming metamorphosed as you lay
Inert upon the ground. Then, on unseen wings, you may
Begin your final, joyous flight—a journey on the way
                    to the stars . . .

                                        D.H.L.

The document that follows was recently found in the secret compartment of an antique bureau bought at auction. Its origin is unknown.

Day 1

Thursday, 19 April 1979

Paul, my very dear Son,

I am finding it difficult to choose the right words to begin this letter. I call it that, but suspect it will develop into a long memoir and is not for you to read until you have heard of my death. That is why, when completed, I shall put it in the hidden drawer of my old desk—where I know you used to hide things as a child—having every confidence that you will not allow it to be sold with the rest of my effects but have it shipped out to where you are living 'on the other side of the world'. You always said it should form a part of your heritage, to be handed on down, and I am sure your curiosity will ensure that you look inside it once again and be surprised to discover an account of a period in my life of which you know nothing. I have chosen this cowardly way, rather than post it directly to you, to make my confession of shame and guilt, as I know I would be unable to look you squarely in the eye in the doubtful, though not impossible, event of our ever meeting again.

You see, Paul, I need to try to clear my conscience, and who better to tell than my only child who might make the effort to understand and be fair in his judgement. I have become wearily conscious of the ills of old age now that your mother has gone, with too much time to reflect on what was and what could have been, the idle reminiscences of a retired, and very tired, headmaster. As I grow older I find I have a clearer vision of the past, which is said to become even more distinct as the years go by while the present fades quickly by comparison.

This unwanted restoration of buried recollections was brought about by an unlikely encounter with Fate yesterday. Before, I had always managed to avoid dredging up memories of that short, yet in retrospect, seemingly long period, the summer of 1929. Some of them are good, as, for instance, it was the year I met your mother, but others must include how I, artless as I was, succumbed to seduction. It must be recounted with the rest as it forms an intrinsic part of the whole horrific tale of haunting, evil and sudden death, of burning shame and lost innocence. It needs to be told, not only to help me clarify the incidents in my mind but also to explain an unexpected gift I am bequeathing you in my will.

I intend to write as much as I can each day until it is done, and that is why this piece is headed 'Day 1'. I know I shall be unable to reproduce the actual words spoken, but will attempt to give an impression. I also urge you to exercise patience with my introspective prose as I try to think myself back into that time—you will need to know all the facts to enable you to decide the rights and wrongs of my part in the events.

Well, here is where I will begin. It was pure chance that caught me off guard yesterday, forcing me to recall the day, fifty years back, when I attained my majority of twenty-one years. Previously, I had experienced nothing other than a well-ordered and happy life, my emotions spared any extremes of feeling, except when my dad had died four years earlier, but in a short span I was forced to grow up and face the realities of love, jealousy, hate, fear and horror.

First I must explain what happened just a few weeks ago. It was your Auntie Joyce who unknowingly brought about the same circumstance as she did that Easter of 1929. You know how bossy she is with me, her 'little brother', and she is still trying to order me around 'for my own good' while exhibiting a surprising excess of energy for her age. Anyway, the telephone rang and her voice burst from the earpiece.

'Bruv? I'm organising a visit to a lesser stately home for a small party of friends—name escapes me at present—but it's one I don't think you've visited before so it'll make a nice change. I've booked it for the Wednesday after Easter Monday—it'll be less crowded then. Pity your Uncle Stephen can't come—golf match.'

I tried to argue, knowing from the outset that I was wasting my breath and it would have to be endured, aware that she was hell-bent on matchmaking, being mistakenly convinced that I am a lonely old codger. In the end I agreed, but lacked the enthusiasm to find out more about the trip except that we would be travelling a fair distance westward.

So yesterday, I dutifully waited outside until a minibus turned the corner. Joyce ushered me in to sit beside a well-preserved and pleasant lady who must have found me quite boring—small talk and chitchat have no place in my repertoire as you well know. The day was fine and sunny and grew warmer as we travelled on our way. Not having slept very well the previous night with thoughts of getting up earlier than usual and further lulled by the motion of the bus, I found my head lolling against the headrest. I made an effort to keep awake, but finally fought a losing battle.

With no idea of how long I had slept, I slowly came back to an awareness of a cessation of movement and a buzz of chatter. After waiting awhile I hesitantly opened my eyes, whereupon the neglected lady beside me began to twitter on rapidly about the bus having developed a fault, how lucky we were to have stopped at a garage that did repairs on the spot and which happened to be situated in a lively

5

place with plenty of shops when we could have been stranded in the middle of nowhere and shouldn't we find a café to have coffee before window shopping? Then Joyce appeared, breaking in to reinforce this proposed programme by saying we had plenty of time, the repair having been estimated to take at least two hours, so we should avail ourselves of the opportunity to seek refreshment before searching the shops.

We all meekly clambered out onto the forecourt of the smart petrol station, its workshops visible at the rear. Standing beneath the canopy, I glanced along the road in both directions, being singularly unimpressed by what I saw—a busy, sprawling suburb similar to the hundreds of others which have sprung up to despoil our countryside, seeping out insidiously, overspills from bulging towns and cities like spreading lava spewed out from a volcano—or from the jaws of hell!

'We'll pop into the "conveniences" and meet back here,' Joyce said diplomatically, 'then decide what to do. I can see several places to have coffee.'

If your Uncle Stephen had come with us I would probably have stayed, but he had wisely committed himself to a golf tournament that could not be missed, so while obeying Joyce's first instruction, I spoke to the man beside me.

'Be a good chap and tell Joyce I'm going to stretch my legs and have a walk, will you? I'll be back within two hours so she's not to worry. Bit of indigestion,' I said, patting my tum, then took the opportunity to slip outside and move quickly behind a parked lorry. Having surveyed the crowded road I turned to my right, away from what I sensed to be the busiest part of the town, but the packed shops were still buzzing with people as I crossed a side road, fancifully called Mill Lane, and noticed a pub sign ahead. That would suit me very well, I thought.

On reaching it, could see nothing to indicate that I might

enjoy its dubious hospitality. Outside, a few tables and chairs, surrounded by wilting, potted plants, occupied a dusty rectangle. The front was swathed in coloured lights and loud rock music coming from the interior beat out a monotonous rhythm. I began to walk on past but thirst got the better of me, so I went through the entrance into a long room that had been favoured with modern, anonymous décor and ordered a drink at the bar. A fit of coughing, brought about by the smoky atmosphere, encouraged me to take my drink out into the questionably fresher air, where I found a table as far from the din as I could. After I had sat down, the pub sign again caught my eye. Newly painted and garish, it depicted the shadowy figure of a man under a star-studded sky who was shining a torch on the pavement before him, the brewer's name printed beneath. This is what the breweries are doing now, Paul, taking over old inns to modernise them and thereby destroying all the charm acquired naturally over the years.

As I sat meditating, a youth, cigarette dangling from his lips, appeared with a tray collecting glasses. 'What's this place called?' I asked, in order to take note of somewhere I never wanted to revisit.

'The pub? Oh, "The Guidin' Light",' he said, moving away.

That was not what I had meant—I wanted to know the name of the area I was in—but his answer gave me pause. It was an unusual name for a public house, though one I had encountered once before . . . But no, this house bore no resemblance to that other I had known, a delightful old coaching inn. I drained my glass and started off again, passing along the front, to find on the further side of the building, and still intact, a graceful, arched entrance designed for stagecoaches, cobblestones leading to the rear where the stabling would be. Cobblestones? Why had I thought of those? My eyes were playing tricks—there were no cobblestones—nothing but cement and paving going through to a car park.

Silly of me. That other inn I had known had been opposite a church with a tower, a new First World War memorial beside its lychgate. As I glanced across the road, my view was blocked by traffic until a sudden lull revealed what lay before my eyes—a church with a tower and a war memorial beside its lychgate . . .

For a moment my mind refused to register that it could be the same, but then, 'The Guiding Light' . . . If this inn sign had been the same as that other—which was merely a translucent, misty glow which faintly illuminated the grassy ground—I would have recognised it instantly. There was a rhyme that went with it, too. I tried to recall the words, but the inhibitor I had once put upon everything connected with that time now refused to raise it from my subconscious.

Surprised and uneasy, and even now hoping I was mistaken, I reminded myself that most early inns had been built in the vicinity of a church, ready for thirsty congregations to wet their parched throats after dry sermons. I looked along the busy main road towards the left of the overgrown churchyard, beyond the stone walls confining the mossy headstones to consecrated ground, and was relieved not to see a humpback bridge straddled across a stream with dirt paths running along each side of it. Where the near-end of the bridge would have been there was merely a side road branching off to the right, apparently giving access to a housing estate, its little boxes covering a rise in the terrain behind the shops where I should have seen fields and Walnut Tree Farm. I sought for evidence of a vast wood beyond, but there were no trees, only more houses topping the rise. Quite different. Yet I remained unsure.

It was then the words of the rhyme flooded, unwanted, into my head.

'The guiding light doth lead the way
For the one who in the churchyard lay
To find his murd'rer, and three times led,
Hangs him high on a tree, by the neck, 'til he's dead!'

The shock of remembrance affected me with a weakness in my limbs and a feeling of dread. Deciding there was only one way in which I could be certain and hopefully push my demons back into oblivion, I began to walk in the direction I had originally intended to follow, striding out quickly past the impersonal buildings. I had to prove it to myself now, one way or the other.

'If there's no school there, then your imagination's been working overtime,' I said out loud, bringing curious glances from passers-by. But of course it was, though only for a short time longer if the active demolition men in attendance had their way.

I stood staring across the road, almost overwhelmed by the wealth of feeling it aroused. There was the playground in front, now full of lorries and bright, yellow-painted vehicles standing over the hopscotch and netball lines marked on the ground, the basket posts gone. The sycamore tree still grew by the far wall, standing like an impotent sentinel, wooden seat encircling the trunk. The lean-to for bicycles, and the ever damp brick housing for the toilets to which, of necessity, the children had to run outside in all weathers, had vanished already. An empty space above the main doors had once held the school bell, its knotted rope dangling down through a hole, its summons now silenced forever.

I dodged the traffic as I crossed over, with no evident volition on my part, disquieted at finding myself there at all and reluctant to begin an unwanted mental journey back in time. It was as if some irresistible force propelled me forward through the gate, where a man, probably the foreman, barred my way.

'D'you want something?'

'I was wondering if I could take a look inside,' I answered. 'I once taught here, many years ago.'

He seemed to be a good-natured, easy-going sort of chap who quickly decided that I was unlikely to cause trouble, so he said, 'We're due for a break and the building's still sound. I can't see any harm in it—but wear this safety hat.' He rummaged around in a van and produced one.

'Thanks. Will another school be built here?'

The man laughed. 'It's easy to see you're not local. Why would they want another when they've just finished that big comprehensive up near the hospital?' He waved a hand in the direction of somewhere further up the road.

'What will be put in this space, then?'

'Car park—another's needed badly.' He saw my face. 'It's progress, isn't it?'

A gentle breeze rustled the fresh, new leaves of the sycamore and my heart sank. 'That tree—are you going to cut it down?'

He shook his head. 'No. There aren't many trees left around here and we're trying to preserve those not actually in the way.'

I felt immoderately pleased—it was an old friend. The children had been forbidden to climb into its branches but I had seen the boys cut the saplings that grew up around it, as generations had done before them, and whittle them into whistles about ten inches long, with some able to produce several varying notes. There was one boy that I remembered in particular . . .

The interior of the school had already been gutted when I entered through the opening where the front doors had been and I walked on into the lobby, the boards echoing under my feet. The cloakroom gaped emptily, its rows of pegs and benches gone. I went on past the head's room, then the staff room, glancing along to the end of the corridor at the large space that had once been the hall, used for assembly and gym, before reaching the classrooms now eerily lacking the pulsating, eager life of the children who had once filled them with noise and chatter.

I stopped when I came to what had been my classroom, leaning against the doorframe, staring inside. It looked bare, so bare, and smaller than I remembered. Gone were the desks with their ink-wells at the top right-hand corners—left-handed children like you, Paul, were discouraged from using that hand, believe it or not—and with benches attached so they could not be shifted about to scrape on the floor. Everything removable had been taken, except the dais that had supported the blackboard and easel and the teacher's desk and chair. With the cupboard doors removed, I could see nothing remaining within their shells, no books, pens, pencils, rubbers or chalk. The only evidence left was that of the big bottles of ink once stored there, the stains caused by their spillage still visible on the dusty floorboards.

Nostalgia hit me with an overpowering sadness. It was so long since I had first walked into this room, arriving for my first teaching post, apprehensive, filling in for a sick teacher. As I said before, it was solely due to the devious machinations of your Auntie Joyce. Older than me, she was already teaching at a girl's school near our home, while I had only just completed a course at a training college and was kicking my heels before taking up a position the next September as junior housemaster at a, now defunct, minor public school.

It was the start of Easter week, and I remembered Joyce, having broken up for the holiday, rushing into the room where I was reading and thrusting a piece of paper into my hand. 'There you are, Bruv,' she said eagerly. 'I've found you a job.'

'Thanks, but I already have one,' I answered, slightly put out at being so rudely disturbed.

'Not for the summer term, you haven't,' she retorted. 'Listen. One of our staff has an aunt who's headmistress of a village school somewhere down in the west country called West Halsey. A small country village in the middle of nowhere, she says. Now, one of their teachers has had an operation and won't be fit 'til the autumn term, which leaves them in a bit of a hole, so I said you'd be delighted to fill in. She's had a word with her aunt, who wants you to ring her today to confirm—they actually have a telephone—unlike us! The number's on the paper in your hand, and the name's Miss Millard—a good old-fashioned headmistress, I believe—one who'll keep you on your toes! Can't have you idling your time away at the swimming baths and tennis courts while I'm working, can we? Besides, it'll be welcome cash in your pocket as well as good practice for you!' She dodged the cushion I threw at her.

I thought it over. It would be foolish to turn it down, especially as I wanted to buy a motor car at the first opportunity. A small legacy, and money I was hoarding from my twenty-first, was nearly enough but not quite. This little bonus could see my dream come true sooner than expected. Also, I lacked friends locally, having been often away at my various seats of learning, so there was every possibility of my becoming bored, and if boredom was to prove my lot then I might just as well endure it in the country—with extra money—as at home. So I telephoned from the post office and it was arranged that I should arrive the day before the start of term, would be met at the station, Halsey Halt, and a Mrs Bessie Marsham would put me up with full board. The loaded die had been cast.

Joyce had invited a new friend, called Babs, to stay with us for a weekend during that Easter. My interest in the fair sex was scanty; girls were, from choice, largely unknown, my father having instilled in me the firm belief that they should be treated with respect—that was when they wanted to be—

12

and the 'love act' kept solely for marriage; dalliance was reserved for the immoral. I felt inhibited and shy in their company. Joyce's friends were inclined to be jolly and robust, displaying precious little femininity and, if truth were told, I was rather scared of them. Babs seemed different and I found I was rather taken with her, but our time together was too short for me to pursue this awareness of compatibility.

It did, however, manage to arouse previously dormant feelings of the 'boy and girl' syndrome, and I looked forward to the possibility of seeing her again. If only there had been more time for us to develop a deeper liking and understanding, if only we had met earlier and I had refused to be tempted into spending the summer of 1929 away from home. If only . . .

Day 2

I had now decided on my venture into the unknown and until the journey began had given little consideration as to what actually might lie ahead. It was only after the farewells, when I was relaxing on the train, that I began to give it some thought.

Why on earth had I allowed myself to be persuaded to teach in what was really nothing more than a 'dame school'? It would have been called that not many years before and had probably changed little, being there merely to provide a fundamental education for children who had no real interest in learning. Here was I, educated up to the eyeballs and coached in modern methods, having to put it all aside for the time being and be content with expounding the basics, English grammar and simple arithmetic. As for history, well, just '1066 and all that'! Should I want to teach anything more it would be way over every child's head and I would have to tread carefully not to be dubbed a 'show off'. These thoughts filled my head for a good part of the long journey so, having laid aside the *Strand*, my favourite detective magazine, I lazily observed the countryside as the train rushed noisily over the rails. I had been told I would have to change trains and board another that ran on a branch line and ask the guard to stop at Halsey Halt, a rural station, as trains only stopped there for those passengers who wanted to get on or off, the drivers looking out for anyone waiting by day or showing a light at night. I had boarded this small train earlier on without any trouble and it was already approaching twilight when we came to rest amid puffs of steam. I heard the guard shouting, 'Halsey Halt' as I got to my feet, and he opened the door, waiting to help me down, my luggage already lifted out on the platform. He slammed the door shut behind me with a 'G'night, sir', and blew his whistle while holding steady above his head a hand oil lamp, its flame showing through green glass, and the train moved slowly away.

I found myself standing alone in the gathering gloom on a platform furnished only with an open shelter. A white-painted slope at one end led down to the track, which had to be crossed to reach the opposite platform for the up line. There was nothing else other than trees that I could see. The air held an April chill, the silence enhanced by the noise of the train becoming fainter as it puffed on its way seemed to take on an eerie quality. I shuddered involuntarily. I think now that the place had been awaiting my arrival, aware with precognition of the moment when my belief in reality would be suspended by the ghastly events that would culminate here. My present uneasiness, though, was centred on the fact that I was expecting to be met and there was no one in evidence.

The next second, to my utter relief, I heard a cheery voice call, 'Sorry to be late, Guv, I'd 'ave brought me motor taxi, but there's a bit o' trouble wi' me spark plugs,' and a round, bouncing, little red-faced man in a bowler hat came up and grabbed a suitcase and one end of my trunk.

'Carter's the name, Guv, Jim Carter. Here—you 'old on t'other end an' we'll be away afore 'ee knows it!' and he led the way over the track and along a path at a fine pace, pulling me after him.

When we reached the road I could see a horse-drawn cab waiting. We lifted the luggage on to the carrier and I got inside while my cabbie climbed up in front. He clicked his tongue and the horse started off without further prompting, hooves clip-clopping on the road. I peered through the window to get some idea of where I would be living for the next few months, but could see only two large stone gate-posts right opposite the Halt, a wide, overgrown driveway beyond them, then nothing other than more trees looming against a darkening sky. These ranged unbroken for about two miles or so until I saw lights shining from several cottages grouped together.

With a 'Whoa, boy', the cab came to rest beside a white-painted gate inscribed 'Clover Cottage' and the cabbie jumped down, let me out, then urged me along the path towards a modest, detached dwelling. 'I'll fetch yer baggage, Guv, never fear.'

The door was immediately opened by a lady of a buxom, bespectacled and rather plain appearance, whom I thought to be in her forties, about the same age as my mother. She relieved me of my attaché case while drawing me inside the shadowy hallway lit only by an oil lamp on a pedestal.

'Come in, come in,' her voice was friendly and warm. 'I'm Bessie Marsham. Did you have a good journey, Mr Parr? I heard train come in on time, as allus—you can set your clocks by 'em—but their whistles an' such-like aren't loud enough to bother you at night!' she hastened to add. 'You'll soon take no more notice than if a cock were a-crowin'. Get that trunk an' the rest up the stair, Jim, and put 'em in the first on the right. Be quick about it! Mr Parr will be wanting 'is supper.'

I became conscious of the delicious smell of food and the emptiness in my stomach. 'Yes, thank you, Mrs Marsham,' I agreed, adding, amongst other pleasantries, how happy I was to be there. I doubt she heard a word as she busily helped me out of my overcoat, while holding my cap and scarf and urging Jim Carter to hurry off the premises. I offered him his fare, but he said it was all taken care of. I insisted on tipping him, anyway—he looked as if he was expecting that.

Mrs Marsham led the way along a passage into a roomy, cosy kitchen, a place set at the table. I was amused to see the lighting to be provided merely by oil lamps—electricity and gas had obviously not penetrated this far. A kitchen range, polished bright with black lead, was set into the chimney breast, the fire door open to reveal bars holding back red coals. Pans bubbled on the hob next to a cast-iron kettle, spout belching steam, lid rattling, and the mantel shelf above held knick-knacks and a photo of a man in Army uniform. The table, chairs, a settee and a tall cluttered dresser furnished the room and beneath the window was fixed a glazed earthenware sink, minus any taps. I am finding that every detail was etched on my mind at the time.

After the meal, my landlady and I shared a pot of tea while she told me about the staff at school. 'There's Miss Millard, the headmistress. A bit strait-laced, but that's as it should be. She gives the children a proper grounding in manners and morals, which stands 'em in good stead later on. She lives in the school house with Miss Hope, who also teaches. They're both older ladies who keeps theirselves close.'

She swallowed a mouthful of tea and resumed. 'Mrs Phillips—who had the operation an' is why you're here—is younger, but you won't be seeing her because she's gone away to get over it. An' you won't see much of Mr Richards, neither—he's caretaker-handyman an' takes the boys for field games, cricket an' such. He stays out o' school mostly an' never has much to say for hisself, but his wife makes up for that! She acts as secret'ry an' general dogsbody, from making tea to keeping order at dinner-time. Some goes home, but others, who live too far away, take sandwiches. I'll make some for you tomorrow. D'you like mustard with ham?'

I said, 'Yes, thanks,' while trying to remember names.

'That leaves Fiona—Fiona Macdonald—the doctor's daughter,' she continued, her face hardening into an unreadable expression before softening again. 'He's a fine, good man, the doctor—been here more'n ten year. His wife left him—some say it were for the best—when Fiona were a child.' The remote expression returned. 'She teaches music and art, games an' the like—so I'm told. She were raised, an' spoiled, by a string o' housemaids an' housekeepers, doing much as she pleased 'til sent to boarding school. After that, she went away to be "finished", whatever that means, in Switzerland, and only come home 'bout a year back. She were taken on at school last autumn—at Dr. Mac's request, I b'lieve—when there chanced to be a vacancy.' She gave a disapproving sniff before eyeing me with a look of some doubt. 'We haven't had a young man teaching here before. Hope you don't find no trouble.'

No more than I do, I told myself, already fearing Fiona.

Mrs Marsham changed the subject by informing me that her husband had been killed in the battle of the Somme in '16. 'We'd planned on having a fam'ly when the war was over, only he never come back. I like children.' She gave a discordant laugh. 'Good thing we didn't, though, because I've had to keep meself ever since. I wanted to be a secret'ry when I were a girl, as I come from a better class o' fam'ly an' studied English an' shorthand an' typing, but never finished the course when I married my Bert an' moved here. Now I takes in paying guests when I can.'

She broke an embarrassed silence with, 'You're welcome to smoke if you want.' When I shook my head, saying I had never felt the need for it, she said, 'Pity—there's naught I like better than the smell o' pipe tobacco—my man used to

18

fill the room with it. Goodness, look at the time! Here I am, keeping you up talking and you dog-tired after all the travelling. I'd better show you the privy. Don't think it's cold enough to need a coat—'less you 'tend staying out for any length o' time, that is.'

I had no idea what she meant, but got to my feet as she picked up a lamp. I followed its light into what I took to be a scullery, but which I afterwards heard her call 'the wash'ouse'. As I passed through I could vaguely see a big sink with a washboard resting in it, and a long, narrow tin bath hanging on the wall.

'There's a storm lantern on that hook,' she said, pointing to a beam above. 'You can take it with you if you stay out there for long—gives a good light if you wants to read.' She opened an outer door. 'This way.'

I accompanied her along a dirt path to a small, sturdy structure, peering over her shoulder when she lifted the latch. The smell of camphor was overpowering, and that I learned was its true purpose, not to deter moths. I could see a polished mahogany board with a hole in the middle put over a rectangular box, my eyes vainly searching for a cistern with dangling chain, and my heart sank. What had I let myself in for? I, who had always enjoyed the facilities of a water closet and bathroom, had been plunged back into the Dark Ages!

'There's a man comes to empty it, so don't you feel obliged to. Here, take the lamp—I can find me way back well enough. You come when you're ready.'

I took it with a muttered word of thanks, but am afraid I watered the flowers that night and it was some time before I was able to approach the privy without a visible shudder. Returning, shivering, I found her with lighted candleholder in hand.

'You'll soon be warm as toast,' she promised. 'I'll show you to your room.'

Once upstairs and on the landing she went inside, setting the candle down on a table beside the bed and lighting another on the mantelpiece. 'You'll find matches on here. If there's anything else you want, give me a call. Oh, an' rather than light a fire, I got this newfangled paraffin heater. D'ye know how to use it?' I said I did.

'That's all right, then. Turn it off before you gets into bed, won't you? I'll bring hot water an' tea at half past six, with breakfast at seven—you'll want to be early on your first day. I'll say goodnight, then.'

I stood taking stock of my surroundings, a fair-sized room with flowery wallpaper, shiny, patterned lino covering the floor and rag rugs by the side of a brass-ended bed. A china jug stood in a basin on a marble-topped washstand, beside it a shaving bowl and a carafe of drinking water, a tumbler over its neck. A dressing table with looking glass and toilet set was next to the window opposite a wardrobe with a full-length mirror in its door. An armchair and an upright chair were placed on each side of a writing desk. I was glad to see that the high bed was lengthy enough for my long legs to stretch out in comfort, but a lump in the middle had me worried until I found it was a stone hot-water bottle. A covering quilt hung down each side, but it was not long enough to hide the chamber pot beneath. The portable heater of shiny black enamel was put inside the fender, its tiny window glowing red. The latticed grille, on which a kettle could be heated, was open, producing a pattern of light on the ceiling which I can only describe as resembling a large, pale chrysanthemum.

Well, I had to accept that this would be my home for the next few months. Thoughts of home brought nostalgia, but moping would not help. I began to unpack my luggage, but the smell of camphor in the wardrobe decided me to hang my suit on a hook on the door. I did not want to give the children the opportunity to make clever remarks about

20

moth-eaten teachers in class tomorrow! I put the rest of my things away and donned pyjamas before going to turn off the heater, and it was only then that I noticed a picture, about two feet by three, on a wall beside the window. Fetching a candle to examine it in more detail, I was able to see an unframed, well-executed oil painting of a girl wearing a long, high-waisted yellow dress set against a background of trees and blue sky, the sun sparkling on a lake. She had flowing black hair, framing a lovely, laughing face radiating happiness. In those days I rather fancied myself as an art expert and wondered who the artist was and how this gem of a portrait came to be hidden away in one of Mrs Marsham's bedrooms, but I would have to wait for daylight to properly satisfy my curiosity.

Just before blowing out the last candle I heard the shrill whistle of a train, demonstrating that there was no need for this feeling I had of being isolated in an unfamiliar world, as civilisation and escape still existed out there, so I got into bed and said my prayers from the luxury of the thick feather bed that lay over the mattress.

I awoke next morning to the sounds of a knock, a 'Good morning, Mr Parr', the rattle of a cup on saucer and the curtains being opened. The daylight made me blink, as I sat up to see my landlady making her way back to the door.

'You've a fine day for the walk,' she said. 'A can of hot water's on the stand, and the tea's beside you. Sleep well?'

'Very well indeed,' I replied, meaning it.

As I sipped the tea my eyes were again drawn to the painting. The beautiful girl was still laughing at me and I mentally entitled it 'Girl in a Yellow Dress', got out of bed and lifted it down, but abandoned the appraisal when I felt the cold morning air. After a wash and a quick shave, I dressed and carried the picture to the window to find I had not been mistaken in my assessment the previous night— the artist had worked with a practised and skilful hand. I searched for a signature, but found only the initials 'J.Q.' within a circle, and 'Armistice Night '18'. That was over ten years ago, so why had I not come upon more of this talented artist's work? There was another puzzle in the fact that the background showed a summer scene, yet the Armistice had been in November—and why 'night' when it was clearly daytime?

A bell tinkled from below as I hung it back on the wall in the shadow, determined to investigate further. An appetising smell of eggs and bacon filled the air as I ran downstairs to the kitchen.

'We usually eat in here.' Mrs Marsham was busily piling sausages and fried bread on to the already full plate. ''Tis warmer by the fire an' less trouble than carrying it through. Here you are, eat up—you'll need it to last you 'til teatime. I've done you a packet of sandwiches, but suggest you try to borrow a bicycle—mebbe Jim Carter at the garage'll have one—and come back here to dinner in future. Sandwiches won't do much for a hearty young man like you, if you'll pardon my saying so, and I prefer to get a hot meal served in the middle o' the day.'

I said I would ask him, enjoying the food while she told me how to find the school, so there was no time left to ask about the picture. I put some fruit and the sandwiches in my attaché case with the books I was taking, donned cap and overcoat, walked down the path to the gate and turned left as instructed.

The sun was beginning to show through the clouds and would soon start to warm up the spring day. I saw that Clover Cottage was in the middle of about half a dozen others, a water pump set between. A woman was wielding the handle vigorously as water gushed into her bucket, and I only then realised that there was no piped water to the dwellings. What drudgery people had to endure in those days, Paul, but I never heard anyone complain.

I walked along the dirt path beside the road, the birds singing and chattering amongst the branches, the pale green leaves fluttering in the breeze, but as I went on towards the village the trees began to thin out. I came to a narrow, rutted lane on my left that led upward over gently rising ground between thick hedges, until it curved out of sight. Fields on either side, stretching down to the main road, showed a sprouting crop of what I imagined to be a type of grain. A few cottages sprawling along the other side of the main road ended with stables and a blacksmith's forge, CARTER'S GARAGE painted on a rickety signboard above it. Behind was open stabling with partial covering for harnesses, a wagonette, a horse-cab and a black-draped horse-hearse. The place was untidy, with bits of motor cars, petrol cans and carriages spread about. Two men in overalls stood by a single-hand petrol pump filling a can, Jim himself not in sight, so I continued onward as horses and carts clattered by, plus a bicycle or two. A motorbus chugged past, making for a small town some eight miles distant according to a signpost, but bustling towns held no attraction for me, who had lived in one or another all my life.

I had now arrived at a row of shops, some with open doors, their keepers sweeping away the dust from the paving in front. One or two nodded as they caught my eye, and I felt that everyone knew exactly who this stranger was. Among the shops I recall was a tiny post office, a draper, a barber, a grocer, a butcher, a tobacconist and confectioner, who sold newspapers, and an oil shop—what wonderful smells wafted out from there! The pungent odours of various oils and soaps, polish, tallow and carbolic teased the nostrils. How I would relish it once again!

On second thoughts, I would not wish to be back in that time or that place, but then I had no idea of what lay ahead as I sauntered blithely on. The shops and paving ended and I once more trod a dirt path, a hedge separating it from more fields spreading out from behind the shops. A lane, branching off on the other side of the road, led to a water mill about a hundred yards distant, its wheel turning rapidly. The mill race came from a fast-moving stream bubbling down from the rising ground to disappear under a hump-back bridge ahead of me, and so on to the mill. I paused as I crossed over, leaning on the coping to watch the water splashing against stones jutting up from the bed of the stream, and noticed a line of flat stepping stones spanning it. I must lack a sixth sense, which could have forewarned me then.

Day 3

I came to the end of the bridge where, on my left, a path branched off down an incline leading to a footpath that ran along the near bank of the stream, to be finally lost among trees framing the top of the hill. The other side of the path was bound by bushes and an ancient church wall, a church tower visible above yew trees, the hands of its clock showing ten minutes to eight, a landmark I had been seeking.

Quickening my pace, I came to a war memorial, the names of the 1914–18 war dead from the village carved deeply into the stone, and glanced across the road to see an inn almost opposite the church, built there long ago for the purpose of swilling down dusty sermons, I imagined! It had a welcoming, mellow air, and I anticipated sampling its ale at the earliest opportunity. The pictured inn sign showed a luminous, misty glow on a path amid tall grasses with the words 'The Guiding Light', and I assumed it to have some religious connotation. Further along, I passed a few large houses set back in their gardens and crossed a side road leading to fresh-looking, recently built semi-detached houses and bungalows.

The church clock struck eight just as I reached the school, which was single-storeyed and smaller than antici-pated. I crossed the playground towards the open door while suffering a frisson of nerves at the prospect at meeting a dragon of a schoolmarm, yet confident of being able to handle anything that might arise in this primitive backwater. Such was my misplaced confidence. I might have been advanced in learning, but still a babe in the academy of life!

I was met by an angular, sharp-faced, middle-aged lady, mousy hair piled on top of her head, who introduced herself as Miss Hope, knocked on a door bearing the label 'Headmistress', and ushered me inside. Seated at a desk, an older, plump woman with greying hair fixed me with a steely gaze through eyeglasses, before smiling with such warmth that I felt enveloped in her obvious benevolence. She rose to her feet and held out a hand.

'You are very welcome, Mr Parr. Indeed, it's kind of you to come here to help us out at such short notice. I'm sure the children will appreciate their good fortune in having the advantage of your teaching—if only for one term. I've written some guidelines to help you—what the classes are studying, our routines and timetables and your duties. If there's anything you need or don't understand, please let me know.'

I took the foolscap sheets from her with muttered thanks; she could not have eased my way more gracefully. Old-fashioned she might have been, with her long skirt, high-necked blouse and pince-nez, but she had good old-fashioned manners.

'I take care of scripture and the kindergarten,' she went on. 'The classes are divided into the sevens to tens and the elevens to fourteens, the juniors and seniors, which will be between you and Miss Hope. I'd like you to take the younger ones—they need the firmest hand.' Her eyes twinkled. 'They'll play you up if you allow it. We try to teach our children to respect authority, but there are potential rebels.'

She rose and led the way to the door. 'You've already met Miss Hope—she'll show you to your classroom where you can study the reading matter I've given you. Later, you'll meet Mr Richards and his wife, our secretary, who helpfully fills in with other duties,' she paused, 'and Miss Macdonald.'

Thus sent about my business and seated at my desk, I read the given items and sorted out books until becoming aware of someone standing in the open doorway. Looking up, I was instantly lost in the vortex of a bewitching pair of green-flecked, hazel-coloured eyes, which held my stare until I gulped and lowered my own to the hemline of her fashionable dress, short enough to reveal the shapely legs of this very modern miss.

'Hello,' she said, the voice soft and melodious. 'You're certainly a nice surprise! I'm Fiona—art, music and games—of all sorts.' She stretched out a hand.

'My pleasure—Edward Parr,' I replied as I clasped it, entranced by her cropped auburn hair, wide smile and piquant face. This was surely the most exquisite girl ever to have crossed my path, and to find her here of all places! What unexpected luck! That was my immediate reaction.

'I shall call you Eddie—but not in school,' she said. 'See you at prayers then, and oh, if you have any trouble during the day, let me know—I'm quite good at keeping things in order.' Then she vanished, leaving a faint perfume on the air.

I was assailed by the thought that this vision, having appraised me, doubted that I was capable of controlling a class so, feeling rather put down, I went to a window overlooking the playground and stood contemplating the children who had arrived early and were amusing them-selves before the bell summoned them inside.

Girls and boys were in different groups, the former mainly skipping, but most of the latter playing a game that seemed to involve two boys standing alone as principals, while the others ran away pretending to be frightened. They were all chanting a rhyme which I could not hear clearly, but suddenly some words were shouted out and the

27

taller of the two, a dark-haired lad, put a handkerchief around the neck of the other, a slender, fair boy, pulling it tight. Alarmed, I was about to rush to the door, when the bell began to toll its warning and they all scattered and ran inside.

I made my way to assembly and was assigned a place between Miss Millard and Miss Hope. Prayers were short, followed by a hymn accompanied by Fiona at the piano. I could hardly tear my eyes away from the entrancing sight of her pert profile as the headmistress introduced me to the school, then it was over.

Fiona gave me a pensive look and an encouraging grin as she passed by. 'See you in the staff room at breaktime. Good luck!'

As I neared my classroom, amid the general noise I could pick out a boy's shrill voice clearly declaiming, 'Mr Parr—should go far—the farther the better—we'll send 'im a letter!' followed by a roar of laughter.

I paused in the corridor before gritting my teeth and entering my personal lion's den. The noise had died down to some extent, but there were still a few sniggers and a shuffling of feet. I stepped on to the dais beside my desk and scanned the room without speaking. I saw girls on one side and boys on the other, some grinning saucily, others serious, not knowing what to expect.

I said, 'Good morning, Class,' which had a limited reaction, sat down, pulled the register towards me and began to read out the names.

'Frank Acaster?'

' 'Ere.'

I remembered that they had not had a male teacher before. 'When you address me you'll call me "sir",' I said, and began again. 'Frank Acaster?'

' 'Ere—SIR!'

The word was grossly exaggerated against a background of giggling and I suspected that this boy, whose shock of dark, untidy hair crowned a pinched, defiant face, had taken the role of 'leader of the pack', and must now justify it. I also thought I recognised him from the playground performance and as the source of the doggerel previously aimed at me, but delayed making any comment.

I continued to run down the alphabetical list, with some voices cheekily over-emphasising the 'sir', while glancing up to mark each child's face in my mind as well as in the book until one response was quiet and polite and had a certain quality about it. I saw a large, impassive pair of dark blue eyes belonging to a slim child with pale gold, curling hair and a warm, sunburned tinge about his fair skin. The words 'golden boy' came into my head, as I noted that both he and the Acaster lad had been the principals in that sinister game in the playground.

'Thomas Piper?' I repeated.

'Here, sir,' he answered, again.

When I had finished, I put down my pen and regarded everybody in a friendly way. 'It seems we have a poet amongst us, very clever at rhyming names. Which one of you is it?'

I watched the faces and settled on the one that had turned a dull red. 'You, is it, Frank? I thought as much. Stand up. You should do well in English and I'll see you have extra poetry to study. For now, though, I have a task for you to do at home. I want you to make up a rhyme on your own name—Acaster—and bring it to me first thing tomorrow. Do you understand?'

'Ay—sir,' he answered, looking discomfited, 'b-but I don' think I . . .' his voice trailed off.

'Do your best—now sit down. You others appear to have found this rather amusing, but I assure you that learning, whether it concerns manners or school work, must be taken seriously and I intend to ensure that you benefit from any encouragement I can provide.'

They might not have clearly understood my words, but I had picked up a heavy ruler from the desk and hit the palm of my hand sharply. It made a noise like a pistol shot, and they all jumped. After that they took notice whenever I picked it up, and I never experienced any further trouble in class during my stay. It did no harm to make them aware that there might be penalties imposed for indulging in rudeness.

I was full of expectation when I joined Fiona in the staff room during break, more than delighted that Miss Hope was closeted with Miss Millard. Mrs Richards was revealed as a bustling, motherly person when she carried in a tray of tea, said hello, beamed a shy smile at me, and hurried out.

'What are you doing at dinnertime?' Fiona asked, after a few prying questions.

I explained that I had brought sandwiches, since it was too far to walk to and from my lodgings in the hour allowed, but I intended to try to borrow a bicycle.

'I might be able to help you there.' She leaned back in her chair, beautiful eyes half closed beneath long lashes. 'My dad's the local doc, y'know. He keeps a bike in the garage in case any of his motor cars of the moment should let him down, as they've frequently done in the past, but the one he has now seems more reliable. I'm sure he wouldn't mind. I'll ask him when I go back at dinnertime— which we call lunch at home. We dine in the evening—like all gentlefolk do!' She smiled mischievously. 'Come back with me this afternoon when school's over and get it.'

The remainder of the day passed in a flash. When the final bell rang I watched the children scramble out as fast as they could without giving me cause to stop and repri- mand them. The one I had termed 'golden boy' did not seem to be in any hurry and was going to be last through the door. I wondered if he was afraid of Frank's contending ways and whether he was being subjected to bullying.

'Thomas,' I said. 'Are you all right?'

He looked taken aback 'I'm us'ally called Tom an' I'm fine, thank 'ee—sir.' Those big eyes seemed to be without guile, but I resolved to find out for sure.

Fiona was waiting at the door as I finished tidying my desk. Her topcoat and hat were as fashionable as her dress and I felt proud to walk with this fascinating creature to her house, which turned out to be one of the larger ones with a drive leading up to it. A small building adjoining was signed 'Surgery'.

'Car's not here, so Dad's out,' she remarked. 'He doesn't often put it in the garage—waste of time. Come in and have a cup of tea—then we'll find the bike.'

I knew I should get back to my lodgings, but wanted to stay by the side of this girl—for ever, if possible—so joined her in the smart, parquet-floored hallway.

'Hang your coat on the hall stand.' Fiona put her own on one of the hooks and walked into a room. I heard a bell tinkle somewhere in the nether regions as I followed her in, finding her sprawled on a sofa.

'Come and sit down.' She patted a cushion beside her as a housemaid entered and received her orders, before turning to scrutinize me and begin her questions. She probed my background, likes and dislikes, plans for the future, girlfriends past and present—which did not take very long—and what I thought of the school, before tea was wheeled in on a trolley. As she poured, I received a potted outline of her academic history, her love of art, music and her father—and how she hated living in this deadly hole but was loath to leave him on his own.

'I have to make do with holidays abroad, and living it up when I can. My mother was part Italian and full of life, and she couldn't stand it either. I'll never end my days here. I spend ages trying to persuade Daddy to move to somewhere more exciting, but he's not keen.' As if in answer to his name a car pulled up outside, and she said, 'Here's Dad now.'

A well-built man, sandy hair balding slightly but face neatly bearded, came into the room. 'Hello, Fio—who's this?' he asked, sizing me up.

'Our new temp. teacher, Dad, Eddie Parr. He'd like to borrow your bike.'

He came over and grasped my hand as I scrambled to my feet. 'I'm pleased to meet you,' he said, sounding as if he really meant it. 'Have it for as long as you want. You must come to dinner—Fio will arrange it.'

'Thank you, sir,' I returned.

'No time for tea, Fio—just came to pick up some papers I left behind. I'm in a rush to get to the hospital. You carry on. Have to go—'bye.'

As I heard the car drive away I said reluctantly, 'I have to go, too,' and together we went out to the garage and inspected the brakes and tyres on the bicycle. As all was in order, I started to wheel it outside.

'Here are some bicycle clips.' She held them out to me, touching my fingers as I took them from her, which sent a thrill running right through me. 'Do call me Fio, like Dad does, when we're away from school.'

I thanked her, and secured my case on the carrier and my turn-ups firmly around my ankles before clumsily mounting the bike, very conscious of her gaze, which caused me an initial wobble or two as I set off. Buoyed up, I flew along to Clover Cottage, jubilant that Fate had seen fit to lead me to that place and that girl! Such is the sublime ignorance of youth; it always expects Fate to show a smiling face.

I arrived back in high spirits, and Mrs Marsham asked me

to put the bike in a shed at the back. She had tea waiting—as it was a cooked meal I suppose I should call it 'high' tea—and afterwards I offered to fetch water from the pump for washing the dishes. She would have none of it, insisting that she already had two buckets put by for use until next day.

'The air still feels cool. Your heater's alight for you to go upstairs if you wish, but if you've nothing special to do then come and sit by the fire wi' me. I shan't bother you if you wants to read, an' I'd be glad of the comp'ny.'

I said I intended writing a letter home to tell them of my safe arrival and would then join her—and could I listen to the news on her wireless set?

I was surprised when she laughed. 'Of course you could, Mr Parr, if I had one. As 'tis, you'll have to make do wi' me weekly newspaper.'

I wondered how she and people like her managed to exist without information about current affairs, and decided I would have to buy a daily paper. Then I went up to my room, said 'hello' to the girl in the painting and wrote my letter home before going back to the greater warmth of the kitchen, a book under my arm.

Mrs Marsham had completed her chores, having hung the tea towel over the range rail to dry, the heat making it sway gently. She sat down in a rocking chair, plainly her usual seat, picked up some knitting and pointed to an easy chair opposite.

'Do sit down, Mr Parr. Written your letter?' As I nodded, she continued, 'You can post it in the village on your way to school tomorrow.' She looked to see that my book remained closed. 'Tell me how you got on today.'

I considered. 'The staff were very helpful, especially Miss Macdonald. She asked her father to lend me the bike I rode back.'

Mrs Marsham's eyes lifted and met mine. 'Did she, now?

33

'Ay, I've heard she can be very helpful.' She dropped her gaze again, busying herself with the needles.

'I've no fault to find with the children, either,' I went on. 'They didn't seem to know how to take me at first. The girls giggle a lot, as girls do, but they're all mostly well-behaved, as, indeed, are the boys—with a little prompting.'

'Some, I know, can be little hellers at times, but there's no real harm in any of 'em. Frank Acaster tries to lord it over the rest and be top dog, but then, his father died in the flu epidemic at the end o' the war, an' though his ma does her best an' dusts the seat of 'is trousers ev'ry so often, 'tis not the same as being under a father's firm hand, is it?'

I said I supposed not, then asked the question that had been on the tip of my tongue ever since I came downstairs. 'Tell me, Mrs Marsham, about that picture in my room— it's very well painted. Isn't it rather a shame to have it hanging where few people can see it? D'you know who the artist is? I don't recognise the initials, J.Q.'

'Ay, I do. John Quinton. He stayed here for a time— almost a year. He'd heard of the village, an' me, because me husband were 'is batman, them bein' in the same regiment. Captain Quinton was his officer an' the handsomest gent I ever saw, with wavy, fair hair an' a small moustache. He told me how much he hated the killing but had to do his bit like everyone else to protect our country. He were gassed after me Bert were killed—that mustard gas were awful, burnt the insides o' yer lungs away, so 'e said. He used to cough something awful. Came to stay wi' me to try to get better and escape from living in a town, an' mebbe his fam'ly, too, though he never said so, and hardly went out at all 'cept to walk by the big lake an' sketch an' paint. There's a path at end of the garden that leads straight to the lake through the woods.'

'Didn't he find life here restricting?' I asked. 'I mean, having so much idle time to fill. He must have felt bored.'

Mrs Marsham increased the speed of her steel needles. They flashed in the firelight as if to indicate by action what she would not have dreamed of saying out loud—namely, that I was more stupid than she had given me credit for. 'He had his painting, see? An' he loved anything to do with nature, did the Captain—'twas all he cared to think of. If he weren't using a brush or pencil then he'd be readin' books 'bout it, an' used to say there weren't enough hours in the day to learn all there was to know. I let him have the use of the room upstairs which faces north, the best light, he said, where he painted that picture and left it on the wall in his room when 'e went.'

'Gave it to you as a "thank you" present, did he?'

'No.'

I waited for some explanation but she kept silent, her mouth firmly closed in an uncompromising manner, and I thought it unwise to press her. Instead, I said, 'The girl who modelled for it—the lovely girl in the yellow dress. Does she live locally?'

Mrs Marsham opened her lips again, releasing a sigh. 'Ay, she do, but life's not dealt kindly with her. I doubt you'll meet her, anyways.' She got to her feet. 'You must be tired, Mr Parr. I'll make a bedtime drink. Horlicks or Ovaltine?'

After I had undressed and was ready for bed I said goodnight to the girl with the long, black hair in the picture. As I stared, another girl with short, auburn hair was superimposed over it and, once asleep, I dreamed I was holding her close in my arms.

Day 4

The next morning, Frank Acaster approached me with averted eyes before the others came into the schoolroom. 'Well, Frank,' I said. 'Did you manage a rhyme with your name?'

'No-o, sir,' he answered, head hung low, then lifted it and faced me with bravado, 'but I tried!'

'That's what I wanted you to do,' I said, 'and with all your lessons, too. You can sit down now.'

He looked surprised, doubtless having expected a taste of the ruler, but behaved himself impeccably in class after that.

During the days that followed I learned more about those around me. Fiona Macdonald remained friendly but seemed adept at keeping me at a distance, my restrained ardour increasing daily. On at least two occasions I thought I caught a sight of her in a sports car with a young man but was too far away to be sure, though I could not ignore the hot flush of jealousy that enveloped me. Tom Piper became a common factor between the two of us, his main school interests being in her subjects, art and music, while in mine he showed promise in English Lit. I felt drawn to him. His physical comeliness pleased my eye and, as we both appeared to be in the wrong environment, I felt we shared the same vulnerability. Country life was strange and new to me, and he appeared to be different in demeanour from the other boys.

The village had its entertainments, though there was little to divert me in the evenings. A cinema film was shown in the village hall every Wednesday, but having studied the list of forthcoming attractions I found I had already seen the best of them. Mrs Marsham, a staunch churchgoer, sang in the choir and attended practices there on Thursday evenings, and whist drives were held in the hall on Saturday nights. On my first Saturday she invited me to join her but the only card game I knew was bridge, so I just accompanied her to the door before crossing the road to where the inn, the dying sun reflected in its small windows, held an inviting look. "The Guiding Light"—I would have to ask how it came by that name.

Walking into the public bar amid a bevy of staring men and conscious of standing out like a beacon on a hill, I forced myself to say, 'Good evening,' which was acknowledged with various grunts and rejoinders. I quietly ordered half a pint of ale from a ruddy-faced man with mutton-chop whiskers standing behind the bar, an apron tied around his ample girth.

'You're very welcome here,' he said, as the amber liquid flowed into the glass. 'I'm Bill Angove, landlord. You'll be the Mr Parr staying wi' Bessie, I'll warrant. My youngest says she likes the way you teach.'

Glad to have met with the approval of at least one of my charges whose appreciation had been expressed in the right quarter, I relaxed and looked around. The men had resumed playing their dominoes and card games, puffing away on cigarettes and pipes. A log fire burned brightly in a huge stone fireplace, necessary for warming patrons standing on bare flagstones. I rested a foot on the brass rail, sipping the ale, enjoying the cheerful atmosphere. Most of the men were farm workers, shown by their dirty boots and leggings, and each acknowledged me when they came up to the bar to replenish their tankards. A door in one wall had 'Saloon Bar' etched on the glass; another door next to it stood partly open so I could observe some better-dressed men that I thought must be tradesmen, and could hear snatches of their chatter and laughter.

The landlord's eyes followed my gaze. 'That's the Snug— you can go in there whenever you want.'

I shook my head, opening out the newspaper I had brought with me. 'Not tonight, thanks, but maybe next time. I'll just catch up with what's going on in the world for now.'

Later, I ordered another drink, but as I took out the money to pay and was preparing to ask the reason for the inn's name, a burly, rather slovenly chap with deep-set black eyes, a stubbly chin and an unruly mass of dark hair, who had been sitting on his own, came unsteadily up to the bar. He pushed hard against me without excusing himself, and thereby knocked my unasked question out of my head. I hoped he might be more civil when sober, but resolved to avoid him in future and make use of the Snug.

When it was about time for the whist drive to end I drained my glass, said goodnight to the company, and went over the road to the hall. Standing just inside, I watched the prizes being presented and was pleased to see a delighted Mrs Marsham receive a tin of biscuits. Leaving for home, we followed behind some people from our nearby cottages, all hurrying along with thoughts of warm kitchens and bedtime drinks. My companion asked my opinion of the inn.

'A jolly decent place,' I answered. 'The landlord's very friendly. By the way, there was a man there who'd rather overdone the drink, a big, dark man, rather surly. Do you know who I mean?'

Mrs Marsham stared at the road ahead, picked out by the light of her small torch. 'Everyone knows him,' she replied. 'His name's George Piper.'

It took a moment to sink in. 'George Piper?' I repeated. 'Any relation of the boy Tom? But he can't be,' I put in as an afterthought.

There was no pause in her stride or movement of her head to look at me as she said, 'His dad.'

I wanted to say that it was beyond my belief, but sensed that she had ended our conversation for the present. I was right—when she made up her mind to it, a subject would be closed.

As the days grew warmer and the evenings lighter I took to wandering in the woods after tea. To me, a town dweller, they resembled a vast forest and for fear of getting lost I only gradually increased my distances away even when I could discern a faint path. Sometimes I would hear a few distinct piping notes and tried to imagine the kind of bird that would be calling. I heard them again one evening as, grown bolder, I had ventured further than before and come upon a partial clearing leading to what looked to be the edge of a large lake. Making my way to it, I peered into the clear water that gently moved the reeds while having an uneasy feeling of not being alone. Then a small voice said, 'There's the biggest carp you ever seen in there, sir.'

I turned in the direction of the voice to find Tom sitting with his back against a tree, half hidden by bushes. 'You made me jump,' I said. 'I hadn't noticed you.'

'Sorry, sir. I come 'ere a lot.' He scrambled to his feet and came towards me, a crude, home-made whistle in his hand. 'If you sits quiet at sundown you c'n see all kinds o' creatures come to drink an' play. Do 'ee like animals?'

I had to think about that. At home, a succession of cats and dogs had been my only contact with them, but I knew I harboured no active dislike. 'Yes, I do.'

'Sometimes there be badgers, an' foxes wi' cubs, an' stoats, an' oh! All sorts. I talks to 'em an' plays me music.'

There was no mistaking his enthusiasm—shining eyes

and face come alive—so different from his usual reticence, more confident and at ease under the open sky.

'Do you have animals at home?' I asked.

'Oh, ay.' He nodded. 'I lives on a farm, anyways, but we don't farm livestock, jest veggies an' fruit an' grain. We've got an 'orse an' chickens an' a dog—an' sev'ral cats in the barns which keeps the rats down. I've got a tortoise, too, called Methy, who's me friend. 'Tis short for Methuselah. He's old—but not as old as Enoch were afore 'e died. He were Methy's father—like it says in Bible. They used to belong to Gran'fer. An' I've got some wild things that've bin 'urt, birds, mostly. I cares for 'em in a barn 'til they're better an c'n fly. Me dad don' like it, but I work roun' farm to make it up to 'im. Me mam helps me with 'em sometimes.'

I was finding it increasingly difficult to accept that the rough and sullen George Piper was this boy's father, hoping that I had misjudged my first estimate of him. Could the boy have been adopted, I wondered?

Anyway, I was glad he was talking so freely, and realised that a little encouragement would not come amiss. 'You know, you need help with your diction—that is, the way you speak—which would help you with your spelling, and as I know little about country matters you could teach me. Perhaps we could help each other.'

He considered this silently, then, 'I'd like that, sir,' and so a comradeship grew between us when we met and talked in the woods. I was surprised that I gained such enjoyment from the company of so young a lad and it had the added advantage of helping to turn my mind from Fiona. I yearned for closer intimacy with her as, though sometimes she appeared to flirt with me, at other times she ignored my very presence, blowing hot or cold as the fancy took her while keeping me on the boil with consummate ease. She had not yet acted on her father's suggestion to invite me to dinner, as I was anxiously waiting for her to do, and it was not until the end of April that there was any indication that I might gain her favour.

It was the first of May, May Day, when the holiday atmosphere of the pagan festival it represented brought excitement and gaiety to the village. The morning began with a parade of the children, the girls in white dresses and the boys wearing white shirts, all carrying bunches of flowers through the bedecked street. They walked behind the parish councillors, church officials and elders, but leading the procession marched the school band, their well-worn instruments rendering recognisable music. The bandsmen were all selected from the upper age group, except Tom. He was playing a recorder as Frank skipped alongside, possibly jeering at him from the expression evident on his face.

The parade ended in a large field known as the Fairfield, next to the village hall, where all outdoor events took place and where several tents and a maypole had been erected. The dignitaries dispersed as the crowd gathered and the band began to play for the younger children to dance. They stood in a circle around the pole, each holding a ribbon attached to the top, before weaving in and out as they danced until the ribbons were plaited down its length. Fiona was in charge, lovely in a loose, pale blue dress with a scarf, the flimsy material floating as she moved. My head swam with the desire to touch her, and when she caught my eye she gave a radiant smile and a little wave of her hand. When the dance was over, she took the bandsmen into a tent to leave their instruments until they should be required again and the crowd started to hurry home to dinner, anxious to return to enjoy the afternoon's entertainment, competitions, sports, cream teas and a dancing display by the girls.

Mrs Marsham and I left together, ambling slowly as it was sunny and hot. I was full of happiness—Fiona had smiled at me most amiably! We passed along the church wall fronting the cemetery until we came to the humpback bridge and the path sloping down to the near bank of the stream, its bubbling water flowing with a soothing, splashing noise on its way to the mill. I glanced upstream to where the path became lost amid the trees and asked how far it went.

'It goes right through the woods to a village over the rise, East Halsey. 'Twas once used as a short cut, but now only as a bridle path since they built a new road further up from school. Cottage Hospital lies halfway along that, which makes it handy for both villages. Jest out of our sight, there's a little wooden bridge over the stream. Cross it and go a bit further, an' you come to a small lake where the children us'ally play, then, if you walk on far enough you'll reach the big lake.'

Beyond the far bank of the stream, fields enclosed by hedges covered the gently rising hill, and what I took to be farm buildings were just visible among trees. I looked over the parapet at the flat-topped stepping stones rising from the water and saw that they connected the paths, overgrown in places by bushes, on each bank. A movement on the far side caught my attention and I saw Frank leap across the stones and on to the path below us. He was red in the face and breathing heavily but began to stroll up the slope nonchalantly, hands in pockets and whistling. As I was high up, I could see something moving along the far side of a hedge towards the buildings.

'What's the name of the place over there, Mrs Marsham?'

'That? Oh, that's Walnut Tree Farm, where the Pipers live.'

'I thought I saw someone running behind the hedge.'

'Prob'ly Tom on his way home to dinner—'tis quicker'n by the main road. George finds it useful, too, fer goin' to and from the inn. If he should happen to fall down behind a hedge he c'n sleep it off in safety, 'stead o' lying where he might get runned over.' I sensed no jesting, only disapproval in her voice.

Dinner over, we returned to the Fairfield. The amusements held no interest for me—I hoped to find Fiona more than anything else. The entire village seemed to have gathered there by this time, and I noticed a few boys behaving in an unruly manner—Frank in particular—which I tried to excuse as being due to the excitement. Later, I saw a tiny, poorly dressed woman I took to be his mother, giving him a talking to—not that he was taking much notice. Tom was nowhere in sight and I was surprised that he was missing the fun, but soon forgot about him when Fiona came and asked me to take her to the tea tent. She hung on my arm, chatting in an animated way, while I clung like a leech to her every word.

By the time we had finished our tea the band was due to play for a singsong, and Fiona left my side to reunite the bandsmen with their instruments. Soon afterwards I saw her anxiously scanning the field, so went to ask if I could help.

'Have you seen Tom?' she queried. 'Everyone's here but him.'

'No, I haven't. Maybe he's with his parents at the sideshows.'

She gave a short laugh. 'They never attend these occasions. The only place where George spends his money is at the inn.'

I thought back. 'Hold on a minute. I'm sure I saw Tom going home for dinner—could be something happened then. Tell you what, I'll run up there and find out. Be quick as I can.'

My long legs covered the ground to the bridge in record time, and I managed to cross the stream on the stones to reach a hedge that divided two cornfields, one stretching upwards towards the farm and the other down to the main road. Narrow paths on either side of the hedge were worn bare with use; by taking the lower one you could be seen from the road, but on the other side you were more or less hidden from view. I did not care which path I took, only to get there quickly, so hurried on to where I met another hedge separating the farm from the fields and found a gap to squeeze through. Facing me were barns and other out-buildings and one side of a squat farmhouse, where I saw a tall, spreading tree growing close, almost dwarfing it, one branch lying across and nearly touching an upper window. I went towards what I thought would be the front but had not moved far before a dog began to bark, so somewhat nervously rounded the corner and thankfully found the animal chained to a kennel and a woman standing in the entrance porch.

'Sorry to bother you,' I said, trying to get my breath back. 'Mrs Piper, is it? My name's Edward Parr, Tom's new teacher. Is he here? I'm trying to find him to play in the band again.'

I was closer now and could assess her more clearly, a pale, lean woman wearing a long, drab, brown skirt and blouse, her untidy, lacklustre hair scraped back into a knot, though wispy strands escaped around her sallow face. Her eyes were reddened, as if she had been weeping, and she had what appeared to be a bruise on her left cheek. I felt embarrassed, intruding on her.

Her voice, though, was quiet and steady. 'I'm afraid Tom won't be playing any more today. He caused an upset at dinnertime, coming 'ome with 'is new shirt wet an' dirty, so 'is dad says he's got to stay in 'is room. I'm so sorry. Would you be kind enough to tell Miss Macdonald?'

I had begun to say, 'Wouldn't your husband relent...' when he suddenly came out from the big barn.

'What's all this ruckus about, eh? Git back inside!' I was unsure whether he meant the dog or his wife, but then he saw me. 'What d'*you* want? Tom is it? Well, he'll be stayin'

44

in 'is room 'til termorrer. Comin' 'ome in the state 'e did—does 'e think I'm made o' money? An' you c'n tell Miss 'igh an' mighty Macdonald, oo's no better'n she should be, that she c'n stop feedin' 'im all the fancy ideas that're goin' to 'is 'ead. Now, you git orf me land!' and he stomped back into the barn.

Although incensed by his attitude there was little I could do apart from inviting a stand-up fight, which I would certainly lose while accomplishing nothing. Mrs Piper had disappeared, too, so I angrily made my way back to the Fairfield with my sorry tale to tell. Fiona received George's message with remarkable calm, an unexpected smile lifting the corners of her mouth, so the band performed without its recorder player though I doubt anyone noticed except, maybe, Frank. I was fairly sure that, jealous of Tom's part in the parade, he had waylaid him by the stream and deliberately dirtied his shirt. I had no proof or any notion of how best to deal with the outcome, only aware that with my inexperience I must tread warily—it would be so easy to make things worse between the two boys. I had intended to discuss the matter with Fiona at a dance to be held in the village hall that evening, but when they were packing up she said she would not be going as she had agreed to go out with friends, which sent another pang of jealousy through my heart and a black pall over my hopes. I was disappointed, having been certain she would spend the evening in my arms, albeit in public, so decided to visit the inn for consolation instead—before the possibility of encountering George Piper for a second time that day changed my mind.

I joined Mrs Marsham on the walk home, containing my despondency as we idly chatted about the day's events. After we had crossed over the bridge and passed the shops, I began to tell her of my visit to the Pipers' home just as we arrived at the rutted lane leading off to our right.

'Did you take this way up to their farm?' she asked.

'No, I didn't know it led up there—I took the short cut on the stepping stones over the stream. Mrs Piper must've been startled if she saw me suddenly appear through the hedge!' I then decided to ask my landlady something that had been bothering me. 'D'you know if her husband ill-treats her? Her face looked bruised, but it could've been an accident, I suppose. She seems such a poor, sad creature.'

'Since no one ever gets invited up to visit, your guess is as good as mine, Mr Parr, but George's reputation don't stand 'im in very good stead an' I have me s'picions. I rarely see Lucy Piper now, but I doubt her life's very happy. What d'you think? Isn't the change in her something wicked?'

'I wouldn't know,' I said. 'I've not seen her before to make any comparison.'

Mrs Marsham's reply was brief and without expression. 'Oh, excuse me, but you have. She's the girl in the painting—the girl in the yellow dress.'

Day 5

We continued walking in silence, Mrs Marsham seeming reluctant to elaborate on her last remark, and once back in the cottage we both found things to do until supper. Afterwards, she relaxed over the usual cups of tea and began to explain.

'Lucy Piper, or Lucy Howard as she were then, were orphaned when a baby an' brought up by her Aunt Sarah who lived above the draper's shop in the village. She served in the shop when she left school, an' towards the end o' the war in '18, was seventeen and a beauty. Most o' the men had gone away to fight, an' two she'd favoured were killed early on, so she were ready for romancing. Captain Quinton'd been staying here for some time afore they saw each other, since he kept away from the village, avoiding folk. Had his reasons, I s'pose.'

She drained her cup and poured another. 'Lucy was a daydreamer, you could tell by her far-away look, liking to wander alone in the woods. They finally met by chance, as I 'member, on August Bank Holiday Monday, when she'd put on her best frock, the yellow one, and set off to enjoy herself—as we all did that day. I saw her in the Fairfield with her Auntie, watchin' the donkey races, but she prob'ly got bored an' went into the woods to daydream her own pleasures. How surprised she must've felt when she saw the Captain! Thought all her wishes had come true, I shouldn't wonder, an' from then on she spent every moment she could with 'im. The summer were mostly fine so he sketched an' painted outside, coming in at dusk to tell me how she'd sit quite still out there, watching 'im work. I could see the trouble he were 'aving not to get fond of her. "I didn't mean for this to happen," he said one day. "I'd purposely kept away from people, but Lucy took me quite unawares."'

Mrs Marsham heaved a sigh and poured me another cup of tea. 'As the days grew shorter she'd come here after tea. She'd often come before as we sang in the choir together. I'd let 'em sit in the back parlour, but they behaved proper—kept the doors open. She must've longed for a cuddle, but he kept 'is distance as he knew how ill he were. Even if he should recover, I suspected, without ever knowin' for sure, that he could've bin trapped in a loveless marriage. Lucy were a loving maid, an' I was afeared she were expecting a future that could never be and end up badly hurt.'

'I can imagine how miserable they were,' I put in, comparing my own feelings at the lack of intimacy with Fiona.

My landlady cast me a glance, indicating her concern at my complete lack of understanding. 'Miserable? They were happy as any pair I ever saw! They were in love, an' jest knowin' it was enough for 'em for the time being without havin' to prove it! Courtships took a lot longer to get goin' then.'

She returned to her story. 'Things went on in like manner past Harvest Thanksgiving and All Saints. News of the war was allus slow comin', so the Armistice burst on us with the suddenness of a shell from one o' them big guns! At first we didn't believe it, then everyone went crazy. It turned into the maddest, most wonderful day I ever remember, only I did feel a bit sad 'cos my Bert weren't there to share it wi' me. The weather were drizzly, but people lit bonfires

48

and danced in the street an' the inn stayed open 'til all hours, so there were a lot o' drunkenness, men—an' women, to their shame—but those of us teetotal organised a party in the hall to do our dancing.' She smiled wistfully, searching into her memories.

'The excitement hadn't tempted the Captain out, the weather bein' bad for 'is chest, anyways. Lucy 'ad put on her yellow dress to mark the occasion and come to the hall, but I guessed she wouldn't stay long an' I soon saw her get her cloak an' slip out the door. Don't know what tale she told Aunt Emily 'cos she'd kept him secret from her, as he'd wanted her to do, and I'd kept me mouth shut. Emily was old an' wanderin' in her mind a bit, so t'was easy to confuse her.'

'She would've been used to Lucy going out on her own, though.'

'Not late at night an' in the wet *and* in her best dress, Mr Parr! Well, when I gets home it were well after midnight and there were still folk singin', shoutin' an' lying dead drunk along the road, despite the rain. I expected Lucy to have gone long since but found 'em both a-comin' down the stair, their faces so bright with love an' happiness that I weren't able to say an 'ard word about it. She already had her cloak wrapped around, an' he was wearing his great-coat. "I'm taking Lucy home," he said. "It's wild outside and she can't go alone." I tried to stop him by saying I'd go with her instead, but he took no notice. Lucy looked to be in a blissful dream, hanging on his arm as if she'd never let go. I waited up 'til he got back and made him a hot drink, seeing as he were a-shiverin' and his breathin' sounding awful. It got worse an' worse as the days wore on, an' I do wish I could've stopped him going out that night.'

'No blame can attach to you, Mrs Marsham,' I said.

'S'pose not ... He were somehow diff'rent from then on—he'd allus been keen to paint but now hardly spared

49

the time to eat—he must've begun her picture then. Also, whenever she visited he decided they should sit in the kitchen wi' me. I sensed that for some reason he didn't want to be alone with her, mebbe 'cos he didn't trust himself or regretted falling in love. They'd sit on that settee there, both restless, Lucy obviously longing to be alone with him while he was fighting his own longing.'

Mrs Marsham's face reflected her pity, knitting idle in her lap. 'A few weeks later, comin' up Christmas, I heard him cough most o' the night, an' when I took in his tea I found the candles guttering. I opened the curtains an' saw the picture hanging where it is now, where he could see it from the bed, and turned to tell him how much I liked it but never got the words out. His pillow were covered in blood and his face as white as a bride's veil, his big, blue eyes starin' wide, an' he give a smile that barely moved 'is mouth. "Seems it's time for me to go home." His voice was faint, and I wondered which home he meant, on earth or up above. "I'll get the doctor," I said, but he shook 'is 'ead. "Nothing he can do—and I don't want Lucy told yet. Will you get the cabbie to pick me up today?"'

'Surely he wasn't fit to travel?'

'O' course not, but what could I do? I helped him pack, but he didn't let me put the new picture with his other paintings. "I must tell you about that one," he said. "I want Lucy to have it, but it can't be varnished 'til it's dry. I've left a bottle of the stuff and a brush, so I'd be obliged if you'd give it a thin coat in a few month's time, about Easter, then give it to her—she might've forgiven me by then."'

Mrs Marsham forcefully tut-tutted to indicate the foolishness of the man. 'I thought that either his mind was befuddled or he knew nothing at all about women! I felt anxious for Lucy. "Have you got a note for her?" I asked, hoping he'd offer her some explanation. "No—what could I say? I don't want her to know how ill I really am and try to find me, as I know she would—I'd rather she thought me a scoundrel! Promise me you'll keep it to yourself." I nodded. "Tell her I'll love her dearly for the rest of my life, but she must forget me and marry someone who can care for her."

'He were a-gaspin' then an' could hardly speak—an' neither could I for me tears. I were so sad to let him go. I did manage to ask for a forwarding address but he kept silent, and as no letters had ever come for him there weren't much point. When Jim arrived, we packed the Captain's goods in the cab, made him as comfy as we could, and I watched 'em drive away. Jim knows where he took 'im, but I never tried to find out in case I was told to mind me own business. I don't know how I got through the rest o' that day—dreading Lucy comin'.' She pulled out a handkerchief and dabbed at her eyes. 'I knew there'd be no way to break it gently, but I didn't have to, anyways. When she saw my face her own set like marble, like the angels in the churchyard. I said what he'd told me to say and she didn't cry, just stared as if tryin' to put meaning to me words. "Where's he gone?" she asked, in a flat kind o' voice. I said I'd no idea, which was true, but I doubt she believed it. "There's nothing, nothing in this world that would've made me leave him," she whispered, so quiet I scarcely heard. "He's a liar and a cheat," and she ran out the back into the woods. Later, I began to fret when I remembered the lake and how all the sense had prob'ly bin knocked out of her, so got the storm lantern and followed without finding nothin'. I finally give up and 'ad a sleepless night, going early to the draper's shop next day to find her behind the counter, her face still frozen and her eyes red, but more or less in charge of herself. "'Tis lucky 'twas only you knew about us," she greeted me, bitterly. "At least the whole village isn't laughing at me for being such a fool!" I longed to hint at the truth to help her understand but all I could do was promise

51

never to tell a soul, though, as it come about, nobody needed to be told.'

'I see what you mean,' I said. 'The Captain put you in a very difficult position.'

'He didn't mean to, an' he obviously had no idea of the trouble he were leavin' behind.' She stood up, then changed her mind and sat down again.

'While I'm about it, I'd better tell it all. Well, it happened that the Piper boys arrived home on leave from the Army for Christmas. Old Tom, their dad, tetchy man that 'e were, had tried to manage farm on his own and let it run right down. George, the eldest by a couple o' year, was wild and unruly, as 'e is now, forever forcing others to test their strength against his, but Robbie, though alike in colour, is of a slighter build and quieter, like his dead mam. His trouble is that he c'n never resist a gamble on just about anything. So, George was bein' discharged from the Army but Robbie had decided to stay on, the farm not bein' big enough for three to work it, anyways, an' there was Lucy on the rebound and there were George an' Robbie—I think Robbie would've won her if he'd stayed home.'

She gazed, unseeing. 'Well, soon after he went back the banns were called. I couldn't believe it, an' tried to tell Lucy what I thought and also tell her about the painting, but she looked right through me—as she's done ever since—saying she didn't want me interfering any more or bringing up the past, so I held me tongue. She an' George were wed early in the Feb'ry, and appeared happy enough to start. Can't say I envied her living with her ill-tempered father-in-law, but she still served in the draper's which got her away part o' the time. She'd left the choir, mebbe to avoid me, rarely coming to church, an' George 'ad settled down, behavin' himself at last, when it became plain there was to be an addition to the fam'ly.'

Mrs Marsham lifted the long poker lying against the brass

fender and poked the fire vigorously before noticing the dirty dishes left on the table, so she started to clear away. I helped with the washing-up, our conversation monosyllabic, thoughts turned inward, until she sat down and picked up her knitting again.

'I'll do a few more rows as I tell the rest. Lucy's auntie died that summer, so she stopped goin' to the shop. George were cheerful and I heard he were treating her proper, proud for the world to know he'd proved himself a man, no doubt. Then, early September, the village buzzed wi' the news that the midwife, who was booked for the end of October, had been called to farm. Eyebrows were raised 'til we were told a boy had been born premature. George were down at the inn that night doing what was unheard of— buyin' a round o' drinks—an' boasting 'bout his fine son to be named Thomas after his gran'fer, poor mite.' She sniffed at the thought.

'The winds blew rough that autumn and Lucy kept the babe indoors for 'is 'ealth, so she said. I visited with a gift but felt unwelcome, only being let a peep in the cot at the boy swathed in shawls. He were quite old afore being taken out in village, when tongues began to wag in earnest. Well, you know what Tom looks like, with 'is fair hair and blue eyes, Lucy a brunette, George as dark as a gipsy, an' both of 'em brown-eyed. There were some who'd caught a sight o' the Captain, too, Jim Carter for one and folk nearby, who could see the lad were the spitting image.'

'I can understand now why Tom is so different,' I muttered, quietly.

'By this time, George 'ad run true to form and gone back to his early way o' ridin' roughshod over everyone, an' the gossip made him worse. Lucy was seen less an' less, wi' no friends left—George scared 'em away. I think he felt he'd been tricked into marrying her, but there's allus the chance that Lucy didn't know 'bout the babe herself when the banns were called and, mebbe, artless as she were, not even 'til after the wedding. She might truly have b'lieved George were the father—'til she saw her newborn an' knew for sure.'

'Did you hear from the Captain again?'

She shook her head. 'I doubt he lived much longer. Well, there's not a deal more to tell, Mr Parr. Old Tom died very sudden 'bout four year back, with the funeral handled in the cheapest way possible. We wondered who'd benefit most by the will 'cos it were rumoured he'd been a bit of a miser, but nowt was heard so p'raps there weren't one, and George, the eldest, took the lot. Nobody knew for sure an' Robbie made no fuss. After all, he'd made his life in the Army so he wouldn' want farm, but we never heard if there were any money left. You us'ally hear things like that in a village, but not this time, though George allus has money to spend at the inn without the bother o' workin' farm as well as he might. He does jest enough to keep things ticking over without makin' too much effort. 'Tis a waste—he should farm all the land which now lies idle.'

My thoughts were on the boy. 'Young Tom, does he know about the Captain?'

Mrs Marsham shrugged her shoulders. 'No idea. The boys used to rag him for seeming diff'rent but he'd take no notice—'twas as if he never 'eard. George did once though, an' give the boy with the loose tongue a good hidin'. That were Frank—an' he's been careful ever since to keep his lip buttoned when George were near. Oh, my—there's the ten-fifteen's whistle—time we were a'bed!'

Up in my room I regarded the picture with renewed interest, now aware of why it was hidden away from prying eyes. I wondered what would happen to it, wishing it could be mine. Lucy would surely never want it, I thought, remembrance would be too painful—though she must be reminded of her lost love whenever she laid eyes on her

54

son—and George was unlikely to give it house room, but what about Tom? If other paintings by John Quinton ever saw the light of day and he became a popular artist, it could become his legacy.

After this, I regarded the boy with increased curiosity, knowing how he had come by his artistic ability. I imagined that Fiona already knew, but when I tried to raise the subject of his father with her she began to flirt with me without listening. As I was still smarting, in my immature way, from her refusal to let me escort her to the dance in order to gallivant with an unknown admirer elsewhere, I refused to respond, so the matter was dropped.

Having little encouragement to be with her as much as I desired, that being the operative word, I spent more time by the lake, sometimes meeting up with Tom and listening to his tales of the countryside. I became familiar with the names of trees, flowers and plants, and the habits of birds and animals. Tom had a rapport with them, so gentle and patient that they allowed his approach without fear, but more wary if I was about, he said. One Sunday afternoon, we were lounging on the grass by the edge of the water as I talked about famous historical figures, when there came a sudden loud flapping and whirring of wings. I sat up, startled, to see ducks flying overhead.

'Ducks!' I exclaimed. 'I didn't know they could fly—they look too heavy and awkward. I thought they only swam!'

Tom shook with laughter, asking me what I thought they had wings for. After that, he amiably teased me whenever we saw them waddling about on the bank. Another time, as we lay quietly looking at the clear blue sky, I saw a bird high up, swinging lazily from side to side, then circling and hovering, and asked what it was.

He shaded his eyes. 'That's a kestrel, lookin' fer food. I'd love to be a bird up there, flyin' above the world, free, able to go wherever I want.' He turned his head to look at me.

'Do 'ee know, their eyesight's so good they c'n spot a vole an' swoop on it in seconds?' He chewed on a blade of grass while continuing his contemplation of the bird. 'Thing is, he's waitin' to pounce so's he c'n eat an' live, 'cos 'e's hungry. Can't imagine me doin' that—I hates killin'. S'pose I might think diff'rent if I were a bird, though . . .' he caught my eye and quickly tried to justify himself, '. . . then I'd do it like 'im, an' kill so fast that whatever it were wouldn't 'ave time to know what 'ad 'appened to it. I shouldn't feel so badly then.'

He gently stroked the back of a beetle as it scurried through the grass before continuing with his theme. 'I once climbed to the top of a tree an' jumped down, tryin' to fly, jest to know what it felt like, but knocked meself out an' hurt me arm an' got a beltin' 'cos I couldn't 'elp wi' the chores.' He glanced again at the sky, fixing the position of the sun. 'Gosh! I'd better git off 'ome—I'm later'n I should be.'

I looked at this small boy's scabby knees showing below the short trousers, noticing the bruises on his legs. He had some on his arms, too, but I knew that all boys are inclined to fall over and knock themselves about sometimes, then suddenly realised that he seemed to have them *all* the time. 'D'you often get . . .' I hesitated over the word '. . . a belting?'

'On'y when I does somethin' I shouldn',' he said with a smile.

'Like when you spoilt your new shirt on May Day?'

The smile vanished and he glanced sideways at me. 'I fell in the stream,' he said, defensively.

'Are you sure you weren't pushed? I thought I saw Frank down there. Does he bully you?'

He coloured up. 'I can 'old me own with 'im. I only needs to see 'im in school. I gen'rally knows when he's in the woods an' then I keep away. I likes to be off on me own,

56

evenin's, when weather's fine. There's allus somethin' to be done on farm 'til then, so when I goes to bed I sometimes climbs out o' me winder an' along an 'andy branch o' the walnut tree, then I'm away to the woods, no matter what time 'tis. Me dad don't like it, case I sees somethin' I shouldn' 'e says, an' if 'e ketches me I gets a beltin' an' 'e nails up the winder, but the frame's rotten an' the nails come out if I shakes it 'ard enough, so I goes on doin' it—an' so do 'e.'

'You know, you must give some attention to your aitches and the ends of your words—try to speak more slowly and think about what you're saying, as I've told you before,' I reminded him, while giving myself time to assimilate what he had said. 'I remember seeing that tree when I called one day—a walnut, you said. Did the farm take its name from that? And tell me, why doesn't your father cut off the branch—that would stop you!'

He grinned as he slowly exaggerated his words. 'Yes, sir. Everybody knows the farm because of the tree, an'—and it is easy to see that you do not know very much about walnut trees. For one thing, they bleed if the branches are cut, and for another, the nuts fetch a fancy price at Christmas jes'—just for the pickin'—picking. That branch happens to be a very good cropper, so me dad would hardly want to get rid of it, would 'e—he? I must go—I'll be skinned alive!'

I saw the logic of his reasoning as I watched him run towards home. The more I saw of him, the more I approved of this well-favoured child who was only separated from my own youth by a handful of years, condemning out of hand the conduct of both George Piper and Frank Acaster with their similar attitudes. And I began to wonder what George sometimes did at night that he did not want Tom to see. Stagger home drunk, probably.

Day 6

The Whitsun holiday was due to take place towards the end of May and would combine with half term, which was only a matter of a day or two then. I was aware of the unspoken approval of myself as demonstrated by Miss Millard and the school in general, although I found my duties, with the limited teaching I was able to offer, becoming tedious. Added to which, the giggling schoolgirls—the moony-eyed ones who had a 'crush' on me and followed me around whenever I was trying to engage Fio, as I now allowed myself to think of her, in intimate converse, were especially irritating. She was being as elusive as ever, either busy with others or nowhere to be found, while each day I steeled myself to reveal my true feelings towards her. I knew that I must take care in my approach—the idea of being rebuffed, of having her laugh at me, was unbearable. I noticed the nervous energy evident in everything she undertook, as if driven by a need to fill each waking moment; even when at rest she seemed alert, ready for anything. I wondered if her mother had been the same and, with little to occupy her in this remote place, had opted for a fuller life elsewhere.

I sometimes had a drink with Dr Mac in the Snug, appreciating his bluff good humour and obvious regard for the villagers. Several times I had been on the verge of asking if he thought Mrs Piper was being ill treated, but had nothing more definite to go on and was pretty sure that little escaped his observant eye. So why had he not seen his own wife's need and moved to a practice offering more social activity? I then recalled the old proverb that the cobbler's family were always the worst shod.

I grew familiar with the locals who frequented the inn. One of the most popular was Wills, the village constable, who lived with his wife in the police house near the Cottage Hospital, and became used to seeing him wheeling his bike about at all hours, a massive man with huge feet and a severe tone of voice which, when he first spoke to me, made me feel guilty with nothing to feel guilty about at that time. Mrs Marsham described him as being the best of men, going out of his way to help offenders if he could—not that there were many of *them*, she said. His very presence prompted prospective wrongdoers to think twice and change their minds. I found him, and most of the others, readily prepared for an exchange of views, which eased my sense of isolation.

Dr Mac encouraged me to talk about Fio. It seemed as if he wanted me to get to know her better and he surprised me one evening by saying, 'You haven't been to dinner with us yet, so how about next Saturday? There's no foreseeable reason for me to be called out then—no immediate pregnancies to come to the boil! Can't answer for Fio, of course, but a word in her ear should ensure her presence. Make it seven thirty.'

I said I would be delighted to come, telling Fio the same when I saw her in school next day. She gave a little laugh and told me not to be late, so I duly arrived full of anticipation on the bicycle and on the dot, only to be met with very unwelcome news by her apologetic father.

'The dear girl had forgotten she already had a date for tonight,' he said, sounding genuinely concerned. 'A friend came to pick her up half an hour ago, so she had no alternative but to go off with him. She asked me to tell you how sorry she is, and looks forward to seeing you on Monday. Now, come and have a sherry or a whisky or whatever you fancy, Eddie, and don't feel too disappointed!'

The only thing I really fancied was Fio, and disappointed I certainly was, failing to fully appreciate the meal or the wine, though both were excellent. I was regaled by amusing stories of the doctor's student days and Fio's accomplishments paraded before me as surely being of interest, but nothing could shut out the sight of the empty chair opposite mine. Having eaten, we went into the lounge to listen to music on the wireless while drinking coffee with a liberal supply of brandy—which went straight to my head—and a little later the phone rang. A maid called the doctor out of the room, and he soon returned to say there was an emergency.

'Sorry about this, old chap. I must go—though it sounds as if it might be a false alarm . . .' But I had got quickly to my feet and nearly lost my balance. 'Steady on,' he continued. 'Look, how about me giving you a lift home? It's on my way. You can leave the bike here and pick it up some other time. It's getting late, anyhow.'

And Fio not home yet, I thought, having foolishly hoped she might turn up before I left. My head was swimming, so I wisely agreed to his suggestion.

After church next day I went back to the house, ostensibly to fetch the bike and deliver a 'thank you' note, but really to confront Fio. The doctor's car was absent as I rang the bell, handed my note to the maid, and asked to see Miss Macdonald.

'I'm sorry, sir, but she's staying with friends and won't be back 'til late tonight. Is there any message?'

I was too taken aback to think of anything to say apart from, 'No—thanks,' and at that moment this worm turned. I rode back to the cottage at a furious rate, arriving there at the same time as Mrs Marsham, who had made her own leisurely way home. She gave me one look before suggesting I take a walk until dinner was ready. My temper had not much improved by the time it was and I doubt she found my conversation scintillating as we ate, but she politely ignored my petulance.

The following day, still beside myself with jealousy, I tackled Fio as soon as I could get her alone even though having to keep my voice lowered, which somewhat cramped my style. 'Where were you yesterday?' I began, gripping her arm, aware that I was hissing like a soda siphon, '*and* on Saturday? Am I so hateful that you take these means to avoid me? You must know how I feel about you, even though you don't give me any opportunity to show it! How d'you expect me to continue in this miserable way?'

A faint smile flickered around her eminently desirable mouth and her lovely eyes narrowed, coolly fixing on mine. The smile widened as she gently disengaged my hand from her arm. 'My, my,' she whispered. 'I *am* surprised! You're growing up. There is some stuffing in you after all.'

Then it was my turn to feel surprise as she kissed me hard on the cheek and was gone through the door, leaving me with my mind in turmoil. She adroitly managed to evade me for the rest of the week

The Whitsun holiday began the weekend after, with a travelling fair setting up various rides and sideshows in the Fairfield. Sunday was a solemn church day, but on Monday the excitement became plainly evident, though I had no presentiment of the effect it was to have on my limited experience of life.

The sun shone in a cloudless sky as bare-armed girls, their young men in light jackets and open-necked shirts like myself, and the more conservative men in stiff collars with their wives equally uncomfortably corseted, flocked to the Fairfield bent on enjoying themselves. I looked for Fio when I arrived but failed to see her in the crowd, so wandered

61

around the sideshows while listening to the shrieks coming from the helter-skelter.

All the pupils from school were there, even the Misses Millard and Hope, and Mrs Richards, I knew, would be in charge of the tea tent. I came across Frank watching the coconut shying, while Tom's attention was taken by the rifle range. A man I had not seen before was shooting, and I noticed that when he finally laid down the rifle he collected a prize and passed it to Tom. They began to walk in my direction when the boy saw me and grasped the man's hand, urging him forward.

'Mr Parr!' he called. 'Mr Parr—this is me Uncle Robbie on leave from the Army, so 'e's good at shootin'—look what 'e's won.' He held up a large woolly dog.

I viewed the fellow with interest, knowing he could have some influence over Tom, while noticing, as Mrs Marsham had mentioned, that he was similar to his brother, George, but fashioned in a less coarse mould, finer featured, of a trimmer physique and better dressed, casual but neat. The strap of a bulky canvas bag was thrown over one shoulder. He held out a hand as they came up to me.

'Mr Parr—Tom's been tellin' me 'bout you.' He gently knuckled the boy's chin. 'He's me best an' only nephew, an' I wants 'im to do well at 'is lessons.'

I responded in kind and we chatted for a while, until they moved away to try their hands at the hoop-la stall. I was glad Tom had company and money being spent on him, and while I was wondering if Frank had any money to spend, a man shouting through a megaphone announced a tug o' war taking place and I saw him running towards it. He would be all right with something to watch, I was thinking, just as I became conscious of someone behind me.

'I'm glad I've found you,' a soft voice whispered in my ear. 'Was that Robbie I saw you talking to just now?'

I turned, my heart thumping, to find her face to face with me, so close that our breaths mingled. I wanted to kiss this lovely pink-cheeked damsel but dared not, stepping back instead to enable me to view her in entirety. She was wearing a silky, green, low-cut dress, which hung straight from narrow shoulder straps to flounce out just above the knees in, to my way of thinking, a provocative manner. I can still recall it in detail, and also that I was resenting the fact that other men could look at her and share the pleasure the sight of her gave me.

Suspecting that she might have an interest in Robbie, my reply was short. 'Yes, it was. Obviously you know him.'

'Grew up with him, dearie.' Her hand had slipped from my arm to my wrist, and gave it a squeeze. 'Don't you find this tinny roundabout music noisy? And it's so crowded and hot. Wouldn't it be lovely just to be on our own by the big lake in the woods? Would you like that?'

I gulped before managing to say, 'Are you suggesting . . . ?'

'I think it would be much, much nicer,' she broke in, 'and we should take advantage of the opportunity while everyone's busy here—don't you agree, Eddie?'

I nodded, too surprised for words.

'Then I'll go home and make my way from there—I can get into the woods from the end of our garden. You leave a bit later and go up by the stream path and over the little bridge—that way we'll avoid sharp eyes and wagging tongues. You know how people talk about the most innocent of actions . . .'

I watched her go, to stop briefly for a word with Robbie, and after an impatient few minutes, idled my way past the church and along the stream path until I reached the wooden bridge, which was out of sight of the village, and entered the wood. Glad of the shade from the trees, I took off my jacket, hoping the cooler air would disperse both the

63

sweat on my forehead and the dampness I could feel between my shoulder blades. Thank Heaven I had taken the weekly bath I was allowed only two days before! An added discomfort was caused, not only by the heat of the day, but also by my extreme nervousness at this totally unexpected tryst. Would she let me put my arms around her? Even kiss her? I thrilled in joyful anticipation.

There was no sign of her when I finally arrived at the peaceful stretch of water, so I replaced my jacket to hide the braces holding up my trousers to observe the rules of respectability. As I sat down to wait I heard a tinkling laugh and got to my feet again to discover the source, moving towards it when the disembodied laugh was repeated. Suddenly an arm reared up and waved from a thick clump of grass and ferns a short distance away, rather in the manner of a snake that had been lying in wait for some unwary traveller. An apt analogy, as it happens! Then a head disclosed itself, with the short, red hair and flawless face that so entranced me, open mouth showing gleaming white teeth bared in a mocking grin.

'Took your time, didn't you? I wondered if you'd taken fright and decided to stay penned in with the sheep in the Fairfield!' A hand beckoned. 'Come on.'

As I moved closer I saw that the green dress had provided a perfect camouflage, so ceased to mentally kick myself for being unobservant. She reached up to pull me down, wrinkling her nose, whether from distaste at the sweaty heat I was generating or at the hindrance of my buttoned-up jacket. I hoped at the latter, because as she pushed me on my back she pulled at the buttons while pressing her mouth hard on mine. I put my arms around her and felt her hands move to other buttons, on my shirt and trousers, her hasty fingers forcing open, fumbling, probing, her mouth panting against mine, while I felt my very being would explode.

All of a sudden she was still, her head resting on my bare

64

chest, then slowly got to her feet. She stood above me, swaying slightly, staring down into my eyes, a strange expression on her face, before kicking off her shoes and deliberately slipping the straps of her dress over her shoulders. I watched as the silk slid down her naked body to lie crumpled at her feet, reminded of Botticelli's picture of the Birth of Venus as she stood motionless, without shame, inviting me to look my fill.

Nothing had prepared me for this—it surpassed my wildest imagining. I had never before seen a female in the flesh and was now past rationalizing my emotions. I was also at a loss to know what was expected of me, stupefied into paralysis. Spellbound, I gazed at her rosy-nippled breasts and firm, taut belly as she loomed above me, legs apart to steady herself. I dared not move—afraid this beautiful goddess might vanish. It must be obvious to you now, Paul, how incredibly naïve I was. She began to walk away towards the lake as I eyed her slim waist with sheer delight, the long legs tapering from shapely thighs to delicate, slender ankles. Then her voice, low and thick and seeming to come from miles and miles away, at last broke the spell that bound me.

'For goodness' sake, Eddie, take your clothes off!'

I complied as quickly as I could and hurried after her, feeling defenceless and foolish in my unaccustomed nudity. She reached the edge of the lake and turned to look back, regarding me with a searching stare.

'You'd better take off your watch, and shoes, and socks, with those silly suspenders. A man always looks so funny wearing nothing but his socks—it makes me want to laugh! Hope you can swim . . .' and with a splash she was gone.

Somewhat deflated, I unlaced my shoes, putting my watch in one and socks in the other, wincing as sharp twigs bit into the sensitive flesh of my bared feet. I was wishing I had studied the subject of carnal passion more fully, read serious books about it or discussed it with others. Indeed, I had deliberately refrained from preparing myself for the act of love-making, intending to wait until I found the right girl to marry so we could learn together—with me as the dominant and controlling half, of course! I was in no way ready for this sudden sexual onslaught.

Walking carefully to the edge of the lake, feeling more foolish than I had ever felt in my life and wanting to be a hundred miles away, yet, paradoxically, vitally aware that there was no other place in the world that I would rather be, I stepped on to some flat stones leading into the water. I was trying to balance myself when a hand shot up and grabbed an ankle, pulling me sideways. I tried to save myself, grabbing at air, afraid of knocking myself out on the bottom, but the water was deeper than I had guessed. The coldness on my hot skin made me gasp as I rose to the surface, spluttering, opening my eyes to see Fio's amused face approach mine. She clutched me to her as her eager mouth clamped over mine, and we trod water in an embrace that ceased only when I fought for breath.

'That's much better,' she said in a mocking tone, swimming away, her body gliding palely through the clear water. 'You're starting to get the hang of it now—you know, practice makes perfect! Let's get out.'

She swam to the side and climbed on to the stones, shaking her head, flinging droplets of water from her hair, smoothing it with her fingers, then lifted her arms and twirled around, laughing, more a mischievous wood nymph now than a goddess, before tiptoeing to where grass and ferns grew in a thick bed and dropped down.

'Eddie . . . Eddie . . .' I heard her call.

I knew exactly what was expected of me now as I pulled myself up on to the bank, only I was not feeling like me any more but like another, previously unknown, licentious person, wild, out of control. There was no concern for saving my feet from injury as I ran to where she lay on her back

66

awaiting me. I flung myself on her, uttering sounds that came from some alien throat until at last we were still, exhausted, and silence fell again. We remained so until she pushed me from her.

'Not bad for a beginner,' she drawled. 'In fact, not bad at all.' She yawned, stretching her arms. 'We should go back—hopefully we haven't been missed. We have to consider your reputation, after all!'

Still wallowing in passion and gratitude, I overlooked being surprised at her concern for my reputation rather than her own. I tried to kiss her again, but she dodged away while stepping into her dress and slipping on her shoes.

'Don't overdo it, Eddie—tomorrow is another day. I'll go back the way I came, and you do likewise.'

I clung to the word. 'Tomorrow, then? Shall we meet here again?'

She paused. 'No, it's another holiday, with nothing for anyone to do this time, so the woods will probably be full of yelling children. Anyway, I'm going into town, shopping. I'll see you at assembly on Wednesday. 'Bye.'

I was reluctant to let her go. 'What about this evening?' I called. 'There's another dance in the hall we can go to . . .'

She waved a hand. 'Sorry . . .' and moved out of sight.

Disappointed and uncomfortable with my person exposed to the world, and suddenly feeling as if I was being spied upon, I collected my scattered garments and covered my clammy skin, picking off bits of grass and leaves before retrieving my watch from a shoe. I strapped it on, but my sock suspenders I viewed with a new dislike and put them in a pocket. Once clothed, I felt more able to piece together the startling transformation this afternoon had brought about, surging exhilaration all but overwhelming me.

I decided not to return to the Fairfield, sure that people would be able to read the triumph on my face, so followed the faint track back to the cottage in order to tidy myself

67

and reflect on how life had changed. On the way I began to make plans, feeling ten feet tall, shoes hardly touching the ground. I had found the girl of my dreams, we were in love, would get engaged and, after a suitable delay to enable me to complete two or three years as housemaster, we would be married. Wet behind the ears, are you thinking? True.

I left a note for Mrs Marsham to say I was resting on my bed with a headache, feeling a pang of conscience when I heard her creeping about so as not to disturb me. With the six-thirty train whistling in the distance, I dragged myself up and stared into the laughing eyes of the girl in the painting.

'I can understand how it happened to you, Lucy—it's happened to me now,' I mouthed, endeavouring to wipe the fatuous grin off my face and replace it with a nonchalant countenance before descending the stairs.

Mrs Marsham was full of concern and, I thought, perhaps I had actually acquired a pallor, but it was not long before I forgot myself and began to bubble over with happiness as we chatted during the meal. I noticed her eyeing me with curiosity—she was very perceptive—and forced myself into solemnity again.

'Going to the dance tonight, Mr Parr? There'll be lots o' maids very put out if you don't turn up. You caused a great upset last time by not going, letting 'em down, I've heard tell. You wouldn't go far wrong with any o' the village lasses, y'know. They're all good maids—ev'ry one.'

I was suspicious of her turn of phrase, but smiled weakly. 'Out of the question, I'm afraid. I need an early night to recover—and don't dance very well, as I've mentioned before, so I'd be glad if you'd pass on my excuses.'

I was aware of her studying my face, which I was trying to avert. 'Hum—you certainly don't look quite like you did, so per'aps you've been sickenin' for somethin' now due to come to an 'ead. You'll have to be watching yerself.'

I silently agreed with everything she had said.

Day 7

I sank into an exhausted sleep that night and the following day caught up with a few chores, one of which was to clean and oil the doctor's bicycle, before returning to yesterday's place of enchantment after dinner. I could not put Fio out of my mind, and lay by the lake reliving every moment of that magical ecstasy. I also planned how, after buying my car, I would take my love home to meet Mother and Joyce, knowing they would approve of her, a doctor's daughter, well educated and lovely with it, plus the fact that we loved each other dearly—the most important thing of all.

Fio had been right when she said the woods would be full of children today, although they were mostly centred on the small lake nearer the village. I could hear distant voices and laughter and the barking of dogs, and hoped my solitude would not be encroached upon, even by Tom, then realised he was probably required to work on the farm even though his uncle was home to lend a hand. As my mind wandered in that direction, I thought it a pity that Robbie had not stayed back after the war for Lucy to have married him instead—he would have made a far more suitable father for Tom—and opened my eyes to find myself looking full into the fellow's smiling face.

'Hello, there,' he said. 'Sorry if I made 'ee jump—you can't've 'eard me comin'. Stayin' wi' Bessie, I b'lieve. I see you've found one o' me fav'rite places—folk don't often come this far into the woods.'

I scrambled into a sitting position, hugging my knees, smiling in return as he sat down beside me while accepting that I would have to defer my daydreaming. 'It's perfect,' I answered. 'You must be sorry you can't be here more often.'

'I spend as much time as I want. Makes a nice change every so often, visitin' me old huntin' grounds, but I enjoys me work, too. I'm attached to a photographic unit in me regiment, an' allus glad to get back to it. Be makin' Corporal any time.'

'That's good,' I said. 'Tom will be pleased—and proud. You seem to get on well together.'

He nodded. 'Ay, we do. I'd like to be aroun' to help 'im more.'

I lifted an enquiring eyebrow, and he shifted his position as he went on. 'I mean, I'd like to take 'im about—show 'im what goes on in the world. He don't go anywheres very much.'

I twirled a stalk of grass in my fingers, considering. 'I imagine there'll be plenty of time for that—nothing for you to worry about. There must be few boys in the village with the chance to travel, and for the time being they can learn a great deal about the world from books. Tom needs other things more, encouragement, friends—and a happy, stable family life.' I awaited his reaction.

He glanced at me obliquely. 'I sees what yer getting' at an' I must say I agrees with 'ee, but I'm not one to interfere in things which don' concern me d'reckly. I does me best for the youngster, but 'ave ter make sure I'll be welcome next time me leave comes aroun'. The farm's allus been me home, the only one I've ever known, and I 'ave no intention of losin' it. Unnerstand what I'm sayin?'

I replied that I realised he was in a difficult position. I found myself liking him and wondered if he would come back here when he finally left the Army, but perhaps he would marry and live elsewhere. He presented himself as being open-minded and caring, and I felt that while he was here he would do his best to protect Tom and Lucy from his brother's violent nature. I noticed his kitbag and a rifle on the ground—or maybe it was a shotgun—I would not have known the difference.

'Have you brought the gun for target practice?'

'Might bag a few wood pigeon or a coupl'a rabbits fer the pot—whatever.'

'I saw you shoot at the fair yesterday,' I said. 'You're a good shot—won that dog for Tom. What does he think about you killing things?'

Robbie shrugged his shoulders. 'He don't like it much, he's too soft-'earted, but he's been brought up on a farm an' knows folks 'ave to eat. Says it's better'n killin' people, anyways—which we 'ad ter do in the war.' He laughed. 'He's right, there, 'twere some waste. We couldn't eat any o' they, could us?'

I supposed that, living in barracks as he did, he was used to such witticisms, so had to be excused for displaying what was, to me, an unfunny sense of humour. I produced a faint smile and changed the subject. 'Tom's doing well at school, but he could be doing better if he didn't have to work so much at home. He finds it hard to concentrate when he's tired.' And unhappy, I nearly added.

'He should'n' be tired.' Robbie scratched his dark head, a twinkle in his brown eyes. 'George sees to it that he spends a lot o' time shut up in 'is room wi' nothin' else to do but rest hisself.'

I did not think it was a twinkling matter, but put it down to that odd sense of humour again.

Robbie levered himself to his feet. 'Best be on me way an' see what I can find fer tea—mebbe nowt. See you in "The Guidin' Light" this even'?'

71

I was reminded to ask about the origin of the name, but not now; I wanted to be left on my own. 'That's a good idea. There's a film showing in the hall that I'm not keen on seeing, so after I've taken Mrs Marsham there I'll come over.'

'Why don't ye call 'er Bessie, same's ev'ryone else? Sure she'd rather. Well, see you later, then.' He picked up his gun and the rather lumpy canvas kitbag, gave a mock salute and went marching off around the lake. There is no mistaking the smart bearing of a soldier, even in civvies.

I lay down under a large tree and tried to resume my contemplation of Fio, itemising everything about her from her glorious red head right down to the toes on her dainty feet, until a sudden, sharp *crack!* very close by brought me to my knees ready to take evasive action. I tried to rationalise it. Was Robbie shooting at me?

A giggle coming from somewhere near allayed my fears but brought anger in its wake. My eyes searched for the culprit and alighted on Frank Acaster, catapult in hand, trying in vain to straighten his face and hide himself. My initial instinct, occasioned by shock, was to grab and shake him, but I managed to restrain myself with difficulty. Instead, I stood up with as much dignity as I could muster and went to where he now stood as if frozen to the spot, a look of alarm replacing the amusement. I snatched the catapult from him.

'What on earth are you doing?' I asked, fuming, though tending to calm down as the shock diminished. 'Don't you know how dangerous these things can be? What were you trying to hit?'

He shifted from one foot to the other, appearing acutely discomforted, cringing away from me. 'That tree—sir,' he said feebly, 'an' I *did* hit it. I didn' see you underneath, honest I didn'—not 'til ye moved.'

'And then you thought it very funny, I suppose.'

'Well, sir, I were s'prised to see you hidin' in the grass like a rabbit.'

Studying his woebegone face I decided he was not intending to be insolent and, having recovered from my fright, had a desperate urge to laugh at the picture he had vividly portrayed so, endeavouring to keep my expression under control, I said, 'I wasn't hiding but meditating, boy, an exercise you'd do well to copy before you make another of these contraptions—as I'm sure you will.'

I knew that the boys invariably kept a catapult in a pocket, a sturdy, forked twig with elastic attached to its arms, plus a penknife used for whittling. These, with bits of string and a few marbles, formed a schoolboy's standard equipment. I waved the catapult in front of his face. 'I'll confiscate this so you won't be tempted into scaring anyone else with it today—or aim at something other than a tree. I suggest you make your way home—it'll soon be teatime.'

Frank's face had lost its anxious look and reverted to its usual cheeky expression. 'That's not what Miss Macdonal' told me jus' now. She said I should stay aroun' an' enjoy the 'oliday. You waitin' for 'er? You like 'er, don't ye, sir?'

My heart missed a beat. Was he fibbing? Fio had meant to spend the day shopping—had she changed her mind? If she were here, I must look for her. Perhaps she was looking for me. Possibilities flew around in my head as my mouth said, calmly, 'I think we all like Miss Macdonald. I hope she wasn't subjected to the annoyance of your catapult as I have been. Go on—get off home with you.' I took a step towards him.

'Yessir—all right—thank ye, sir,' and he went.

I mentally berated myself for not having asked exactly where he had seen Fio. Had he, in fact, not seen her at all and was simply being mischievous? He had implied that I had a special liking for her, which was true, but it was not a fact I wanted bandied about amongst the children. We

73

would have to be doubly careful to hide our feelings before their sharp eyes detected our increasing passion—children picked up on emotions so quickly. I walked a short way around the edge of the lake hoping to come upon my darling, but saw no one. I listened for gunshots to indicate that Robbie had chanced upon something for the pot, but heard only children's voices shouting in the distance and at last gave up and strolled home for my own tea. I had to be patient and wait until tomorrow before getting an explanation—and also to discuss Frank's precocity with her.

Mrs Marsham was looking forward to seeing the film—'going to the pictures' she called it. Some of our neighbours were also going, older people, having little in common with me, but we all went off to the village together. I was in two minds whether to call round and ask Fio how she had spent her day, but as it was nearing the time when they usually dined and she had been pretty decisive about seeing me next in school, I went straight to the inn.

The public bar was fairly empty, partly because it was early and also because of the film show—the younger men had their screen idols as well as the women. I ordered my drink there so I would see Robbie when he arrived.

Bill Angove was his habitual jovial self as he drew the ale. 'Not going to the picture show, Mr Parr? You generally gives it a miss, don't you?'

'I've seen most of them before—all those I've wanted to see. Tonight's show appears to be too sickly sentimental for my taste. I'd rather live my romance than watch other people go through the motions.'

He pushed the tankard towards me, his eyes staying on mine. 'I see. How d'you get on with your fellow teacher, Miss Macdonald? Now, there's a girl anyone might want to share a little romance with.' He was quick to follow that up before I could answer, by saying, 'I mean, just looking would make any man want to master her—she's such a well-bred beauty, isn't she?'

Not quite the way I would have put it—he could have been talking about a horse. The man spoke well, his diction good, but it was easy to turn a phrase in the wrong direction and so lose its intended meaning. Anyway, instead of bridling and saying it was none of his business, I countered his question with one of my own.

'You don't sound like a local man. Where are you from?'

'Surprising what a bit of education can do for you—but you should know all about that, sir. As a matter of fact, I was born in the vicarage just along the road—me father were vicar then. When I was 'bout eleven he took another living, and you're right, I was brought up in a town and destined for the Church, but soon became aware that I'd been mistaken in that vocation, though me faith stayed intact, and when this place come on the market I was happily in a position to take over. My purpose now is to try to steer my customers into the ways of moderation while still enjoying the fruits of God's bounty.'

'I haven't seen the present vicar in here,' I said.

'No, 'tis sad. He's a good man, the Reverend Hillman, and entitled to his opinions, but he seems to think that if you drink anything other than Communion wine you're heading for the jaws of hell! Speaking of that . . .'

He broke off, as I heard the door open and looked to see who had come in. George Piper slouched to the other end of the bar, distancing himself from me, though I was conscious of his insolently amused stare. I nodded to him, about to ask if his brother was on the way, but he ignored me, turning his back as he ordered, so I began to read my evening paper while he slumped heavily down on a settle.

The room began to fill and chatter increased, as did the smoky atmosphere, only slightly dispersed by the open windows. Catching sight of the inn sign through one of them, and having the landlord at my elbow, I delayed my enquiring no longer. 'I'm curious to know how the inn got its name and what the sign represents.'

Bill mopped the top of the bar. 'Well, all I know is that a few hundred years back there was a large house, Halsey Manor, on the far side of the big lake—the gateposts at the entrance to the drive leading up to it are still there. You might've seen 'em opposite the railway Halt when you arrived. The lord of the manor, Sir John Crispian, was, by reputation, ruthless and cruel. He was a widower, left with one son who was little more than a youth, and this son had fallen in love with a fair young maid and wanted to wed her. His father, sadly, desired her for himself and went so far as to abduct and imprison her in the manor, so the son, overcome with rage, took a battle-axe to him with the intention of teaching him a lesson, but giving, it seems, insufficient time for him to learn it.' He grinned. 'Yes, Jim—the usual?'

Jim Carter shared a few words with me while his tankard was filled, before taking it away to play dominoes with one of his cronies. Bill then returned to his tale.

'Where was I? Oh yes. The son dealt Sir John a mortal blow and released the maiden he loved. It seemed that nobody cared much about the murder and Sir John was duly buried in the churchyard opposite here, while the son took over both manor and maid. As soon as they were wed, however, a man leaving here one night described watching a strange glow, staying just above the ground, which moved slowly from the churchyard, went down over the stream and across the fields before disappearing in the woods. People said he'd had one too many and took no notice, but the next night others said they'd seen the eerie light, too, and this led to a watch being kept on the third night, when many people saw it but were too scared to go near. The following day, servants came from the manor with the news that their young master had been found hanging from the great oak in front of the house and his bride was demented, crying and screaming that the ghost of his father had come from the grave and carried his son off into the night. The way I see it, is that the boy hanged himself in a fit of remorse, but why the bride went mad I don't know. Anyway, it got about that the place was haunted and no one would venture there, until the bravest villagers decided to raze the place and fell the tree. They hoped that'd keep the ghost in its rightful place and remove any further temptation for it to wander about—it can't've been a very comfortable feeling having a corpse-candle lurking on your doorstep, y'see.'

'A what?'

'Oh, a corpse-candle—originally so called because it was the name given to a flame with a soft glow which moved along the ground without scorching it, generally seen in churchyards and over graves and thought to be an omen of death. Could be a kind of marsh gas, actually, but folk keep well away from the Old Manor even now, believing the place is still haunted—and that's the story, Mr Parr. Same again?'

'Just a half, please.' I mulled over his words as he served others before returning. 'I don't see why the inn should be called "The Guiding Light", though.'

'It was called "The White Hart" at the time, I believe, but the innkeeper felt that changing it would help to record the circumstance of a strange happening, that a ghostly light had guided the victim to his killer *and* keep the thought of Divine Retribution in everyone's mind. However wicked the father had been, the son was still a murderer, after all. They made up a rhyme to remind those who might be contemplating similar sinful deeds, and every new generation of children has played a game that imitates the events as they chant it. You must've already become familiar with it. It goes this way:

"The guiding light doth lead the way
For the one who in the churchyard lay
To find his murd'rer, and three times led,
Hangs him high on a tree . . . *by the neck 'til 'e's dead!*"'

I jumped as I felt hands from behind grip my throat, and found that Robbie had arrived in time to join in the final words and startle me. Everyone laughed, and someone shouted, 'Teachin' the schoolmaster now, are ye, Robbie?'

He looked contrite. 'Sorry if I gave yer a fright. Let me buy 'ee a drink. Same again, please, Bill, an' a pint an' a packet of twenty Gold Flake cigs fer me. Is that today's evenin' paper?' he asked me. 'Mind if I look? Must keep me eye on 'ow the gee-gees are doin'. Ta.' He skimmed through the Stop Press as Bill pushed the drinks and cigarettes towards him with his change.

'Still betting on the "also-rans", Robbie? The Derby'll be run in a coupl'a weeks. What's going to win?'

'There's one or two I fancy. I'll tell ye which I'm puttin' me money on when I've made up me mind.'

'Robbie can never resist a gamble,' Bill said to me with a wink. 'He's a poker player with a poker face.'

''Tis well 'e c'n afford it then, in't it? Give us another pint, Bill . . .' the gruff voice came from beside us, George already leaning heavily on the bar, '. . . as yer buyin', Rob.'

'Sure. Give it 'im, Bill.' I glanced at Robbie's smiling face with no trace of annoyance on it, just good humour, and wished again that he had been the one to care for Lucy and Tom.

He returned my paper as George stumbled back to his seat. ''Tis best take no notice,' he offered by way of an apology. 'So, you've been hearin' the tale o' "The Ballad o'

78

Halsey Manor", have ye? I were up there today wi' me gun, but didn' see no ghosts to shoot at.' He grinned. 'Somethin' more solid, in fact.'

'Did you have any luck? I listened for your gun but heard no shots.'

Again that grin. 'I 'ad me usual luck, ay, Mr Parr,' he said. 'An' I did manage to shoot me gun, on'y it made no noise when it went orf.' He winked, left it at that and walked away.

Day 8

I greeted the next day with a great sense of well-being, glad to be returning to school. As I dressed, I was thinking that Fio would be feeling the same and how hard it would be to hide our pleasure in each other's company, but necessary because of Frank's remark if we were not to become the subject of whispers and innuendo. While brushing my hair in front of the mirror, I noticed a bulge in my jacket pocket and pulled out Frank's catapult. He had already shown that he had not yet learned enough prudence to be trusted with it, and I hoped its loss would make him think twice about playing with one—though doubtless he would soon replace it with another.

A bell tinkling downstairs reminded me that I would soon be with my darling, so I said adieu to 'Girl in a Yellow Dress', sharing with that happy face the joy of being in love. Having hurried through breakfast, I jumped on the bike, pedalled fast and furiously past the shops and 'The Guiding Light', which no longer posed a query now I had learned its gruesome history, and arrived early at school.

After setting out the books, I kept watch on the gate through the window hoping to see Fio as she arrived. Staff and children were crossing the playground, but she was obviously not going to appear until the last moment. I was not best pleased, because it meant I would have to wait until break before I could warn her to be on her guard. The children were forming into groups, some of the boys re-enacting 'The Ballad of Halsey Manor', while others raced about playing 'He', and the girls either demonstrated their skills at hopscotch or skipped furiously to the chant of 'Salt, mustard, vinegar'n PEPPER!' I have never been able to find the origin of that particular phrase.

As the bell began to clang, I heard the children running into the cloakroom before filing noisily up the corridor and entering the classroom, when a certain calm descended as they said, 'G'morning, sir.' The monitor then topped up ink-wells, lids of desks were raised as personal belongings were put inside, and books and writing material taken out before being closed again, some quietly but others slammed down, with always an apologetic look on the face of the offender whether it had been accidental or not. I noted that both Tom and Frank appeared to be as usual, with the latter trying to stare me out, and we filed into assembly to find Fio already sitting at the piano. She flashed a bright smile at me, making my heart leap, but the smile I returned was lost to her as she bent her head while sorting out the music. Soon it was over and we were back in the classroom opening history books, when I absent-mindedly put the chalk in my pocket and encountered Frank's catapult. I held it aloft.

'Stand up, Frank,' I ordered. 'This is yours, I believe. How many of you boys have one?' I glanced at the hands hesitantly lifted by every boy—even Tom. 'Well, this is going into the cupboard with the other confiscated items because of its misuse.' I put it inside and turned the key. 'You boys must realise that these things are capable of causing damage and hurt, so be careful at what you are aiming when you use one. Understood? Now, sit down and we'll begin with the Battle of Hastings.'

My own battle of the day, which was managing to be alone with Fio, was only just beginning. Miss Hope and Mrs

Richards drank tea and chatted about half term for the whole of break, and at dinnertime I was delayed in the classroom. When at last I escaped, it was to find that my quarry had already left; it was no use following her—there was little enough time to ride home to dinner as it was. I rushed through my meal and back again and was just able to intercept her along the road, my bike coming to a screeching halt at her side. She showed surprise as I jumped off and took hold of her small hand, standing as near as I could in order to smell the faint, delicious perfume that always enveloped her.

'Eddie, Eddie,' she murmured, endeavouring to free her hand. 'What are you doing? Anybody could be watching us.'

I was past caring about other people, just eager to hold and kiss her, to feel her body against mine. 'What does it matter, my darling?' The new endearment sounded strange, coming from my lips. 'Everyone will know soon, so why not now?'

'Because we are both teachers in the school and Miss Millard and the parents might not understand—might be concerned that we are neglecting the children to favour ourselves. We mustn't be impetuous. It'd be far better to wait 'til you leave at the end of term, which won't be long now, will it? Don't you agree?'

I did not, but could see the point she was making as I remembered Frank's saucy remark, and supposed she might be right in wanting to delay our news until the holiday when neither of us would be in evidence to be stared at and questioned. I reluctantly let go of her hand, wondering how I could possibly continue to conceal my feelings for—how long? Another six or seven weeks? Well, if it had to be done . . .

'Yes, of course, anything you say, but it'll be very difficult. By the way, I wanted to ask you about the holiday. Will you come home with me to meet my family? I haven't written to

82

tell them about us yet—I want it to be a surprise. I'll have my own car by then and able to take you to visit my other relations.'

She seemed rather taken aback by the suggestion, hesitating. 'Didn't you know I've arranged to go to Italy for a month? I leave just after we break up. Sorry—it's been booked for ages.'

I remember the bitter disappointment I felt, and obviously registered.

'Eddie—cheer up—the time will soon pass 'til I'm back, and for the present we have several weeks to enjoy being together before I go.' Her voice cooed in my ear as I regarded her entrancing face, the hazel-green eyes fixed on mine with a promise I could not mistake. A craving for her filled me.

'When?' I asked huskily. 'When shall I see you alone again? Tonight? By the lake? Like before?'

Her eyes half closed, I hoped at the thought of my embrace, and then, to my delight, 'Yes, all right, after dinner, 'bout eight thirty, then you can be home in time for your night-cap of Horlicks, or whatever it is you have.'

'But—should you go swimming on a full tum?'

Her eyes opened wide again, a wicked little smile playing around the corners of her mouth. 'Who said anything about swimming? Is that all you want to do?'

I shook my head, feeling foolish. 'No, of course not.' Then a thought intruded, reminding me of the branch on the walnut tree. 'What if someone, like Tom, for instance, could be in the woods tonight and see us?'

'I can guarantee that he won't. You worry too much. Is that all?' She briefly squeezed my arm. 'Now, hurry back to school so we don't arrive together.'

Once again I flew along on wheels of joy, words of love ringing in my head and hardly able to restrain myself from singing out loud. I understood the reasoning for the late hour—children would be in bed—and that hopefully included Tom, whom she seemed to be so sure about, with their elders engaged in evening pursuits. Most of the village was habitually tucked up by ten to ensure a good night's sleep before rising at dawn. Bother! I had forgotten to ask if she had been in the woods yesterday.

The remainder of that day crawled sluggishly on. Tom appeared to be sluggish, too, almost falling asleep until reprimanded, but at last the four o'clock bell rang. He was slow to put his books away and hung behind, while most of the others were through the door before the last clang had finished reverberating; I wondered if he was waiting for Frank to get well on his way. I could see several girls lingering in the corridor to follow me across to the cycle shed, giggling as always, hoping I would stop and chat with them and show favouritism, but I was not that stupid—just stupid about everything else. Then Tom asked if he could have a word with me, about a bird, he said, but I had no time to spare for him.

'Sorry, Tom, it'll have to keep 'til tomorrow. I'm busy this evening so don't expect to see me in the woods. You stay home for once. Get off to tea, now.'

His face fell but he did not argue, though I could feel his eyes burning into my retreating back.

I tried to hide my anticipation of the evening from Mrs Marsham—it might arouse her curiosity. As we were finishing the meal I told her I would be going out later, so while she washed the pots I went upstairs and washed myself, changing into clean clothes—omitting the vest and sock suspenders. The soiled things I hid in my trunk—my landlady might wonder what was prompting me to exhibit this excessive cleanliness! Thinking back now, I have no doubt at all that she knew exactly what was going on as I sometimes let my guard drop by mistake, humming tunes and whistling. I was never normally that cheerful.

Going downstairs just after eight and without entering the kitchen, I called out that I was leaving and would be back by bedtime, slipping out through the front door, full of guilt at deceiving the good lady. I walked to the stone bridge and turned off on to the path alongside the stream with a glance up to Walnut Tree Farm when I passed the stepping stones, hoping that George and Robbie were already safely settled in the inn. Once over the wooden bridge, expectation increased at every step until I saw the fading sunlight flickering on what I now thought of as 'our' lake. I was feeling hot, so knelt down to dip a corner of my handkerchief in the cool, clear water to wipe my forehead, then behind my reflection another face appeared and I felt her hands on my shoulders as I turned, but she sped away around the edge of the lake, looking back with a glorious expression of abandon, daring me to follow.

The undergrowth began to thicken as I chased after this sure-footed woodland nymph, with no hope of catching her until she would allow it. She was forced to stop when she reached a dense barrier of thicket, pressing her arched back against the ivied trunk of a tree as she raised her arms high above her head, the movement lifting her seductive, pointed breasts under flame-coloured silk in a consummately provocative way. When I reached her, I thrust my mouth hard on hers and was enveloped in joy, but it was barely a moment before she pulled away.

'There's no need to rush through the meal,' she rebuked me, passing the tip of her tongue over her white teeth. 'Each course should be savoured to its fullest extent. Come and see my special place—where we'll be safe from unwanted eyes.'

I longed to make love to her there and then but she had made her way into a seemingly impenetrable tangle of bramble and shrubbery, though as I hunched myself over and reluctantly pushed my way after her, I found myself in a dark, twisting tunnel of greenery that neither scratched my skin nor tore my clothes. It continued on for some way before we came out into a light, open area, and I could see we had skirted around the rim to the furthest side of the lake that now lay before us, its sloping bank shrouded by hanging foliage.

Fio took my hand and led me towards some moss-covered mounds and the remains of collapsed walls, obviously the ruins of a place of habitation, but what affected me instantly was the utter silence, as if nothing lived or breathed there— no sounds of birds or insects. I have always been sensitive to mesmeric atmosphere, easily influenced by pervading impressions, but had never felt such an overpowering sense of . . . what? I failed to identify it, just briefly wished I was somewhere else until I did hear a sound—the shrill whistle of a train—and was relieved by the thought that civilization was not very far away.

As if reading my thoughts, or perhaps because of the whistle, Fio said, 'Getting here wasn't half as bad as you thought it was going to be, was it? You're all in one piece and you're not in the middle of nowhere. Over there is a definable pathway through to the main road and the Halt, though it's never used now.'

She was pointing as she sat down, resting her back against a large mound set some yards in front of the others, bare knees bent up with her skirt fallen around her thighs, regarding me with a quizzical stare. She popped something into her mouth and chewed on it as she patted the ground beside her.

'Come and join me here. I heard you had a discussion about the Old Manor in the inn last night, so I thought you should see it.'

So that was where we were! I should have guessed when I saw the ruins and when Fio mentioned the pathway to the road that would have been the carriage drive, but I had been diverted by my inner thoughts. Then, 'Who told you I discussed it?' I asked. Had her father been in the Snug without my seeing him?

'Never you mind!' Her tone was bantering. 'We're wasting time. Here, eat these—they'll do you good.' She put a few berries and a piece of something soft, white and fleshy in my hand. 'Go on—eat up like I'm doing. They won't hurt you—they grow here.'

Totally enamoured, I would have done anything she asked of me, so knelt beside her and put the things in my mouth as a child obeying its mother's request, becoming surprised to find how tart the one and earthy the other tasted.

Fio was studying my expression and laughed. 'Maybe they're an acquired taste, like olives. In a minute you'll find you have enjoyed them, though.' She lay back and her eyes held mine. 'Well, what are you waiting for?'

My mood had been slightly dampened by the haunted quality of the place, but as I leaned towards her a surge of my newly found, lascivious ardour overpowered me and I threw myself on her, covering her with kisses as I closed my eyes. Opening them again suddenly, I saw a look of aversion marring her lovely face, which was instantly replaced by another look, bland and unfathomable. Assuming I had been too rough I started to apologise, but it seemed it was not that at all.

'These clothes,' she said, beginning to unbutton my shirt. 'Don't you find them inhibiting? Here, you're able to do this better than me.'

She slipped from under me and had her frock off in a second, at once beginning to twirl and dance naked since she had been wearing nothing else. My fingers trembled and fumbled and I silently cursed the amount of clothing I was discarding, feeling as uncomfortable and foolish as I did that first time.

'Eddie, look at me—dance with me,' she invited, but I hung back, sitting with shoulders pressed against the mound she had recently vacated, watching, entranced.

It was a wild, abandoned dance, though graceful and adroit, which whipped up an intense longing in me. It also conjured up half-imagined, swirling visions of what I thought must be pagan rituals, of unclothed men and women, the latter having long, long hair which flowed out around them, at times concealing their voluptuous, coveting bodies and at others revealing the stark promise of fulfilment—the effect stimulating me almost to the point of madness.

Without being aware of how it happened, I found I was dancing too, amongst those others, not conscious of any embarrassment or awkwardness but as if it was the most natural thing in the world to do. My loved one touched and teased me until I responded in kind, following her lead, sometimes close, then apart, but always aware of ever heightening rapture, until I was aflame amid sudden flashes of light, burning with a fire that was consuming me. Then, abruptly, it was over, and we were lying on the ground with the universe exploding into millions of stars and I was a part of that explosion, flying inexorably through space, a finite segment of creation . . .

We lay side by side until the pounding of blood in my head had quietened. I raised myself to reach across to caress her but found I was fearful, wanting to claw at her flesh and draw her to me again in a renewed, frenzied spasm. This was not the gentle, loving passion I had imagined as being the ultimate in affection for my future mate, but different, a violent, lustful passion that drummed in my body with an increasing urgency that was impossible to resist. We lay thus until I became aware of being chilled and the sky had darkened, then saw Fio on her feet and searching for her discarded frock.

'Get dressed, Eddie,' her muffled voice exhorted me, which I did my best to do, my head thick and muzzy and my whole body feeling exhausted. These mournful ruins, viewed in the twilight, tended to oppress me with a sense of black depression. Also, I had the uneasy feeling that we were not alone, that there were watchful, unseen eyes. I sat on the edge of the mound where Fio had sat and, shivering, hastened to put on my shoes.

'Why do you come to this eerie place with its unsavoury history?' I enquired, endeavouring not only to stop my teeth from chattering but to bring rationality into play.

'I told you why—because it's so private. Don't you like it? I love it. By the way, d'you know you're sitting on the tree.'

I leapt to my feet. 'Tree? What tree? What d'you mean?'

Her laughter filled the air. 'It's the stump of the oak on which Sir Crispian hanged his son,' she said. 'They felled it when they pulled the house down, trying to lay his ghost, but I don't think they succeeded. Don't worry—it can't kill you! Come on, hurry up, otherwise it'll be quite dark and you'll be frightened to death when I leave you in the woods on your own!' Her face was full of mischief; I hoped she had no idea how closely she had touched on the truth.

I followed hard on her heels back through the tunnel of shrubs, though my legs felt treacherously weak. All my strength had gone, and there was a pulsating pain in my skull that threatened to shatter the bone and break loose. We came out by the edge of the lake where our tryst had begun and I could see the sky again, stars already twinkling and nightfall nearing, fire-flies moving like sparks through the air. Fio appeared not to be suffering such dire effects from our exertions as were affecting me and almost skipped along, stopping only when we came to where our paths divided and she turned to face me. I tried to kiss her, but although she pouted her soft, red lips, she put a hand in front of mine.

'Haven't you had enough? There's no time for more. Hurry home to Bessie before the phantom gets you!' And she was away.

With my head still spinning and feeling that I might be sick, my amorous fires were cold ashes by now and I was glad to be alone. Alone. Was I? Could I hear footsteps? An owl hooted from somewhere nearby, and I moved as fast as I could along the barely perceptible path towards the cottage, not daring to look behind me, only stopping once to heave up the contents of my stomach, then continued as quickly as possible on trembling and shaking legs. I only felt safe when I had the back door open and shut behind me. It was later than I had imagined, and I found my landlady waiting, unsmiling, undressed and ready for bed.

'S-sorry . . . I'm so s-sorry, B-Bessie,' I remember mumbling, as I staggered through the kitchen. I know I called her that without meaning to. I'm sure she had been intending to make some acerbic remark, but one look at the state of me must have decided her otherwise and she was at once solicitous and fussing over my welfare. She probably thought I was suffering the effects of too much alcohol, and I said nothing to dispel her delusion. I felt awful, undoubtedly looked worse, and went straight to bed without having to utter one untrue, deceitful word of explanation. Tomorrow would be another day.

I drifted into an unwelcoming sleep that brought no refreshment, only horrific dreams and nightmares seeming more frighteningly real than reality itself. Had I already become ghost-ridden and haunted by the shape of things to come?

Day 9

I awoke next morning to a taciturn landlady and a thumping headache, feeling drained and lethargic as if having forgone sleep for days. I longed to turn over, close my eyes to shut out the light and forget about the rest of the day, but knew that simple way of escape to be unacceptable. I was in something of a quandary about how I could excuse my behaviour of the previous night to Mrs Marsham, sneaking out of the cottage by one way and returning by another—after having apparently been involved in some disreputable revelling!

A quick glance at my discarded, crumpled clothing littering the floor seemed to confirm this. During her walk from door to window to draw the curtains she must have stepped over them, a fact indicating the extent of her disapproval—normally, she would have picked up anything lying on the floor—and no use my saying I had over-indulged at the inn, she would soon find out that I had been nowhere near. I felt like a naughty boy caught out while participating in some forbidden sport, but is that not exactly what *had* happened?

I then unintentionally punished myself by getting out of bed too fast, to find the floor less firm than expected as the room spun around until I sat back on the bed, which succeeded in pinning everything down to its rightful state of stability. After that I was more careful.

Breakfast presented further trouble. I did my best to eat under Mrs Marsham's steely gaze, but my stomach rebelled to the extent of repulsing the enemy and I was forced to retire to the privy. Some vestige of pity was showing on her face when I returned, weak and shaking, to find her stirring a thick, white potion in a glass. She insisted I should drink the noxious-looking mixture.

'There—that'll settle your stomach if anything will. Whatever possessed you to drink so much?'

With my mouth full, I shook my head while managing to swallow. 'No,' I finally gasped. 'I didn't drink anything last night.'

Disbelief clouded her features, but she refrained from comment.

'No, really, it's true.' I was anxious not to be thought guilty in her eyes of the heinous crime of drunkenness, even though aware that what I had actually been doing would have offended her far more. I tried to justify myself.

'You see, I could've popped into the inn when I left here but didn't, having decided to walk in the woods instead. Then I strayed off the path and into parts where I hadn't been before and foolishly ate some berries, which made me feel so fuzzy-headed and sick that I must've sat down and dozed off. When I awoke it was nearly dark and I found it hard to find my way back. I can't apologise enough for giving you this aggravation—and presuming to call you by your Christian name as I seem to remember doing.' I blushed as I recalled it, hoping my apology would suffice.

She tut-tutted, continuing to look askance at me as if unsure she had heard the whole story, but her expression had softened. 'You were very foolish to eat something without knowing what it might do—remember what happened to Adam when he ate the apple? The most innocent seeming things can be bad for you, and as for straying off that narrow path ... I must say I had credited you with more sense. But there, you can't put an old head on young shoulders or wisdom into a newborn babe, so I trust you've learned enough this time not to put yerself in danger again.' She just stopped herself from wagging a finger at me. 'An' as for callin' me "Bessie", well, most folk do an' you're welcome to do the same if you feels easy with it.'

I mentally heaved a sigh of relief at having cleared the air, while regretting her choice of similes. Did other meanings lie behind her words? Had she made a calculated guess as to what really happened? I decided to leave well alone.

'Now, you're looking a mite better,' she continued, 'but d'you think 'tis wise to go to school today?'

'Your medicine's done wonders—I'm sure the worst is past.' I tried to sound cheerful even if not feeling it. 'Staying here and moping won't help. Work would be best—Bessie. My name is Edward, you know, if you'd like . . .'

'Oh, no!' She hurriedly brushed that aside as she would a wasp on her arm. 'Dearie me, that wouldn' do at all, not proper, Mr Parr, thank ye all the same.'

The upshot was that I finally wobbled off on the bicycle, arriving ten minutes late to find that Mrs Richards had already shepherded my class into assembly. I waited in Miss Millard's room until it was over.

'I'm so glad you're here, Mr Parr.' Her voice evinced genuine concern when she came in. 'We wondered what had happened to you. Nothing bad I trust? You look pale—are you not well?'

I explained that I was recovering from sickness brought on by having eaten something that disagreed with me. She was kindly, saying I should go home and take the day off if I felt any worse.

I thanked her while noting her intent stare, which seemed to pierce through my eyes and into my brain as if seeking any secret knowledge hidden there. Was she, too, suspicious of my involvement with Fio? Or was my own awareness of improper conduct rendering me liable to suspect anyone who held my stare for longer than a second as censoring me? I became even more anxious for the day when the two of us could announce our betrothal to the world.

During break I had to endure Mrs Richards' fussing, asking pointedly if Bessie was looking after me properly, while my beloved viewed me over the rim of her cup, revealing a Mona Lisa expression whenever she lowered it to the saucer. We managed to exchange a few formal words, but I longed to pour out my heart. I knew I was not worthy of her—she had many more accomplishments than I—but she had chosen me and I loved her to distraction.

The following days brought no further intimate contact and I kept very much to myself, avoiding the woods and staying home to read, while Bessie—I was glad of the new informality—went to the film show, then to choir practice and finally to the whist drive. My next outdoor appearance, apart from school, came in church on Sunday, when the pinch-nosed vicar, with particularly huge teeth, preached a sermon on the value of chastity before marriage, his beady eyes peering over the top of his specs, straight at me. I wondered, rather unreasonably, whether he had been granted supernatural information to enable him to aim his darts in my direction, every syllable being addressed solely to my conscience. I also noted an alert Bessie in the choir stalls observing me and I began to sweat, but the rest of the congregation appeared to be lacking interest, unresponsive to his exhortations, fidgeting, gazing up at the fine, vaulted roof above or gently snoring with eyes closed.

As evening approached I felt the need for a stroll in the cool of the woods, the day having been warm. The lake drew me like a magnet as it invariably did, and I spent some time watching the dragonflies skimming over the water on transparent wings, their bodies shining with a variety of brilliant, translucent colours reminiscent of the fairies pictured in books I remembered from childhood. Those books had also been peopled with the creatures of nightmare, witches and goblins, ogres and ghosts, and I thought it fitting that the lake should be encompassed by this veritable magic wonderland of joy and fear.

My reverie was broken when I heard the notes of a sycamore whistle and saw Tom approaching. He ran the last few yards and threw himself down on the springy ferns beside me. 'You've not come 'ere fer days, sir. I 'eard you bin poorly, an' you've bin lookin' bad so I dursen't take yer time to talk to 'ee in school.'

Memory flashed through my head. 'Oh, of course, I remember. You wanted a word with me. What was it about? Birds, was it?'

He gazed down at his feet, rather shamefaced. 'P'raps I shouldn' say—I don' want to git no one in trouble but . . . Well, y'see, it were you talkin' 'bout catapults. I found a pigeon with a broken wing an' I'm sure t'were a stone what done . . . I mean, I think a stone broke it, sir. I put the bird in the small barn an' it's doin' all right now. It'll be flyin' high agin soon, you mark me words.'

I tousled the golden, curly hair. 'Well done. What d'you want to be when you leave school? A vet?'

He pondered the question with a serious expression before shaking his head. 'Naw, don' think so. I'd prob'ly feel too sorry fer the animals if they was poorly—but I'd love ter paint 'em or make models of 'em—'specially the birds.'

'Perhaps that'll be the way you'll make your fortune,' I said, knowing it to be very possible with his father's genius in his veins. 'By the way, who d'you think hurt the bird? Was it Frank?'

He turned a dismayed face to me. 'Oh, I wouldn' like ter say that fer sure, sir. Could've bin anyone. Only, I have seen 'im aimin' at 'em, an' 'e's a good shot. Mind you, I can shoot stones jest as well, but I never shoots at nothin' but tin cans. Could you 'appen to say 'ow cruel 'tis to 'im, quietly like?'

'Tom, do you realise that when you're concerned about something you cause your words to suffer? Both at the beginnings and ends of them—and sometimes in the middle! Try to concentrate on what you're saying. You can, you know. It's a matter of getting into the habit of speaking correctly—try to listen to yourself. I could take you to Constable Wills and have *you* charged with cruelty, you know!'

He stared at me with those solemn, dark blue eyes, mouth dropped open, endeavouring to see if I meant what I said, and when I was unable to hold my face straight any longer and burst out laughing he joined in, punching one hand into the palm of the other in his relief.

'You had me there, sir, fer a moment. I'll remember better now.'

A movement in the grass held my attention. 'There's a snake!' I cried, in alarm.

Tom leant back on arms stretched out behind him. ' 'Tis only a grass snake—can't hurt 'ee. You're more likely to hurt him—an' he knows it.'

I took his point and relaxed. 'I'll do what I can about Frank,' I promised. 'I won't be hard on him because there's no proof that he hurt that bird, but I'll keep an eye open. How's your uncle?'

'Oh, he's gone back—he's never here for long. He don't—doesn't—get along wi' me dad very well at times.'

I was tempted to point out that neither did anybody else, but refrained.

So the days passed. I had a quiet word with Frank, who protested innocence as expected, but I sensed an increased intensity in his rivalry with Tom, though it was never overt

96

enough for me to take punitive action. I kept an achingly aloof distance from Fio, as she had suggested, and there were no more invitations to meet at the lake. Curiously, although I became ever more desperate to embrace her, there was also relief that she was not immediately expecting me to return to the haunted manor—my stomach revolted again at the thought. I was anxiously awaiting the time when the two of us would be together for always—and a long, long way from this village.

On my own, I was aware of being morose and bored, occasionally playing a few sets of tennis at the recreation ground with some of the older pupils who would be leaving at the end of term, while aware that I could have beaten them easily had they all been facing me together on the other side of the net. For that reason I found no enjoyment in it, and had to force myself to lose sometimes in order to bolster their morale. I also watched cricket played on the village green on Saturday afternoons, helping out the local side once or twice when asked. Some evenings were spent in the Snug, chatting to Dr Mac whenever he made one of his rare visits, or to the regulars, having become on friendly terms with most of them. I found I enjoyed their somewhat jocular company and waggishness.

Derby Day in June came and went, bringing great excitement to the inn on that Wednesday, as Bill held a sweepstake that was won by Jim Carter. Delighted, he told me about it the next morning as I cycled past his garage.

'Never won nothin' afore. I only ever bets on the Derby an' the National. Not like Robbie. 'E must've lost a packet yest'day, 'cordin' to Bill. Told 'im 'e were a-goin' ter put 'is money on one wot's still runnin', 'stead o' "Trigo".' He clicked his tongue and winked. 'Good job you ain't a gamblin' man—Bessie wouldn' approve!'

The next day of note was Sports Day. I did my grudging stint of overseeing running practice at the recreation ground, doing my best to keep the unruly crocodile formation in some sort of order as we journeyed forth and back. The actual day turned out to be overcast with a sprinkling of rain, but it cleared by noon and the sun shone by two o'clock. Parents able to be there crowded into the Fairfield, their children grouped apart with the teachers and, as with all such occasions, the competitive atmosphere brought a charged, lively tension.

Races were run, and even though handicaps were imposed, Frank, being bigger, won the most, though when it came to the sack race his size had little effect. Unfortunately, Tom accidentally knocked into him, sending him off balance to fall in an ignominious heap. His reddened face expressed his anger, his eyes darting resentful glances at his imagined adversary, obviously believing it was done on purpose, then, during the egg and spoon race which I was stewarding, I saw him deliberately bump into Tom and send his egg flying. I ignored the incident as he lost his own egg in the process, thinking that justice had been done.

The afternoon ended with prizegiving. Frank, flushed with success, received his prizes and I hoped that would be enough satisfaction for him. I saw him giving them to his meek and colourless mother, leaving her to carry them home while he ran off.

It had been difficult to keep my gaze from straying to Fio's graceful figure as she busied herself. She was so good at organising, seeming to be everywhere at once, taking over duties from Miss Millard and the other teachers, myself included, monopolising the limelight, the star of the show. I wondered how the others viewed this upstart, this gifted, beautiful newcomer who had been their colleague for less than a year. Were they pleased or resentful? Their faces betrayed nothing of what they were feeling, and after helping to clear up, which Fio did not, I noticed, I stayed back to help Tom search for his lost shoe bag, which we failed to find.

'It's bound to turn up,' I told him, 'and in the least likely place.' Prophetic words as it turned out, but I was not really bothered about it as I went back to Clover Cottage for tea with Bessie who, uninterested in children's sports, had stayed home to polish her brass.

As it was a Friday evening, I took myself to the inn. The Snug was soon full of smoke, laughter and ribaldry, some fathers and grandfathers extolling the successes of those of their kin who had managed to win a prize, while surreptitiously trying to trick me into disclosing whether or not they were making progress with their lessons. I parried them by saying that Miss Millard was the one who put the final remarks on the end-of-term reports, but I was well satisfied with my own class.

It was about half past nine when Constable Wills came in, nodded to everyone, fetched his ale and sat his large frame down next to me. He began packing tobacco into his pipe and, after puffing furiously to keep it alight, blew out the match and turned to me with his back to the others.

'A word, Mr Parr,' he said. 'Had a bit o' bother awhile back, after tea.'

'Did you?' I queried warily, wondering why he had singled me out to impart this information.

'Ay, quite a little dust-up t'were. Thought you might be able to shed a bit o' light on the circumstances—on the q.t. mind you—nowt official,' he ended hastily.

'Of course, I'll help in any way I can.'

He drew deeply on his pipe to make the wad of tobacco glow, and tamped it down with the horny tip of one finger. 'Well, y'see, it concerns one o' your pupils. He's suffered a deal o' punishment from George Piper.'

My thoughts flew to Tom. 'What happened? Has he been hurt?' I asked, in some alarm.

'Oh, ay, he's rather poorly. Had a right good thrashin'—more'n 'e deserved, be all accounts—seeing as how boys allus will be boys. George seems to have taken that old saying to heart—you know: "A woman, a dog an' a walnut tree, the more you beat 'em the better they'll be"—while changing "dog" to "boy" to suit 'is own thinkin'.'

I half rose to my feet. 'Is he badly hurt? I'd better go and see him. What a way for a so-called father to behave!'

The constable regarded me with some surprise. 'He hasn't got a father . . . Oh, I get it! You thought t'were Tom, did ye? Now, sit down an' rest yerself—t'weren't 'im but Frank Acaster that were assaulted.'

I seated myself again, feeling relieved but still angry.

'I'll tell it from the start,' he continued. 'I were finishin' me tea when Kate Acaster, they lives close by, comes a-hammerin' on the door. She had Frank with her, all bloody an' snivellin', an' asked if I'd take a look at 'im as she couldn't afford to pay Dr Mac—not unless there should be somethin' badly wrong. She couldn't get a word out o' the boy, she said, not where it hurt, who did it, nothing, an' thought 'e might've been attacked by some gang. I could see he were shocked an' frightened, which in itself is unusual fer Frank, an' I got nowheres with him, neither, 'til I threatened 'im with the law for hidin' the truth.'

'Could you do that?' I asked.

'He weren't to know I were bluffin', poor lad. Anyway, his story was that George came upon him up at farm, where he'd gone to take back a shoe bag he'd found with Tom's name on, an' began walloping 'im fer no reason. Frank thought 'e were a-goin' to be killed, an' screeched so much he were finally let go.'

'It was lucky, then, that he did screech,' I put in.

'Frank said for me to forget about it, he were all right, didn't hurt nowhere special, an' could he go home to his

100

tea, please? Well, I got his clothes off an' looked him over, and apart from a very red backside, bruises on his arms where he'd been held and more on his face next a swollen, bloody nose, there was no lasting damage done that I could see—though I'm no expert. Mind you . . .' he gave a half smile, 'he's going to 'ave a beautiful shiner tomorrer!'

'What are you intending to do about it, Wills?' Though suspicious of Frank's altruistic action, I was still concerned about him. 'Piper must be charged with assault. What does Mrs Acaster say?'

'Oh, she don't want no fuss made, jes' wanted to know that Frank weren't hurt bad, but I went straight up to see George. He didn't deny hitting the boy—said he'd caught him in a small field where he's raisin' cabbage an' carrots an' such. It lies higher up the rise, out o' sight o' farm. He says the lad were pullin' 'em up an' gen'rally creating one 'ell of a mess. After he'd got a hold on 'im he says he saw a shoe bag lying on the ground, an' Frank squealed out that it belonged to Tom so it must've been *'im* what done it, so George told 'im to pull the other one—not a cabbage, as ye can guess!—an' proceeded to teach 'im a lesson. I went an' inspected the field and t'were as George said, so no wonder he were wild, though 'e went a bit over the top, I agree. I cautioned 'im, whereupon 'e said he'd do the same if he ever caught the little beggar at it again. Thought you should know the details, Mr Parr—rumours'll be all round village afore dawn.'

I mulled over his words. 'Frank was feeling resentful against Tom, mistakenly thinking a wrong had been done to him during sports this afternoon. I imagine he planned revenge by taking Tom's shoe bag—we were looking for it afterwards—meaning to damage the crops and leave the bag there to incriminate him, only he was himself caught in the act.' The constable nodded his head as he drained his glass. 'Though what I can't understand,' I went on, 'is how he risked going there in the first place—he couldn't rely on George not seeing him. Can I get you another?'

'Ay, thank ye. Frank wouldn't expect George to be there, because early every Friday he delivers his veggies to our local shop before driving the cart to sell to another in East Halsey. 'Tis market day there, so he sells what he's got left afore visitin' their local inn to spend what cash he's made, an' never gets back 'til late. Today, though, the market closed as soon as it opened 'cos there was a fire, leavin' George with 'is cart full of unsold veggies. He went and got a bellyful anyways, prob'ly to console hisself, an' got back early afore tea somewhat the worse for wear and even more ill-tempered than usual. Good thing the horse knows its way home 'cos George sleeps most o' the way, so t'were Frank's bad luck that he were there unexpected like to cause the lad's little game to misfire on him.'

And Tom's good luck, I told myself.

Day 10

I said nothing to Bessie about it before going to bed, but she was all keyed up when she brought my morning tea. 'What d'you think was done yest'day, Mr Parr? Seems Frank were attacked by George Piper. He's black an' blue, so they say, an' could be his nose is broke. How about that, then? S'pose 'tis a change from Tom gettin' the beating but it shouldn' be allowed anyways. The constable had to call at farm to see what George'd been up to. Will 'e be put in prison?'

I raised myself on an elbow. 'I doubt it, Bessie. He'll probably be warned to keep his temper under control. He might've been provoked, you know—the boy could have deserved it—though to a lesser degree.'

'I'm s'prised to hear *you* saying that, of all people, Mr Parr, taking George's part.' She opened the curtains and turned to glare at me. 'People don't often make excuses for 'im, but then, you're not from these parts. We've allus said 'e might kill somebody one day with all the fights and ruckus he causes, an' Heaven knows what he'll do with 'is temper if he's stopped from using 'is fists!' She stomped out huffily.

As it was a Saturday, I felt duty bound to call on Mrs Acaster to survey the damage done to her offspring, so after an immersion in the tin bath in the wash-house and break-fasting, I cycled off, stopping at Miss Millard's cottage first.

Both she and Miss Hope, not knowing the full facts, were overly shocked by the incident, but when I relayed what had actually happened, they agreed that it was not the chastising but the extent of the assault that concerned them. For my part, in my relief at knowing Tom had escaped the beating that Frank had intended he should have, I had secretly applauded the punishment meted out, deeming it to be justified, and thereby tending to overlook the fact that no child should be subjected to such violence. This was made more obvious to me when I saw the result of George's handiwork.

The Acasters' rented cottage made no pretension of being other than a poor, dilapidated building, but the front garden was neat and tidy and so was the interior of the dwelling. Though worn and shabby, everything was spotlessly clean, a smell of carbolic soap still hanging in the air. This was only to be expected as Mrs Acaster earned her living in a like manner, and I had been given to understand by Bessie that she was much sought after as a charwoman, called a 'daily' in the bigger houses, and also 'did' for the doctor. She opened the door when I knocked, ushering me into a front room that was seldom used, as indicated by the musty air, visibly embarrassed by my presence and wringing red, work-worn hands as she stumbled over her words.

'Th-there were no n-need ter come, sir, Frank's all right. Shouldn'ta' bin up farm in first place. I'd 'ave given 'im an 'iding meself, but felt 'e'd 'ad enough.'

'I'd like to see him. Is he here?'

'Oh, ay, he's 'ere.' The sad, sharp face, framed by thin mousy hair scraped back into a tight bun, nodded vigorously. 'I've a-warned 'im that if 'e dares put a foot outside 'til Monday, 'e'll get a clout an' a dose o' caster oil. That'll make 'im mind as well as keepin' 'im reg'lar. Frank—come in 'ere at once!' she called.

As I waited, I idly wondered how Mrs Acaster would

manage to administer the nauseous oil, should it become
necessary to carry out her threat if he refused to take it. I
had only previously been aware of it as a purgative, not a
punishment. Then Frank shuffled in, eyes downcast, though
I could not be sure he might be incapable of lifting the
swollen lids. One eye was distinguished by a huge purple
bruise, with the other not much better. His normally small
button-nose was more than twice the size, with the rest of
his face marked by sore-looking, fiery patches standing out
angrily on the skin. There also appeared to be a tuft of hair
missing and I could see his right wrist, which dangled from
a too-short sleeve, disfigured by bruises. I was horrified. It
was far worse than I had imagined.

'Frank . . .' Lost for words to express my feelings, I finally
came out with a foolish banality. 'Does it hurt much?'

The eye with the least damage became visible and fixed
on me. 'Naw, sir.'

I tried again. 'It might be as well to see the doctor . . .'

'Oh, we did, this mornin',' his mother broke in. 'I went
to work there, but couldn' leave me boy by hisself so took
'un with me. Dr Mac came by an' looked, an' didn' charge
a penny piece fer seein' to 'im. Said 'is nose were busted
but it'd get better on its own. Sent us straight 'ome an' paid
me full wages—proper gent 'e is!'

I agreed, and went on: 'Are you going to see the constable and get something done about the assault—have
Piper charged?'

She shook her head. 'That's what doctor said, but naw—
I don't want no trouble, sir. Frank were doin' wrong an'
'e's bin taught a lesson, haven't yer, son?'

Frank, head bowed, muttered something unintelligible. I
decided to leave, to release him from this irksome
discussion.

'Think very carefully before you decide to ignore it, Mrs
Acaster,' I said. 'The man had no right to hurt him so

105

badly. By the way, Frank, Miss Millard says you are not to come back to school until you feel well enough. I'll bring some books here for you to study if you like—give you something to do.'

' 'E'll be back Monday, never fear—'e's not that bad.'

His mother, I could see, wanted him out from under her feet and into the care of the school, regardless of how much pain he was suffering. She might love him dearly, but she was too wrapped up in her need to provide necessities and a roof over their heads to show it. That was probably why Frank had developed into the envious and insecure bully he had become, having to gain approbation in the only way he knew by becoming 'leader of the pack'. He had become angry at Tom's refusal to kowtow to him, which was made worse by what he surely deemed to be the favouritism shown by the staff at school. It could not have been Tom's home life, more harsh and threatening than his own, that he envied, but the quality of spirit that helped Tom to make the best of everything without demur and so induce approval.

As I regarded Frank's black eyes, I had no idea what dark thoughts were germinating in his bruised and bloodied head, but knew for sure they would involve some form of retaliation for somebody.

'Frank,' I said, hoping to pacify him. 'You wouldn't have been hurt if you hadn't gone to the farm to cause hurt to someone else, would you? You've none to blame but yourself, really, so the best thing you can do is try to behave better in future. We're all sorry to see you this way and trust you'll soon feel better.' With that I left, wishing I had been able to find the right words to cure his inner wounds and knowing I had not even reached them.

For the next few days the village buzzed with rumour, which soon died down when it was realised that no action was to be taken. Frank duly arrived on the Monday, displaying his fast-yellowing bruises to his peers with pride like a returning soldier with war wounds. His reputation was enhanced, with Tom being treated as a pariah by the other children, indignation against the absent parent being transferred unjustly to the attendant son now shunned in the playground. I hoped Tom would prefer it that way, rather than having to defend himself in conflict.

Fio was showing equal interest in both boys, praising Frank for his stoicism in suffering and Tom for . . . being Tom, I supposed. I was made more aware of the attention she was showering on them as I was longing for her to show me the same favour, while mindful that she was unable to do so because of the secrecy we shared.

We were nearing the longest day of the year as June progressed, after which they would begin to shorten as autumn approached. There was no hint of it then, in the glorious, warm, sunny weather that made my life bearable as I waited impatiently for term to end and Fio to openly declare our love. The 'nine days' wonder' of Frank's mishap was all but forgotten before another thunderclap came out of a clear, blue sky.

I was having breakfast when there came a rapid knocking on the rear door of the wash-house. Bessie went to open it and I could hear voices pitched high and low before she came back, her expression troubled, an arm about Tom's quivering shoulders as he clutched a large tortoise to his chest. They both stood silent, sheltering behind their unreadable faces, gazing at me as if waiting for me to put to rights something that had gone badly awry.

Apprehension filled me. Tom's cheeks were grimed and puffy, streaked by tears that dripped from his chin on to his dirty clothes and the tortoise. His breath was coming in great, painful gulps as if his throat was constricted, but it was his eyes, the wide-open, tortured eyes, that wrung my heart. As I stood up he suddenly flung himself at me, face pressed into my stomach, the hard shell of the tortoise between us, sobbing out jumbled words that I was unable to put into any sensible order.

I held him to me, stroking his head, murmuring things of no consequence until the paroxysm began to lessen and he moaned with long-drawn out, muffled cries. I took the tortoise from him and put it on the floor, looking enquiringly at Bessie, who shrugged in a helpless way, her own sympathetic tears starting to fall. My compassion began to turn to anger at whatever had caused this child his pain.

'Tom . . .' I kept my voice low. 'What's happened? Are you hurt?' I noted a slight shake of the head pressed against me, as if I shielded him from something fearful. 'Then what? There's nothing I can do to help if I don't know.' I sat down, cradling him in my arms. He had gone limp, like a rag doll, his chest heaving.

Bessie had poured out a cup of tea, heaping in sugar, stirring so hard that she slopped it in the saucer. 'Here,' she said, 'drink this. It'll do ye a power o' good.'

He pushed it away, looking at me with a blank, frozen expression. ''E killed 'em all . . .' His face crumpled as he burst out crying again, beating his fists into my chest.

I gripped them. 'Calm down, Tom. Who killed what?'

After a moment he managed to control himself, though unable to stop rocking from side to side in his anguish. 'Me dad—me hurted creatures an' everythin'—an' 'e said 'e were goin' ter kill Methy, too, an' I knows 'e will!' Tears welled up again and began to fall, but it was gentle weeping now.

I felt cold, as if I had been stabbed, allowing all my blood to drain away to leave only emptiness inside. 'Why?'

''Cos he caught me climbin' out down the walnut tree last night. 'E said I were wilful an' 'e were fed up o' tellin' me, an' 'e couldn' beat me as 'ard as 'e wanted in case it showed, 'cos of Frank bein' 'urt, but I 'ad ter be punished.

So 'e shut me in coal cellar ter sleep on floor. When 'e let me out this morn 'e took me in barn an' made me watch while 'e did it . . . an' 'e punched me mam when she told 'im to stop, an' when 'e let go of me I grabbed Methy an' ran. I wish it were *'im* who was dead!'

The sobs almost choked him, hiccupping in his throat. I put my arms tightly around his shivering body and he buried his face in my jacket. The cold within me was being replaced by a burning rage directed towards this man, whose vindictiveness, I suspected, had been nurtured over the years by constant brooding on his belief in his wife's treachery and his own humiliation when Tom was born.

Bessie was hovering, wanting to be of use but not knowing how, wringing her hands and tut-tutting. Glancing at the clock, I knew I must get things moving.

'Tom's not in a fit state for school, Bessie, and he obviously can't go home yet. I want you to give him half an aspirin tablet—you'll find a bottle on my dressing table— and let him have a sleep up there. He'll be all right 'til I come back for dinner. I'll have a word with one or two people and see what's to be done—though not a great deal, I fancy.'

'George Piper should be horse-whipped!' Bessie expressed her indignation by viciously poking the fire, before asking, 'Like some breakfast, Tom? No? Then I'll just wash your face an' hands and take you upstairs. You can have your aspirin with a glass o' milk.'

The small, tragic figure stayed motionless. 'What about Methy? I dursn' take 'im back.'

I stared askance at the tortoise clambering awkwardly over the hearth-rug until Bessie came to the rescue. 'Don't you worry 'bout him. I had one once. He'll be safe in the glasshouse in the garden for the time being—we'll put him in there now. I'll look after him for you, Tom. Come along, now.'

I left them, pedalling as hard as I could, but was still late for assembly so I waited for Miss Millard in her room. Her look of disapproval soon changed to concern after I explained the reason for my belated arrival, and she showed that she was similarly appalled. We agreed to discuss it with the others at break to see what action to take, and after I had recounted the events to them there were exclamations of dismay, only Fio remaining quiet as if distancing herself from any censure.

''D'you think I should telephone the constable?'

'I can't really think what he can do, Headmistress. Tom hasn't been injured, the brute was too clever for that,' Miss Hunt answered, regretfully. 'Lucy seems to have been harmed, though. It's not for the first time, but she's never made any previous complaint against him so she's unlikely to do so now.'

'I feel Wills should be informed. He is a kind man and won't turn a blind eye to such cruel behaviour. George Piper must be taken to task for this!' Miss Millard banged her cup down. 'What d'you say, Fiona?'

Fio lazily raised her eyelids and glanced at each of us in turn. 'As you have said, what good would it do? Tom has been warned many times not to climb out of his window and he's disobeyed once again. He'll soon get over it—children quickly forget. To my mind it's best left alone.'

'And if George feels he's being harassed, who knows what other wicked things he'll find to do?' affirmed Mrs Richards.

I was oblivious to further conversation for a short space as I contemplated Fio, my adored one, wondering how I could reconcile her words with the loving, caring person I believed her to be. How could she possibly ignore the mental injury done to that small boy? Then, reasoning, I found myself excusing her as being more experienced and wiser from her close contact with her professional father, though still remaining uncertain as to which of us was right. However, being me, with my zealous regard for justice, I knew I would be unable to leave it there.

'In all conscience I suggest you do inform the constable, Miss Millard. I'll take Tom back home at tea-time and have a word with Piper.' I was angry enough not to feel unnerved by the prospect. 'Would it be an idea for your father to check Tom over sometime today, Fiona? After all, he did spend a frightening night on the floor of a cold, dark cellar.'

She responded slowly. 'I doubt it's the first time that's happened and it's not caused him any harm before, so wouldn't it be wasting Dad's time? The boy hasn't been physically hurt. I really don't see what all the fuss is about.'

A certain silence settled over the room as we absorbed her words. I was acknowledging that she could possibly be right in her assessment, but only possibly. She seemed so cool and detached, while I was feeling what I thought was justifiable anger at the treatment meted out to a small child who, I knew, would never forget.

Miss Millard broke the heavy silence. 'Very well. I shall telephone Wills and put him in the picture then it'll be up to him to do whatever he decides. You, Mr Parr, have said that you will take Tom home later. I would wish he could be kept away, but we have no option—I'm sure he would choose to be with his mother no matter what hazards await him. I advise you to keep your own temper in check—in fact, it might be best if Wills goes with you.'

I saw the wisdom in that, agreeing for her to arrange it, and before I left at dinnertime I had received a message that the constable would be waiting for us at the bottom of Walnut Tree Lane at five o'clock. Arrived back at Clover Cottage, I found Bessie alone, with the table laid for three. 'How's Tom?' was my first concern.

'There's not been a sound from him since I tucked him

in your bed. I was jest wondering if I should go up an' fetch him down.'

'He must be tired out—I doubt he slept much in the cellar. Better let him sleep on 'til he wakes. He'll have to face up to recalling it all again then.'

'Poor little chap—he can have his dinner later. I washed his clothes. They soon dried an' I'll iron 'em this afternoon. Everyone's saying George shouldn't get off scot free this time. Putting the boy in the cellar with the coal an' all! What's to be done about it?' She mashed the potatoes so angrily I feared she might break the fork.

I told her what was planned, that the constable would deliver another warning and make sure Lucy was all right. There was little else anyone could do.

I left for the afternoon sessions, hurriedly returning after school to find Tom dressed, clean and tidy, and sitting at the table before a half-empty plate. He was more composed now, the only indication of his earlier distress showing in his red and swollen eyes. Bessie clearly had something else bothering her and avoided meeting my gaze, insisting that I sit down and have a cup of tea before taking Tom back home.

'By the way, Mr Parr, when Tom here woke up, he saw that picture on the wall in your room an' wants to know all about it. I'm afraid I said that *you'd* be the best person to tell him . . .'

Now, that was a tale I was quite definitely unprepared to tell.

Day 11

Today I resumed writing rather late, having to collect my thoughts as to what happened after Bessie had taken the wind out of my sails yet again. I needed time to meditate on the situation where I left it yesterday, at the point when I knew Tom had seen the painting. Having grown so used to it being in my room I had forgotten that he might notice it and start asking questions, and had not been best pleased that she had left me to provide an explanation. Caught off guard, I remember, I was momentarily silent, wondering what to say.

Tom made it easier. ' 'Tis a lovely picture. When I woke up I jest lay an' looked at it for ever such a long time, an' the lady looked back at me, kindly like. She seems so real. Wish I could paint like that.'

I was not surprised he had failed to recognise his mother, so completely changed from that happy, carefree girl on the canvas. 'Perhaps you will be able to some day,' I replied. 'I've seen your watercolours—they're very good.'

'Did you paint it?'

The words were there in my mouth, and I longed to answer, 'No, but your father did.' Instead, I gave a brief laugh. 'Me? No—I'm not clever enough. A real artist, who was staying here, painted it. Bessie promised to look after it for him.'

'You remind me of him, Tom,' Bessie said, her voice soft,

and I noticed the tender way in which she was regarding the boy. 'I'm sure you'll do as well when you're older—if that's what you want.'

I felt it would be prudent to change the subject. 'Finished your tea? Then it's time we went to meet the constable and got you back home.'

An expression of dismay spread across his face, and I felt angry with myself for having been thoughtless enough to come out so bluntly with what must have been, to him, a grim proposal. 'You do have to go home, you know,' I added, lamely.

He nodded, his face clearing. 'Ay, must look after me mam, any road—she'll be worried sick as 'tis, not knowin' where I am—an' there's chores to be done.'

Bessie was cautioning. 'Mind you do as you're told in future, Tom. No more sneaking out at night to anger yer dad an' give him cause to punish you.'

He stared at her for a long moment, his face solemn. 'Naw, don't 'ee worry, 'e'll never ketch me doin' it again, and 'e'll never do nothin' like 'e did *then* again, neither. I promise ye—I'll kill 'im first!'

The vehemence of his reply shocked me, but why should it have done? It was a natural reaction to want to lash out and be revenged on his tormentor—the trick would be for him to keep that emotion under control.

'I'm sure you don't mean that,' I said, 'but I do understand how you feel.'

The dark blue eyes, like the deep waters of the lake, were unfathomable. 'Do ye?' he asked. Then, 'What about Methy? If he should get away from here 'e'll come to farm, lookin' fer me.'

'I've told you I'll take care of him.' Bessie smiled in a patronising manner. 'He can stay here for as long as you want. I'll feed him an' keep him shut in. You don't really

114

b'lieve he'd find his way back through the woods, do ye? It'd be some terrible long way for 'is poor little legs.'

'He'd get there—'specially if 'e hears me whistle. We loves each other lots.'

Five o'clock found us approaching the end of Walnut Tree Lane. I could see Constable Wills already waiting, leaning on his bike. He had a question or two for Tom, writing his answers down in a notebook before we went up the uneven track, deep-rutted from hooves and the wheels of carts, which meandered between blackthorn hedges with their white flowers already fading. I heard the dog bark a warning as we turned the last bend, and put a hand on Tom's shoulder to steady us both. I had to be careful to keep my temper in check and not be tempted into rash action.

'Best if I do the talkin'. George knows 'twouldn' be wise to come to blows with me in the King's uniform.' Wills grinned, and winked at Tom. 'I 'member I allus used to win when he an' I had fights at school, boy.'

We moved towards the dusty forepart of the house, chickens scratching the dirt, a cockerel strutting and the dog barking, until a rough voice ordered it to shut up— which it did at once, aware, no doubt from experience, of the peril of disobeying its master. George came out of the big barn and stood watching, arms akimbo, his dark, beady eyes alert. The moment I saw that brutish, bearded face I wanted to smash my fist into it.

''Art'noon, George.' The constable wheeled the bike towards him while Tom and I hung back, the lad pressing against me. 'Been expecting a visit?'

'Naw.' The answer was short and unequivocal.

'Bit of a surprise for ye, then.' He leaned the bicycle against the barn and turned his attention back. 'We've brought Tom home. He had quite an upset this morn, be all accounts.'

115

'By jest one account.' George had neither relaxed his stance nor his stare since we arrived.

'Mebbe. Any road, it didn't fall easy on the ears. How's Lucy?' He raised his voice. 'Tom, go an' fetch yer mam.'

'I'm here.' She came swiftly from the house and held Tom close. 'I'm so glad you're back—I've been very worried about ye.'

I looked hard at her, trying to distinguish any signs of injury, but her pale face showed no recent marks, only the yellowing of old bruises. I assumed that George had cleverly punched her where it failed to show, but I knew the constable was making his own assessment.

''Ow do, Lucy,' he said. 'You all right?'

''Course she is,' George broke in roughly. 'Can't yer see? She's not complainin'. Tell 'em, Luce.'

Her eyes were hooded as she gazed blindly over Tom's head. I hoped she would find the courage to tell us how badly she was being treated, to get this ruffian put behind bars, but wives rarely accused husbands in those days and this poor woman had her own special reason for suffering penance as a way of expiating what I'm sure she considered to be her sin. She fixed her lips in a mirthless smile.

'That's so—I'm not complainin'. Tom shouldn't've done wrong, then he wouldn't've needed punishin' an' no one upset.' She was stroking his head as she spoke, as if asking his forgiveness for apportioning the blame.

'There y'are, what'd I say?' George looked smug. 'If that's all yer come for, yer can go.'

I saw Wills take a deep breath and noted the intense hostility in his eyes. 'Don't fool yerself that I don't know what goes on, George. I'd cause to caution you on another matter not long since, an' I'm doing it again now. You knows what you've been at an' so do we, so you'd better not lay another finger on anyone, understand? Next time you mayn't be so lucky as to get away with it.' He went to the

116

barn and wheeled his cycle away, heading for the lane. 'I'll look back in a few days, Lucy,' he said, 'but I'm available any time you needs me. Comin', Mr Parr?'

Lucy had been having a whispered conversation with Tom, acknowledging the constable's words before turning to me as I began to follow him. 'Thank ye—an' thank Bessie—for all yer kindness to Tom. We're grateful.'

I murmured something appropriate as Tom ran into the house in front of his mother. George had not moved away from the barn doorway, but he now came further out, nearer to me, a self-satisfied smirk on his face.

'You needn' be so "holier than thou", Mr namby-pamby Parr. Butter wouldn't melt, would it? What d'you git up to in the woods in yer spare time, eh? Same's me, it seems, if yer did but know it!' His low tone was mocking and derisive.

I stared him straight in the eye while managing to keep my mouth clamped shut and quickly made to stride after Wills' retreating back, but his taunting voice carried far enough to reach my ears.

'What about them fancy things you keeps yer socks up with? S'penders they'm called, ain't they? Like women 'ave for stockin's. Odd sorta fella you are.' A burst of raucous laughter pursued me as I thankfully rounded a bend in the lane.

Hastily picking my way over the ruts and potholes, I had nearly caught up with Wills as the words began to have meaning. Suspenders. How did he know I wore them? They had never been exposed to public view, except once . . . I froze. Wills was talking but I heard not one syllable, finding myself lost in an indescribable moment of disbelief and incredulity. The only person who had seen and remarked upon them had been Fio, and she would hardly have noised the fact abroad to anyone, let alone George. But . . . I felt the skin on my scalp tighten with mortification. Suppose he had been there to see for himself, to witness what had taken place the first time I had been with her, absorbed and clumsy in my ignorance of lovemaking. It was possible—he had not been in the Fairfield with the other men—but the coarse, graceless presence of George as voyeur? It did not bear thinking about! I felt the shame of it, the fire in my cheeks burning them scarlet. I wanted to bury myself in the deepest, darkest pit I could find and stay there for ever!

'You all right, Mr Parr?' The voice of sanity saved me from my insanity. I gulped and pulled myself together.

'Yes, Wills—fine.'

'You mustn't get too worked up over the boy, you know, he's tougher than 'e looks—got a good head on 'is shoulders. Reckon he'll find ways o' dealin' with whatever 'e comes up against—does well to defend hisself 'gainst Frank's meddlesome ways. I worries more 'bout 'is mam— seems she's goin' downhill fast.'

We emerged on to the main road and he prepared to ride away. 'See you in the inn this even'?'

I said possibly, while still inwardly cringing. Could I ever show my face anywhere again? I was pretty certain now that George must have spied on us, and before reaching Clover Cottage I had mentally peopled the woods with crowds, all silently enjoying and applauding the spectacle of me, naked, cavorting and indulging in amorous, erotic activity! And what about Fio? How dared he feast his loathsome eyes on her nude beauty? How upset she would be if she knew! And further, what had he meant by saying that we both did the same things in the woods? Was he insinuating that he and Fio . . . No! But the thought had presented itself and would not be dismissed. Was that why Tom was sometimes kept in his room? Questions rebounded around the inside of my skull with no hope of answers and I found I had walked past the cottage and reached the Halt without realising it, having then to turn back to where my meal was waiting. After I had forced it down my unwilling throat

118

neither the inn nor the woods cast an enticing, beckoning finger in my direction.

Sleep, though invited, remained absent that night, the unseen presence of George Piper replacing it. Loathing for him filled me and loathing makes no easy bedfellow, so I came to breakfast in a foul mood, thinly disguised, and Bessie, ever sensitive to atmosphere, figuratively walked on eggshells. It must have been pretty obvious in school, too, for my class behaved with unusual attention, even the girls transferring their wandering thoughts from me to their books. Tom showed no outward signs of distress but, truth to say, he was no longer my main concern—Fio was—and a quick word from me convinced her that we needed to talk. I must have appeared feverish, because she asked if I was ill before agreeing for once to let me accompany her home after school finished.

As we walked she seemed distant, reluctant for serious discussion, and I found it difficult to find a way to broach my pressing subject. I began by describing Tom's return home, and asked her opinion of George. She briefly moved her eyes from the road to mine, without altering an expression of what I took to be tedium.

'Why ask me that?' She hesitated in her stride. 'We both know what he's like, don't we? Born to the soil, rude, earthy, crude and unpolished—out of place anywhere but where he is. That do you?'

'I'm entirely in agreement. I just wondered if you'd spoken to him recently.'

'And if I had—what business would it be of yours?'

I was taken aback by her asperity of tone and hostile attitude. 'None,' I hastened to say. 'It was something he said and the way he said it that puzzled me. I thought he was trying to stir up trouble, but maybe I misunderstood.'

She stopped, facing me squarely. 'What did he say, then?'

I searched for the right way to convey the doubts he had

119

raised in my mind. 'Well, he implied he had seen us in the woods, and I was afraid he might spread it around. But what is worse is . . .' I faltered, 'that you had debased yourself with him.' I was amazed that I had actually managed to say it, but the pain of uncertainty had forced it out to give me some relief, no matter what the consequence.

I waited for her reaction as we stood face to face, a look of guilt, humiliation, even fear of having been exposed, but it was like regarding a closed book with a blank cover until she startled me with an unexpected response. She threw back her head and roared with laughter, so forcefully that she fell against me, her head resting on my chest, which gave me so much pleasure that my devil was temporarily driven out as I clutched her to me, not caring who might be watching.

When her paroxysm ended, she tapped me on the chin with a finger. 'Oh, you silly boy,' she reprimanded me, with a throaty chuckle. 'You didn't take any notice of that, did you? George is so disliked that if he did see us and told, nobody would believe him, knowing how untruthful he can be, and if he also saw how wonderful it was for us, then he's so jealous he's only wishing himself in your place. I'll make sure he stops provoking you. But, do you honestly think that I . . . ?' She stared into my eyes, eyebrows raised.

'No! No, of course not.' I could not show my belief in her fast enough. 'But it was a rotten thing for him to say. What would your father do if he knew?'

'What he doesn't know won't give him indigestion! That reminds me. We're going out to dinner with friends after surgery and I have to get ready, so off you go to your tea and don't worry any more.' She squeezed my arm and began to move away, whirling around to wave a hand. 'Bye, now, 'til tomorrow.'

I stood watching her go, my joyous mood beginning to deflate.

The next few days passed without incident. Everything and everyone was subdued—Frank, Tom, Fio, me. I put it down to the fact that Frank was still nursing his physical injuries and Tom his mental ones, while we two were lovesick. Also the end of term was fast approaching, with school tests imminent, the children apprehensive that the results would show how they had applied themselves over the term. It meant more work for the staff, setting the questions and marking, and would also indicate our own ability to impart knowledge. Although it could not affect my future, as that had already been determined for the coming September, my pride was such that I wanted it to be seen and remembered that I had done well while helping out in this back of beyond. Fio would have to stay on here for a couple of years while we were engaged, so I would often be returning here to visit her.

Saturday was a very hot and boring day, as I remember it. I bathed in the long tin bath while Bessie shopped, then wrote letters in my room until she returned. Every time I happened to glance up I saw 'Girl in a Yellow Dress' watching me, and wondered what was to become of her. Did Frank know about Tom's real father? Gossip must have been rife when those two were toddlers, but after a time it would have faded from people's minds when no longer a subject for discussion. Forgetfulness, too, might have been induced by a fear of George's reaction if the subject should be broached. I roused myself—contemplation had crept up on me again. I told the girl in the picture that the sooner she went to her rightful owner the better, while acknowledging that it was unlikely to occur for a long time yet.

After dinner, Bessie and I strolled to the green to watch cricket, reclining in deck chairs. During play, in which Wills hit a couple of sixes, I pondered on how the villagers could endure such a boring existence where nothing out of the ordinary ever happened, one day following another with

121

predictable accuracy. Thank goodness, I was thinking, that in a few weeks I would be far away with a new car and a new life with Fio ahead of me, when polite clapping signalled the end of the match and we left for home. Later, I walked back to the village with Bessie, who was eager for the evening whist drive, and took myself into the Snug. The usual groups were already there and I settled down at my ease, until I happened to glance into the public bar and saw George Piper. He caught my eye, and I seemed to detect a sly leer directed towards me before I looked away. My stomach quaked and bile rose in my throat.

I left at about half past ten and crossed the road to the hall, ready to escort Bessie home. Noisy, uneven footsteps behind me disturbed the quiet night, so I turned around as I reached the door and by the pale light of the moon was able to make out George lurching along the road. Others began to follow him, talking and joking as they went their various ways, then Bessie appeared, bemoaning the fact that she had lost by only a few points. We walked along past the church, chatting with some neighbours, and came to the bridge. As we went across, I thought I heard indefinable sounds from below that mingled with the noise of the splashing water. Could it be George, swearing as he tripped over his feet as he stepped over the stones? He was prone to do both at this time of night, but I was not tempted to peer down past the coping for another sight of him—in any case, a gusty wind had arisen, blowing heavy-laden clouds across the moon, which brought visibility to less than a few yards.

'There'll be rain, sure 'nough, mebbe a storm,' someone said, so we put our heads down into the wind and hurried towards home. We had barely reached the cottage when the heavens opened and the rain poured down amid flashes of lightning and a sharp crack of thunder. Thankfully, Bessie and I shut the door on the wild night outside and had our bedtime drinks, stretching out the time until the storm had abated enough for restful sleep. The whistle of the eleven forty-five coincided with the last of the thunder as I got into bed, the air now much cooler and less charged.

The morning dawned bright and clear, fresher for the overnight rain. Bessie prepared the vegetables, put the joint in the oven and we set off for church, finding more traffic on the road than was usual for a Sunday in late June. A car turned up Walnut Tree Lane as we reached it and I saw vehicles parked down by the bridge, with some activity taking place beneath it as we arrived there, to find, amongst others, Jim Carter, his bowler hat perched on the back of his head, leaning over the parapet.

The church bells began to ring out their call to worship as Bessie poked him in the ribs. 'What's to do, Jim?'

He jerked his head sharply around at the sound of her voice. ' 'Tis George Piper. 'E were found dead—face down in stream this mornin' . . .'

Day 12

I heard Bessie's indrawn breath as we cast an involuntary glance down to where the interest was centred. There was little to see, just a few official-looking men, some in uniform, with two or three walking up alongside the hedge edging the cornfield towards the farm. There was no sign of a body.

'Seems he's been moved,' said Bessie, in a subdued voice.

'Ay.' Jim Carter was equally muted. 'They'll 'ave took 'im to mortu'ry at Cottage 'Ospital.' He suddenly brightened. 'I wonder if she'll want the motor 'earse or the 'osses? The 'osses makes a finer show.'

'You should be ashamed of yourself, Jim Carter, thinkin' on that at a time like this! Come along, Mr Parr—if I don't hurry I shan't have time to get me surplice to rights,' and Bessie swept on her way clutching her hymn book, her well-rounded, well-corseted rear exuding her disapproval, as the bells summoned us urgently to forsake the temporal and seek the spiritual.

Jim Carter gave me a sly look and winked, saying under his breath as I prepared to follow, 'Can't 'magine a better time ter think on't, can 'ee, Mr Parr?'

My own thoughts were in turmoil, until one took precedence over the others. I felt glad. Try as I might I was unable to feel anything other than that, neither pity nor regret, nothing but thankfulness. Destiny had decided that

124

this man's reign of terror should come to an end, and it was meet and right that he had been taken now before he could wreak more harm. I wondered what kind of reaction Lucy and Tom would have—shock, of course, perhaps relief— and guilt? I had heard Tom wish him dead, and Lucy would not be human if she had not done so at some time or other. I understood that you always feel some guilt when a person close to you dies, either because of things done or not done, and I hoped those two would not feel too badly.

The church was humming with excitement as I took my place in the pew next to Miss Millard. She raised an enquiring eyebrow and I nodded briefly in return. There was no time for speech before I made my obeisance, giving thanks to the Lord for His wisdom and mercy, and when I raised myself from my knees the clergy and choir, including a rather flustered Bessie, had already begun to process along the aisle.

The service over, once we were outside tongues were loosened and discussion rife. The common denominator was the surprise expressed that such an accident had not occurred before, considering George's condition whenever he left the inn.

'Them stones is slippy. 'Tis easy done to lose yer footin' an' get fell in.' So Martyn, the miller, a grey man with a drooping moustache, was saying to the world in general, and then to me, 'Them two at farm'll 'ave an easier life now 'e's gone.'

I agreed, chatting to him as I waited for Bessie, who was taking longer than usual to reappear, possibly exchanging views on the subject with the rest of the choir.

'They're saying that Mr Graves—you know, the builder— has already been approached,' was how she greeted me. 'Not wasting any time, are they?'

'A builder? Whatever do they want a builder for?' I asked, in my ignorance.

'Oh, sorry, you wouldn't know. Mr Graves is also the undertaker. They knock up coffins in the carpenter's shed, very plain, no satin linings—but they do have brass handles. If you wants anything more fancy you have to get somebody out from town, but people here rarely bother.'

'I don't think I've met him. Graves—what an appropriate name! It'd be right on the tip of your tongue if you were planning a funeral.' I looked to see if she shared my half-concealed amusement, but her thoughts were elsewhere.

'Wonder how Lucy and the boy are taking it? Seems she'll have to identify the body—as if everyone don't know who 'tis! S'pose Robbie'll get leave an' come home. Wonder when funeral will be?'

We had walked until reaching the bridge where children and youths were leaning over the coping, Frank not amongst them, I noticed. A few cars remained and a police officer wearing a peaked cap stood by the stream, hands behind his back. The slope down to the footpath had been cordoned off and a group of local men were foregathered at the top. One of them heard Bessie's last remark and prepared to show off his scanty knowledge.

'The funeral, Bessie? Dunnow—there'll 'ave to be an inquest first. A chap said the coroner's already bin told—sudden death, y'see. George'll 'ave ter be cut up so's they can find out what caused it.'

' 'Tis pretty clear what caused it,' interjected another loiterer. ' 'E got drunk, fell in an' drownded 'is silly self.'

'Wouldn't 'a thought water were deep enough,' said the first man. 'But p'raps 'e jest passed out cold.'

'Come along, Bessie, let's get home.' I took her elbow as she had gone quite pale at the thought of George having to undergo a post-mortem. I had no such qualms about what was to happen to that evil man, merely pondering on whether Dr Mac would preside or a pathologist be called in. In the event, it was the latter.

126

Bessie, for once, only picked at her dinner but I tucked in with relish, thinking how Lucy and Tom, and even myself, were at last free to lead happier lives. Then I remembered something else. 'You'll be able to give Lucy the painting now.'

'All in good time,' she answered. 'She'll have enough to do getting over the awfulness 'o being caught up in all this.'

'I can't see what's so awful about it,' I protested. 'I look upon it as a day when we should put the flags out and sing from the rooftops. It couldn't have happened to a more worthy person.'

'You mind what you're a-saying.' Bessie pushed back her chair while giving me a warning stare. 'You're tempting fate—and the good Lord—by speaking ill of the dead, however much you think 'tis deserved. How do ye know his shade's not right here in this room?'

'Bessie!' I was taken aback. 'I'd no idea you believed in such fanciful things—and you a pillar of the church! Anyway, even if it was hereabouts, it couldn't do us any harm.'

'I'm glad you feel so sure, Mr Parr.' Bessie was in a huff—a rarity for her. 'Me, I tend to tread very carefully about these things, though I find it 'ard to believe in that old "guiding light" story that led the ghost back for revenge. You must've seen the children play that game. They believe it, though, as do all the folk who were raised around here, and who are we to argue with them?'

With a confidence supported by a bright, sunny day, I laughed. 'That was merely the village people's credulous imaginations working overtime to account for the son's suicide from remorse. And George killed himself—without intending to, of course—so what has he got to come back for? Now he's gone, he's gone.'

Bessie stacked the plates with such vigour that I feared she might break them. 'You believe what you want 'bout the afterlife, Mr Parr, but there's no need to call down retribution on yourself in *my* home!'

Having duly been put in my place, I began to have second thoughts about it as I recalled the night I visited the ruins in the woods. There was no denying that the place had a weird atmosphere. I did my best to soothe Bessie's ruffled feelings by apologising, but it took her some time to forgive me and resume normal conversation. It was then I suggested I should go to the farm to offer help, but she was against it.

'What can anyone do at the moment? The place'll be crawling with folk trying to learn all they can so's they'll be able to be first to spread it around. Why else would they be there? The Pipers have no close friends to bring real condolence.'

I accepted her reasoning though I would have liked to see Tom. Later, I walked in the woods while Bessie was at Evensong, hoping I might find him there. I heard a cuckoo call and recited aloud as Tom had taught me, 'Cuckoo in May sing all day, in June change its tune, in July away fly.' I had hoped to hear an echo provided by a childish voice or hear some notes played on a sycamore pipe, but was disappointed.

On my return I found Bessie also arrived back, having gleaned more news. It transpired that it had been Mr Kinsman, the small, chubby milkman with bristly cheeks, who had noticed the body as he drove his milk cart over the bridge. He owned a dairy farm and delivered milk daily, dispensing it by ladle from churns into metal cans with lids which were left on doorsteps for him to fill with the rich, creamy liquid, often still warm from the cow. Sometimes, when it arrived I would see Bessie half fill a glass jar, screw on a top, and sit shaking it as we chatted and, after a time, as if by magic, a golden ball would appear in the white

128

liquid and she would say, 'There y'are—we'll have this nice bit 'o butter on hot scones with our tea.'

I pulled my thoughts back from the milk and butter to hear her tell, shuddering, that a pathologist would perform his duties tomorrow with Dr Mac in attendance, and the inquest would probably be held on Wednesday, with the funeral on Friday. Further, she said, inquisitive people who had gone up to the farm had been refused entry by the constable, who also reported that Lucy and Tom were in shock but recovering, with Tom obviously not expected back at school that week. There was nothing more for us to do but go to bed early and, as I bade goodnight to the girl in the picture, I wondered how soon she would be taken from me.

Monday was filled with the same pervasive curiosity that was infecting the whole community, anxious to hear any minor detail. Everyone was talking about the grim misfortune that had overtaken George, with much tongue clicking but little regret, all acutely aware of what was taking place in the mortuary. My darling Fio, seeming reluctant to pursue what she called 'this morbid topic of conversation', refused to be drawn and was reticent for the rest of the school day. The children, on the other hand, appeared to find it vitalising and were more alert than usual, one notable exception being Frank, who was restless, not paying attention and apparently unable to focus his thoughts. I had a suspicion that he might be jealous of the spotlight now fallen on Tom, which was bound to continue until after the funeral.

On the Wednesday, as I cycled back to tea after school, I stopped to pick up my newspaper and a magazine from elderly, white-haired Mr Hillman. Standing behind his counter, he verbally distributed all the local news as well.

'G'day, Mr Parr. Inquest's over. Robbie arrived back on leave jest in time fer it. There was one or two witnesses, like

Bill Angove, but the verdict were as expected—accidental death. They'll be able ter bury 'im now. Seems there were some discussion 'bout a wound on the side of 'is 'ead, but the path—the pathol'gist said that were prob'ly caused as 'e fell an' hit one o' them craggy rocks that stick up in stream. Even if he hadn't bin dead drunk—an' coroner said 'e'd 'ad enough drink in 'im to sink a battleship—then 'e'd prob'ly 'ave bin knocked out an' lay on 'is face an' drownded. That'll be sevenpence ha'penny, sir, if you please.'

I duly informed Bessie of the verdict and the fact that Robbie was home. I felt pleased about that—Tom and Lucy would have someone to help stabilise their disrupted lives. I was still resisting the impulse to call on them, knowing that any sympathy I might offer would sound hollow, and vainly hoped to come across the boy in the woods. I had managed to pen and post a note of sympathy, tongue in cheek.

The inquest over, a kind of tedium fell over the village. The children drifted back into their normal pattern of resistance to learning, Fio appeared disinclined to agree to a meeting alone with me, and I was disinclined to do other than lust over her and ponder on those in Walnut Tree Farm. I asked Bessie if she was going to the funeral and she said of course, it was her Christian duty to say a prayer for a soul expected to sup with the Devil and who would, therefore, hardly be resting in peace.

It rained heavily on the Friday. I cycled back to a cold dinner just ahead of Bessie returning from the burial, and hung her dripping mackintosh with my own in the wash-house before drying the rest of me in front of the kitchen fire.

'How did it go?' I asked.

She handed me a packet of ham to open as she rendered

her account of the proceedings. 'Well, it would've gone better if it hadn't rained,' she began. 'The 'osses' plumes got very bedraggled an' so did Jim Carter, the bearers an' the rest of 'em—one can hardly call 'em mourners—and there were quite a few nosey-parkerin'. Lucy and Tom, nor Robbie, showed anythin' at all on their faces an' stayed dumb, letting Vicar deal with the hymns and service on his own. I think he found it difficult to find the right words to say over coffin, hummin' an' hawing a bit, but it were done at last.' She divided the ham on to our plates amid the salad. 'I didn't follow coffin to the grave to see it lowered, but I did see it were bein' put right against the wall overlookin' the stream where 'e died—an' there were only one wreath. All in all, I did me duty and went, but I didn't feel good about doing it. Kate Acaster were there, too, which surprised me, saying she felt the same, as if God were turning a blind eye.'

The meal over, I had an idea. 'We've got end-of-term tests next week and there are some points I'd like to discuss with Miss Macdonald. I'd consider it a favour if she could come to tea with us tomorrow or Sunday. It looks like being a wet weekend with nothing much else to do, anyway.'

Bessie, at the sink with her back to me, stopped what she was doing before resuming with an increased burst of energy. 'You've taken me by surprise, Mr Parr, not having heard you mention her name lately. Of course, if you want her to come she's welcome—just let me know which day.' The cutlery rattled noisily in the bowl.

I received the impression that Fio would not be welcome and I could not really understand why, although one reason could be that, being the doctor's daughter, she would be considered as belonging to the upper middle classes even though a working girl herself, and that might put Bessie, whom I knew to be very class conscious, at a disadvantage.

The class system here, Paul, was already under threat but tenacious, and in those days people looked upon doctors as gods, with the power of life or death.

I had to bite my tongue to prevent myself saying, 'Bessie, I want you to be the first to know that Fiona and I love each other and, when I've asked her father's permission, we'll get engaged and eventually marry.' What I did say was, 'Good, I'll ask her which day will be the most convenient.'

She sneezed sharply. 'Oh dear, Mr Parr, I do hope I'm not getting a cold. I'm liable to, whenever I gets me feet wet. Should've changed me shoes d'reckly I come in, but stupidly forgot.'

I was putting on my damp mac in the wash-house before returning to school when I heard a knock at the back door. I opened it to find Tom standing in the fine drizzle holding his tortoise to his chest, a wide smile brightening his wet face.

' 'Allo, Sir,' he greeted me. 'I've come ter take Methy.'

'Tom!' I was surprised by the rush of thankfulness that made me want to throw my arms around the both of them, hesitating as Bessie asked who was there.

'It's Tom—he's got Methy.' Then to the boy: 'How are you and your mother getting on? Is there anything I can do to help?'

He shook his head. 'We be all right, thank ye,' and as Bessie arrived at the door, inviting him inside, 'best not—I should get back. Want to thank 'ee fer lookin' after Methy. He's fine, but he's missed me—I can tell. See you Monday, Mr Parr,' and he went off happily along the path and into the woods.

I stopped Fio later as she was leaving her art class, and as I touched her arm that familiar thrill enveloped me. 'Will you come to tea with Bessie and me tomorrow—or Sunday?' I whispered. 'I need you near me for an hour or so—if nothing else.'

132

'Please be patient a little longer,' she whispered back. 'I can't manage this weekend—I'm staying with friends.' She gave me a lovely smile, which compensated slightly for her refusal, while I tried to be glad she had so many friends, but found it irksome that she did not try to spend more of her time with me.

Bessie's voice was croaky next day. As it was still raining she decided not to go shopping, so I had my bath, took the list she gave me, and went along to the village to shop for her. 'An' when you buy your paper, ask Mr Hillman to 'pologise to Vicar an' say me throat's bad, so I'm staying indoors 'til it's better,' she said, hoarsely.

After moping around listlessly until after tea, I braved the rain in the evening and hurried along to the inn to relax with a pint, reminding myself that there would be no need to avoid anyone in the public bar any more. Despite that, I had got used to chatting to the fellows who frequented the Snug, so was making my way towards that door when I felt a hand on my arm.

'Hey, Mr Parr.' The voice was quiet and friendly, and I met Robbie's earnest brown eyes. 'I wondered if you'd be in tonight. We got yer note—thanks.'

'It's been a bad business for you all.'

'Ay. Nobody to blame but hisself, though.'

'That's true. When he left here that night I saw him stumbling along.'

He glanced at me sharply. 'You saw him? But you weren't called as a witness at inquest, were ye?'

I shrugged. 'There were several others who saw him after I did, because I went across to the hall to pick up Bessie. I regret not having looked over the bridge as we crossed, but it was dark and I doubt I could have seen anything. If I had, I would've gone down and pulled him out.' Would I have wanted to, though, I asked myself?

'But you didn't.' It was a statement.

133

'No. I thought I heard something—a noise, a voice—but there were several of us talking, the wind was blowing hard and a storm threatening, so we made for home.'

'That's a pity, then, but it's hardly your fault,' he said, giving it some thought. 'George swore a lot to hisself—s'pect you heard 'im doin'that.'

'Might have.'

Robbie lifted his tankard, emptying it. I felt sorry for him—he must find it hard coming to terms with losing someone who had been a part of his life since birth.

'Have another?' I enquired, and when he agreed I ordered, then continued the conversation with what was concerning me most. 'What about Lucy and Tom? How are they dealing with it?'

'Oh, all right. They're getting over the fact that they're on their own an' can do much as they please. They're finding it some diff'rent.' He gave a short laugh.

'Will you be staying long? I mean, long enough for things to be settled. Someone will be needed to run the farm. Will you arrange to hire a man? Or does Lucy intend to sell up?'

He laughed again. 'So many questions with answers not yet thought on! Don't 'ee fret—it'll be took good care of. I'll be here awhile to get things ordered.'

Others had come in by now and were crowding round for a word with Robbie so I went into the Snug. Jim Carter was there with Martyn the miller and Constable Wills. There was no mention made of George, I noticed.

After a while, Dr Mac joined us. This evening he brought his drink over and came to sit beside me. 'You haven't visited us lately,' he began, wreathed in clouds of smoke from his pipe. 'I had thought to see more of you, having hoped that you and Fio might've hit it off with each other.'

His pointed remark took me completely by surprise. I searched for the words to deny something of which I was

134

terribly proud, but what came out of my mouth was, 'Well, actually, sir—we have!'

He dropped his glass down on the table, staring momentarily into my face before a smile softened his own. 'You have? Then I must beg your pardon because Fio has said nothing—but I'm really, truly delighted to hear it! Not having seen you with her at the house, I'd foolishly assumed . . . But it's always a mistake to assume anything, isn't it? Assumptions can be so wrong, my dear chap.'

Yes, I now know very well just how wrong they can be.

Day 13

Having made that incautious admission to Dr Mac, I did my best to be careful not to be drawn further even though increasingly anxious to acknowledge my overweening pride in being loved by Fio. As it was, I had the uncomfortable feeling of already having said too much, and endeavoured to dampen down the flame I had unwittingly ignited.

'I think Fio might prefer to tell you about it herself,' I put in hastily. 'She wanted to wait until term ended, so it might be as well if you try to forget anything I've said for the time being.'

He tapped the side of his nose with a forefinger, his broad grin not lessening by an inch. 'Very wise of you. She knows how much this will mean to me and I expect she'll want to choose the right moment to spring the surprise. I understand, Eddie.'

His understanding was not accompanied by a similar amount of discretion, however, as he grew more and more convivial, buying drinks freely for everyone, which I feared might arouse speculation as to the reason for his benevolence while in my company. The evening became slightly riotous and nobody left until closing time.

The next day, Sunday, I nursed a thick head. Bessie was not very well herself, unhappy about having to stay indoors and thus miss the gossip-of-the-day in church, while I was glad of her indisposition in case the chief topic should possibly refer to yours truly and Fio. She refrained from remarking on my own gloomy expression, which was accompanying a thumping head, but her look said volumes about my deserving it. I had no doubt she was right and that I merited whatever was my due. Why had I been so stupid?

A curious numbness infected the atmosphere around me on Monday morning. To begin with, the weather was sultry and overcast, which was conducive neither to clear-headedness nor to good temper and, furthermore, I was suffering from a certain amount of apprehension. I would know by Fio's attitude whether she had become aware of my indiscretion on Saturday night—and I did—or thought I did.

On the way to assembly she floated past me, pretty dress flaring out to offer an occasional glimpse of knee, pert nose in the air. I held my breath when she looked in my direction before seating herself at the piano, feeling a wave of thankfulness as I saw the bright smile, white teeth gleaming in the red cupid's bow of her mouth. I murmured a thankful prayer that either she did not know or felt no vexation about my having exposed our secret, little realising that those gleaming white teeth were really desirous of sinking into my jugular vein.

My class was complete again with Tom returned. He was more at ease than I had ever seen him, eager to learn, the ideal of every schoolmaster. Frank, on the other hand, was inattentive, his thoughts divided as if he had something on his mind. I had noticed him behaving like this for a week or so, but it became more obvious when seen beside Tom's industry. In addition to this, a feeling of—was it expectation?—was looming over the entire class, and in my naivety I failed to understand why. Smiling faces held a saucy knowingness that I did my best to ignore, the girls whispering behind their hands. The end-of-term tests were due to begin next day, so I tried to capture their attention and guide them into studying the relevant pages of the books which would help them most in revision.

At break I found Fio closeted with Miss Millard, so had to kick my heels on my own with no chance to talk with her before the form bell rang and we were back in our class-rooms. The rest of the morning dragged away, while I longed for the dinner bell to ring out its call to freedom as much as any child there. When it came I dashed out, almost catching up with my darling before being intercepted by Miss Hope.

'Miss Millard would like a word with you before you go,' she said, primly. 'She's waiting in her room—now.'

I could not ignore this irksome summons. Miss Millard, well mannered and composed as always, gestured to a chair. 'Please sit down, Mr Parr. I felt I should speak with you as I have just done with Miss Macdonald. I don't hold with idle rumour, but as this publicly affects you both it must be inquired into lest it should reflect upon the school.'

What did she mean by 'reflect upon the school'? Had someone other than George observed us as we cavorted in the woods? My stomach went into a knot, but I endeavoured to relax and present a carefree appearance.

'Please forgive my seeming to pry into your private affairs, Mr Parr, but I heard via a reliable source that you plan to enter into an alliance with Miss Macdonald. This has come as something of a surprise as you have not been seen openly together, and I wondered at the reason for your pursuing what must have been a clandestine romance in order to avoid notice. There is usually a period of apparent interest between two people when courting.' She smiled fixedly, awaiting my reply.

I bitterly regretted my careless lapse in the Snug—some-one had obviously guessed aright and spread it around. I had no idea how Fio had reacted to the summons or to what she had admitted, so hesitated over my own response and in the end prevaricated. 'As you've already spoken to Miss Macdonald, she must've told you how things stand between us.'

Miss Millard innocently fell into the trap. 'She surely did.' Her level gaze bored into my face. 'She said there is nothing at all between you both, never has been and never will be, and that someone has made a mistake.'

I doubt she could have missed the involuntary tightening of my facial muscles caused by the shock of hearing what was, to me, an incredibly cruel and untrue statement. If Fio had wanted to continue keeping our secret, though I could see no purpose in doing so now, she might have done it more diplomatically and without being so plain spoken. I swallowed, while carefully choosing my words in reply.

'There you have it, then,' I said, as calmly as I could. 'You've had your answer from her mouth. I can't see why you need it confirmed by mine.'

'Because rumour named *you* as the original source, Mr Parr, but it seems you must have been misunderstood. I am very glad to have cleared it up to enable us to know where we stand. In school, as you are aware, teachers must be above reproach. Thank you for your time.'

She gave me a piercing stare, getting to her feet as a sign of dismissal. I went, with the impression that I was a naughty schoolboy leaving after being chastened—but it was more than that. It was a warning as to how I should conduct my personal life and I resented it. How dared she! Did she think I had been 'showing off' by suggesting this beautiful girl was attracted to me? I peddled fast and furiously towards Clover Cottage as I tried to flee from my embarrassment and annoyance, wondering what everyone else must be thinking of me.

Once arrived there I found that Bessie had been taken by the same surprise, probably having heard about it from a neighbour, or the milkman, or postman, or all of them.

What did it matter which one? I hated being the target of gossip and felt unreasonably ill-tempered towards her. Recovering from her chill, she was evidently feeling irritable herself and disinclined to mince her words.

'You're rather late, Mr Parr, so I'm hoping dinner isn't ruined. Been spooning with your intended, have you? I do think you might've told me what's been going on instead of letting me find out—the last to know!'

'Mrs Marsham,' I countered angrily. 'If there had been anything for you to know, I would've told you. As it is, whatever you heard has come about by way of a misunderstanding, so I'd be grateful if you'd kindly deny anything further that may be sloughed off into your no doubt waiting ears—and I don't want anything to eat, thank you!' With that I went up to my room, leaving her with her mouth hanging open.

I slumped into my chair in the utter despair of injured youth, my world in tatters around me, the laughing-stock of West Halsey. How was I ever going to face anyone again? What were they saying about me? Worst of all was remembering how blatantly Fio had denied our love; I wanly contemplated catching the next train home.

A hesitant knock on the door a little later roused me from my wallow in self-pity. 'Come in,' I responded, albeit reluctantly.

Bessie entered, looking contrite. 'I'm sorry for what I said, Mr Parr. Suppose me feelings were hurt. I should've known you'd behave in a proper manner and not set out to deceive me.'

I felt even more ashamed because that is exactly what I had been doing at Fio's insistence, though I could not put all the blame on her—I could have refused. What a mess I had landed myself in!

'Bessie . . .' I stood up and went to her, taking her hand. 'I'm sorry for what I said, too, it was unforgivable, and I'm just as shocked by all this fuss as you are. I wish it had never happened but it has—and I don't know what to do about it.'

I must have looked suitably contrite and worried, because she patted my hand in a motherly fashion, saying, 'Come down and have some bread an' cheese an' a cup 'o tea fer now, we'll have our meal later on. Don't you be upset—things are never so bad as they seems to be in the beginning—an' folk soon forget.'

'That's true. Thank you. I'll come when I've had a wash.'

After I had sluiced my face and hands in the cold water I felt a little better. 'Girl in a Yellow Dress' and I faced each other. 'You had your time of trouble and shame, much greater than mine, Lucy, but you carried on, so I suppose I must do likewise,' I mouthed, and went downstairs.

I forced myself to return to school that afternoon, trying to act as if nothing was wrong, and met Fio alone in the corridor for a fleeting moment. 'Fio,' I said urgently. 'We have to discuss this . . .'

She put a finger to her lips, her expression unreadable. 'Not here—not now. When the children's tests are over we'll arrange to be together again. It's best to go on pretending we're nothing to each other for the time being.'

I gulped with relief. There was no trace of hostility in her manner, though it was not displaying love, either, merely amiability. My mind was eased with regard to her forgiving me for opening up to her father when she had said 'pretending'. What a terrific girl she was—taking it all in her stride! I was happy and relieved and foolish enough to try to embrace her, but she neatly evaded me.

I somehow got through the rest of that week and the next, though only by gritting my teeth and facing up squarely to the knowing stares of the villagers, but word soon got around that I was *not* becoming engaged to Dr Mac's daughter and interest flagged, as Bessie said it would.

141

I saw nothing of Lucy and no more of Robbie, but Tom seemed happy enough, working hard at his revision while keeping away from the woods, and I was glad his home life had changed for the better.

The day finally came when the tests were finished and the children heaved sighs of relief—but not the teachers who had to mark their work. I had been staying behind after school, whittling down the piles of books and papers while hoping that Fio would do the same, but she was not so involved with written work and what she did have she took home with her. I went back that Friday evening and carried on until quite late, finally finishing the task on Saturday morning. That afternoon, Bessie and I watched Wills hitting his usual sixes and winning the match, then I stayed home, avoiding the inn with its speculative customers, while she went off to the whist drive.

It was on the Sunday morning that a field day arrived for the gossips, lifting any remaining pressure from me. The July day was perfect as my landlady and I stepped out for church, arriving just as the bell-ringers began to exert their full energy on the ropes. Bessie left me to join the rest of the choir while I went to my usual seat beside Miss Millard, ignoring any eyes that might fall on mine. We chatted quietly about the results of the tests, until becoming aware of a sudden hush that had settled on the pews behind us. Heads turned and necks strained, mine included, in order to see what was happening, and at that moment the choir and clergy began their solemn march. There had been time enough, however, for me to notice three strangers in the back pews, strangers to the church but not to the worshippers.

Robbie, Lucy and Tom were rising to their feet with the rest of us as we swallowed our amazement and began to sing praises to the Lord. We had to contain our impatience and curiosity until the service was over, but then, when the congregation moved outside, tongues got busy. The three Pipers were arrayed in smart new clothes, with Lucy in particular changed almost beyond recognition once more. She could no longer bear comparison with the girl in the painting, but showed a mature beauty and serenity and, wonder of wonders, happiness in her face. She was dressed in a pretty frock and strappy shoes, a small hat tilted at an angle over hair cut short, appearing to be nearer twenty than thirty. Before this, she could have been mistaken for Tom's grandmother. It was obvious that she was feeling shy by the way in which she clutched her son's hand with downcast eyes, staying close to Robbie, who held an elbow protectively. Tom waved to me so I went up to them.

'I'm so pleased to see you here,' I enthused. 'It helps to get rid of the cares of the week, doesn't it?' at once wishing I had said something less banal, but as I searched for a better phrase, others joined us. I saw Bessie waiting on the steps, so politely excused myself.

'Well! How about that?' she greeted me, 'But only to be expected, I s'pose. It'll be good for Tom—just seems a bit soon to be in good taste, don't ye think?'

We had reached the lychgate while I was still trying to puzzle out what she meant. 'Er—a bit soon for what, Bessie?'

'Oh, come on, Mr Parr! You surely noticed how they was making sheep's eyes at each other. 'Tis an ideal thing to have happened to Lucy—I hope we can be friends again now. An' aren't they dressed nice? I've just been told Robbie took 'em to town yesterday an' bought new outfits. He must've had a big win on the gee-gees.'

Mrs Acaster and Frank caught up with us as we went through the gate. Bessie was still bubbling. 'I was just a-saying, Kate, how nice the Pipers look in their new finery. I hear Robbie took 'em shopping an' bought a whole lot o' diff'rent things—even a wireless set!'

143

Mrs Acaster nodded her head, which invariably displayed a worn, anxious expression, in agreement, while Frank gazed down the road, scowling. 'Lucy's lucky,' she murmured. 'Seems like 'er ship's come 'ome at last.'

Lucy's luck formed the chief topic of conversation amongst everyone we met on the way home, with extra snippets of information being bandied about.

' 'Tis said that Robbie's took on a chap from East Halsey to manage farm an' 'elp with 'arvest. Man called Mitchell, 'tis—don't 'member 'im rightly.'

'I b'lieve Robbie's plannin' ter get a discharge from Army an' take over farm hissel'. S'pose it belongs ter Lucy now, since there's been no talk of a will.'

'He knows which side 'is bread's buttered on if he's started a-courtin' 'er.'

'Or is she a-courtin' 'im—like she did George?'

The last remark was followed by laughter and a knowing wag of heads. I was wishing the couple well, glad for Tom's sake and my own now the spotlight that had briefly shone on me had been swung around in the Pipers' direction.

I wrote letters home that afternoon, one in answer to a query I had received from your Auntie Joyce. The summer holidays were almost upon us and she had been offered the use of a beach house, sleeping four, at a seaside resort for a month. She was taking a boyfriend she hoped to marry, your Uncle Stephen as it turned out, and Babs, the girl I had been so taken with at Easter. She had faded from my thoughts the moment I laid eyes on Fio, and I now found it difficult to recall what she looked like. Lacking any real enthusiasm to go with them, I wrote that I would decide later, my main desire being to take Fio home to meet the family before she left for Italy. If only the dear girl would discuss things with me so I could finalise the arrangements! Also, time had to be found for familiarising myself with the car I intended to buy, the later model Austin Seven, a type in which I had previously been able to have practice runs.

I posted my letters when walking Bessie to Evensong, then, hoping to find Tom—or perhaps Fio—in the woods, I left her and walked back along the stream path to the small, wooden bridge, but as there was no sign of the two persons I most wanted to see when I reached the big lake, I continued on to the cottage, having made up my mind that I would no longer be put off with Fio's delaying tactics.

Monday morning, unusually, had quite an ebullient feeling about it. We had reached the last weeks of term and nobody was too concerned about cramming knowledge into heads, though interest and discipline had to be maintained. I noted that the children in the playground seemed to be more unruly, especially Frank, who dominated the others without showing open aggression to watchful eyes, except when he played his part in 'The Ballad of Halsey Manor'. He then seemed to be overly heavy-handed with Tom, who was invariably the chosen victim, and I suspected that Frank's jealousy lay behind it, newly inflamed by the Pipers' good fortune. That morning, after seeing Tom pushed about, I called him in for a quiet word.

'It was good to see you in church with the family, Tom. We haven't had that chat you wanted yet, have we? How are things at home? Everything settled down?'

'Ay, they're all right, thank 'ee, sir.'

'Your mother looked well, I thought.'

The large, dark blue eyes regarded me without giving away one iota of information. 'Yessir.'

It was like talking to a cardboard cut-out. If something was bothering him, if Frank was being too overbearing, I would have to discover it some other way. I found it surprising that one so young was capable of such self-containment.

145

Fio was still keeping her distance, too, arriving at the very last minute, dashing in and out of assembly without catching my eye, and failing to join us for break. My annoyance was rapidly increasing. I did not intend for this avoidance to continue any longer, and left my classroom at dinnertime with such alacrity that I was outside the gate and along the road by the time she came hurrying out.

'I'm going to walk you home,' I announced, with as much firmness as I was able to muster, the longing for her beginning to take hold again.

She appeared slightly disconcerted, but it was quickly masked by a bland expression. 'Are you sure that's sensible? It could give the tittle-tattlers more ammunition.' She lifted her adorable face up at a fetching angle, smiling at me, and I was unable to resist bending to kiss that tempting mouth. She jerked her head away and walked on, gazing straight ahead while saying, 'And that would be most unwise.'

I hurried after her, staring down on the top of her close-fitting cloche hat. 'I'm sorry, Fio, but I'm so madly in love with you. How can you expect me not to show it? You mean everything to me and I'm sick and tired of pretending otherwise. Can't we be honest with ourselves and everybody else?'

She slackened her pace, raising a pensive face to mine. 'You know I want that as much as you, but think of all the fuss there's been already. It took me ages to explain to Daddy when you let the cat out of the bag. He also thinks it best to keep quiet for the present, so I advise you not to mention it again if you see him.'

I put out a hand to hold her back. 'There's so little time left before school breaks up and I have plans we must talk over. When will you come home with me and how long will you stay? And I need to know when you're going away and when you're coming back—and an address where I can write to you, my love. If I don't resolve these details soon, I think I shall lose my mind and *really* spill the beans!'

146

I saw real concern in her eyes when I said that. 'Oh, Eddie—you won't do anything rash, will you? We've had such lovely times together—and I've an idea for something even better if only you'll have patience for a few days more. Look, it's the rounders match on Friday—maybe we can slip away as we did before and settle your worries then—and make love. Now, go home to your dinner.' She squeezed my hand briefly and stepped quickly away.

I went back for the bike with renewed hope in my foolish heart, and as I cycled over the humpback bridge I saw Tom ambling home alongside the hedge bordering the corn-field. I felt some satisfaction that his life was taking a turn for the better, and it was not until I was seated at the table that Bessie once again knocked the stuffing right out of me.

'There's a new rumour been flying around today, Mr Parr. I've no idea where 'tis come from—or who started it.'

I took the plate from her. 'Oh? What's this about, then?'

'They're saying that George Piper didn't die accidental—somebody meant to kill him . . .'

147

Day 14

I nearly dropped the plate Bessie was handing me. 'But that's ridiculous,' I said, angrily. 'Nobody queried it at the time and the coroner decided it was an accident. Who on earth is trying to cause the Pipers more trouble? They'll now have to suffer from this idle talk. Why can't they be left in peace?'

Bessie shrugged her shoulders. 'Can't say it's come as any surprise to me. No one liked George—an' quite a few detested him—so the idea must've crossed a few minds. 'Tis said that if somebody did drown him they should be given a medal.'

I lowered my knife and fork. 'You don't honestly think anyone did, do you?'

She shrugged again. 'It don't much matter now, one way or t'other. He's dead an' buried an' no love lost. 'Tis Tom an' Lucy I feels sorry for.'

'I'm sure it was an accident.' I tried to reason it out. 'He'd had too much to drink, overbalanced and fell in the stream. I'm only amazed he managed to keep on his feet for so long without keeling over.'

We ate in silence as I wondered if, perhaps, rumour had it right. I considered who stood to gain the most by his death—only Lucy and Tom directly. Who had hated him apart from them? Frank? Mrs Acaster? The constable? I recalled his look of aversion when we took Tom home. But speculation was absurd—it could have been anyone or nobody at all.

'Has a particular name been mentioned?' I asked.

She shook her head. 'No, but if someone did know something, they'd hardly be going aroun' sayin' that so and so 'ad murdered George, would they? Why not speak up at the time? I've simply heard it said that George were killed deliberate.'

'It sounds to me as if some malicious person merely wants to liven up village gossip.' I cleared my plate and eyed the plum pie.

Bessie fetched the pudding dishes. 'I'm sure you're right. It's been done to whip up a bit of excitement like it were when he was found, and to liven things up again now they've gone a bit flat. Mebbe it'll soon die down and be fergot.'

I heard nothing of it myself and it did not appear to have affected the Pipers, as once or twice I caught sight of Lucy in the shops looking radiant, making the most of her newly found freedom with Robbie in attendance. One evening I strolled to the lake, enjoying the fresh, scented air. There was no breeze, everything hushed and calm, and as I neared the edge I saw Tom standing with his back against a tree, staring out over the water to where it shimmered amongst the overhanging trees.

' 'Evenin', sir,' he said, without moving his head.

'How did you know it was me, Tom?' I asked, with a laugh.

'I knows yer step, an' you cough in a pertic'lar way.'

'Quite the young detective, aren't you? You'll have to read the stories in the *Strand* magazine about Sherlock Holmes—I'll lend you some of mine if you like.' I sat down near him. 'What else is there you can tell me?'

He shifted his position slightly. 'There's nowt else—'cept Uncle Robbie's goin' back to barracks soon.'

149

'You'll miss him, won't you? Still, I don't suppose he'll be away for long. I hear he's applying to leave the Army.'

The boy gave me a quick glance before transferring his gaze back to the lake. 'Ay. He says he's going there to fix it an' then come back fer good. Farm don't b'long to him, though.' He kicked a clump of grass before coming out with, 'I think he wants to wed me mam.'

It was a flat statement, with no expression. 'That would be a good thing to happen, wouldn't it?' I queried, tentatively. 'She needs someone to look after her.'

'I c'n do that.'

I tried to read his face, which had become flushed. Was he jealous of his uncle? He had been the only one to have his mother's love while George was alive and could now be resentful at having to share it with someone else. Robbie would have to tread very carefully to keep the boy's affection if that were so.

'I'm sure you can,' I agreed. 'But you have to attend school and leave her on her own for much of the time, and there must be heaps of work to do on the farm. Harvest time's near, isn't it?'

'Comin' up. I'll manage that easy wi' the man from East Halsey 'cos I'll be on holiday for weeks.'

I admired him for wanting to take on George's neglected duties and assuming it must be his place to do them, though with no idea of the responsibilities involved. He had obviously not reckoned on Robbie moving in to take over the reins.

I stood up, dusting off my trousers, and changed a subject I did not feel able to advise on. 'Have you any special friends, Tom?' I enquired.

'Only Methy—oh, and the 'oss. I calls 'im Joshua, but nobody else bothers wi' names. 'Tis the same wi' the dog— I'll have to think o' one—mebbe Prince. That's a smart name. I've never been let make friends with him as 'e's s'posed to be fierce—but I makes a fuss of 'im on the quiet when nobody's about. I'm goin' to be able to take 'im off the chain when Robbie's gone and give 'im a long run—'e don't know what 'is legs is for.'

I noted that Robbie seemed to be taking over already, but that should have been expected as it had been his home all his life. 'Watch those aitches and your grammar, Tom,' I suggested. 'Your written work is better than the way you speak,' and then mentally berated myself. If he should manage to perfect his diction, as I had been encouraging him to do, he would become the butt of everyone in the village for giving himself airs and graces; I should have thought of that before. I returned to my earlier question about his friends. 'What about the boys in your class?'

'I gets on with 'em all right, 'cept Frank, who wants to boss us all the time. I don't mind that, only he makes me join in when I'd rather be left alone.'

'It's no bad thing to be part of a team, though, like when you play cricket, or football or rounders.' I did not go on to say, because I had not yet realised it, that while some people adapt to be part of a team, others remain excluded by reason of their individuality. 'What about the end-of-term rounders match against East Halsey on Friday? You'll be doing your best to win for the school, won't you?'

''Course,' he replied, without sounding at all convincing.

I wondered whether to mention the gossip about George, but decided to leave it unsaid. If Tom had already heard it, it did not seem to be what was bothering him.

The sun was sinking low in the west, the birds flying home to roost as the boy had once told me. 'Time I was going and you in your bed—you're too often sleepy in school. Besides, your mother will be wondering about you.'

'Oh, I don't think so—s'pect she's too busy with other things to think about wi'out wondering 'bout me.' He pulled his whistle from his pocket and tapped the side of

151

his face with it, his mind elsewhere. 'D'you *really* believe she needs 'im? That he'd be good fer 'er?'

What curious questions. 'Why, yes—she obviously enjoys his company.'

'I never thought it'd be like this. It were going ter be so diff'rent wi' me dad gone,' he said absently, blinking his eyes and staring as if seeing me there for the first time. 'G'night, then, sir.'

'Goodnight, Tom.' I watched him wander off, unwillingly, I thought, and listened to the notes of his whistle as I followed the beaten path to the cottage, full of feelings of unease that I could not define.

When Bessie returned from choir practice she reported that the rumour seemed to be petering out, possibly because an accusing finger could not be pointed at any individual so it seemed to be passing into oblivion, and I was truly thankful.

Having finished marking the books, I felt free to look forward to tomorrow's match, remembering that Fio had promised we would try to slip away while everyone was engrossed in watching the game. Unfortunately, the day dawned cloudy with a threat of rain that boded ill for us, since it meant the crowd would be thin and our absence, therefore, noticeable. What was worse, I found I had been deputed as an extra referee in the event of a dispute, an inconvenient arrangement since I had planned on not being there at all.

I found Fio alone in the changing tent just before the start and took her hand. 'Doesn't look too hopeful for us to get away, does it, darling?'

She shook her head, disengaging my fingers. 'Somebody may come in. No, we'll have to give it a miss today. You do understand, don't you, that as we break up on Thursday week and I leave for Italy on the Saturday, it'll be the end of August before we see each other again?'

152

Put into words that our separation was so close and inevitable I felt totally devastated, grasping her arm and trying to draw her to me as she resisted.

'Edward—let me go at once!' There was no mistaking the authority in her tone that made me obey without question, and if only I had been able to see beyond the end of my nose I would have realised how much she really despised me.

Contrite, I begged her forgiveness. 'I love you so much, Fio, that I can't bear the thought of not seeing you for such a long time—though I'll write daily.' A new idea flashed through my mind. 'I know—I'll come with you!' Why not? I could use the money saved for the car. Where would be the pleasure in owning one if my love were not sitting beside me as I drove?

Quickly, and obviously composing herself, she said forcefully, 'Silly boy, that would be quite impossible—I'm touring with friends and our car is already full. We're not staying anywhere in particular, either, so I can't leave an address for you to write to. You'll just have to wait until I come home.'

'Then for pity's sake tell me when we can be together again before you go—and when we can declare our engagement?' I could hear my voice sounding loud and thick and frantic, rising up from the swirling, black depths of my stomach.

I suppose she could see I was reaching the end of my tether and put up a hand to touch my cheek. 'Look—we must go. Next week—I promise to fix a time when we can make our plans. Tell you when and where later.' As a whistle was blown on the field, signifying the start of play, her lips met mine in the briefest of encounters and she pushed out through the flap, leaving me once more in mental turmoil.

A fine drizzle had begun to fall, hurrying up play on the

153

field, though I hardly noticed it—or anything else for that matter. The whole of that dull, miserable weekend remains a blur of nothingness, except that I recall writing to Joyce to say I had decided to spend my holiday with her and her friends in the beach house after all.

Monday morning was fair and blue-skied, my spirits lifting at the prospect of meeting with the elusive object of my passion. You no doubt remember from your own school-days, Paul, how the period prior to breaking up has a special 'feel' to it, as of having almost won through to a goal once far distant but now within easy reach. This time my emotions were torn, anticipating the purchase of the car but regretting the empty weeks without Fio. My class held such an air of expectancy that it was no use hoping they would settle down to any serious work, so I gave them a chapter of a book to study with the promise of questions to follow. Tom was quiet and listless, seeming unable to concentrate on a task he usually enjoyed, and I called him back as he was leaving for break.

'Things all right at home, Tom? You didn't manage the lesson very well.'

His face reddened. 'Sorry, sir. Ay, everything's fine.'

I was not so sure it was but let him go, hastening to the staff room for a word with Fio, only to find everyone gathered there to discuss the prizegiving planned for the Wednesday of the following week. I managed to whisper, 'Tonight?' in her ear as we emerged.

'No, can't make it tonight,' she answered, and stopped me as I opened my mouth by saying, 'See you outside at dinnertime.'

The remainder of the morning passed slowly as I tried to curb my impatience. I noticed that Tom sat unmoving, his eyes fixed on the book before him without turning the pages, while the other children were fidgety and restless—in tune with my own mood. When the bell rang, I was as eager as any of them to get away and not best pleased when Tom came forward and tried to detain me.

'Not now, Tom,' I said, while resisting being overruled by those appealing eyes. 'Won't it wait 'til this afternoon?'

I saw him hesitate, then nod somewhat reluctantly as I skirted around him and caught up with Fio at the front gate.

'Why can't you see me tonight?' I queried, accusingly.

'Because I've already arranged to play tennis with some friends.'

I thought I detected a note of annoyance in her voice and wondered why, if she loved me, she was unable to cancel the game.

As though reading my thoughts, she said, 'You know we have to be careful not to be seen together, so I'll do my best to fix up something which won't arouse suspicion.' She pursed her lips and made a kissing noise, before hurrying for home.

The week dragged itself away as I waited impatiently for some sign from her. Although I carried out my schoolwork satisfactorily on the surface, writing reports and finding tasks to interest the children, underneath I was preoccupied with my own dreams and plans and had completely forgotten Tom's request to talk. He did not approach again to remind me, maybe put off by my air of detachment.

When Friday came without further word from Fio, I went to tackle her in desperation as she returned in the afternoon, but she was the first to speak.

'I was just coming to find you. Forgive me, I've been so terribly tied up this week, what with preparing for my holiday and one thing and another, but we could make it tonight, Eddie, if you agree. Some friends of Daddy's and mine who work at the hospital are coming to dinner and we're playing tennis afterwards. Did you know that we have a tennis court at the end of our garden? It's better than those you use at the recreation ground—where I've heard you boast that you beat the older boys easily!' She paused. 'Would you like to join in after dinner and beat us?'

Like to? 'Of course I would!' There was no uncertainty about the enthusiasm of my response. My frustration at not being able to shout out our love across the rooftops would be considerably offset by this unexpected opportunity to gain her admiration in showing my prowess at the net in front of her and her friends.

'All right, then. We'll be dining early so our guests can chat to Dad before he leaves for one of his boring meetings. I know you wouldn't be interested in medical matters, so what about eight thirty? We'll be able to get in a few sets, and when the others go we can take ourselves into the woods.' The promise hung there between us.

The afternoon flew by as I concentrated my thoughts elsewhere, wishing I had been given more notice of the evening's activity, anxious to remove my white flannels from the camphor-impregnated wardrobe and hang them in the fresh air. I did this as soon as I got back, telling Bessie of my invitation and pointing out that a heavy meal slopping about in my stomach might do worse than just cramp my style. She said we were having rabbit and pork stew and I could eat as little as I liked.

I was ready and waiting at eight o'clock, white pullover slung jauntily around my shoulders and wearing the flannels that yet retained an odour, though not as strong as before. I almost neglected to don the bicycle clips, afraid that creases would show, but changed my mind. Better to suffer creasing than come a cropper. My racquet, in its case, was tied to the saddlebag holding freshly whitened plimsolls and I was eager to go. Would it matter if I arrived early? Bessie stood watching me wheel the bike along the garden path, the non-committal expression on her face indicating disapproval of my visit, which caused a spark of anger to

156

flash through me. What business was it of hers? What possible reason could she have for opposing it? Would she relax her attitude and give me her blessing when she was made aware of the love we two shared? I liked Bessie and wanted her approval.

On arrival at the Macdonald house I found a flashy sports car in the drive which cost more than I would be able to afford. It was only a quarter past eight, but dinner must be over as Dr Mac's car had gone. I put the bicycle in the garage and changed into the plimsolls before ringing the doorbell, which brought a housemaid to guide me through a rear door leading into an extensive garden and tell me how to continue on.

I could hear faint laughter, voices, and the sounds of tennis balls pinging on racquet strings as I made my way via a rose garden, before passing a lily pond with spraying fountain and then through an area of fruit bushes and trees terminating in a high, thick hedge. I went through a gate to find that the hedge hid protective wire netting surrounding the court, and on the other side stood a few chairs and tables. The whole area was concealed and shielded from any unwanted onlookers in this perfect arboreal setting, and as for the court, there was no comparison to be made with the bare patches of grass and sagging nets of the recreation ground! At the far end of the garden I could see the woods, held back by tall hedges centred by a partly open gateway.

My eyes lingered briefly on the surroundings before settling on the players serving and volleying, two men, a girl and Fio. She waved to me and spoke to the others, and they all turned and waved in a friendly fashion before she indicated for me to sit at a table on which jugs and glasses were set.

'Help yourself,' she called. 'Nearly finished this game— we're making heavy going of it after eating too much.'

157

I poured myself a full tumbler of what I took to be a fruit punch and sat watching them. The other girl was vivacious, with brown hair cut short, older than Fio and of a fuller figure. Hazarding a guess, I put her in her late twenties with the men about the same age. They were both energetic and personable young men and able players, as I noted with displeasure, then decided it would be foolish to allow a moment of jealousy to put me in an ill humour. Why be jealous? My tennis was as good as theirs, better in fact, and Fio loved me and she was mine!

I felt thirsty, having forgone the usual cups of tea after my meal, so as soon as I had emptied one glass of the deliciously refreshing punch I poured another, swallowing it down in a few gulps. A great feeling of bonhomie enveloped me as I waited for the game to finish—beginning to float on a cloud of sheer happiness, friendliness and love. When I noticed the four players converging on me I stood up, as men used to do in the presence of ladies and which I continue to do out of habit. Well, I attempted to stand up, but something pulled me back in my seat, head swimming, as Fio made the introductions. I seem to remember that the girl was a ward sister at the hospital—or was she a sister of one of the men? It hardly seemed to matter, and neither did the identities of the other two—junior doctors, I think, with names I never heard. As I shook each hand from the confines of my chair, I noticed Fio regarding me quizzically before my love for her began to overwhelm me.

'Fio, my darling,' I believe I said, as I attempted to pull her on to my lap. She disengaged herself while fixing me with an unreadable expression, neither loving nor disliking—but purposeful. Of that much I was aware, before her face began to swell large and then shrink as I bent forward to embrace her—to find I was clasping my arms around nothing. Undeterred, I managed to grasp my racquet and stand, anxious to show I could beat 'em all and prove my ability to my love.

'Have a drink, darlin',' I heard myself say, and without awaiting an answer I plunged on, heedless. 'C'mon, let's have a game,' and stalked, stiff-legged to keep my balance, on to the court. 'Rough or smooth?' I threw the racquet into the air and idly watched it fall at my feet, not caring which way up the strings were, but as I bent to pick it up I joined it, head first, on to the soft, sweet-smelling, newly mown grass.

Events thereafter were blurred, but not unpleasant to begin with. I know my clothes were removed, I presumed by Fio at the time, and erotic actions performed with her that seemed to go on into infinity, with the sight of naked white bodies invading my senses as I drifted in and out of consciousness until blackness finally enveloped me. I suspect now, that I was the main attraction at a planned orgy in which they all played a lusty part with me, taking full advantage of my helplessness.

The next thing I can call to mind was an awareness of movement, that I was somehow in motion, though where I was going and how I had no idea until sometime later, when I knew by the soreness of my bare feet that my own legs were carrying me as I blundered along. I know I was trying to puzzle out why they were bare without finding any satisfactory answer, uncertain of where I was coming from or going to. What I was sure of, when my splitting head allowed me to be sensible of anything, was that I hurt, hurt all over, and in places where I had never hurt before.

I also felt unclean, with a filthy taste in my mouth as of having swallowed some foul, unfamiliar liquid, gall and wormwood drunk with the Devil. I longed to cast him back into the depths of hell where he belonged and from whence he had come, and if I could not . . . ? Had he already

159

dragged me down there with him? Would God ever be able to receive me again with His grace and goodness and finally allow me into heaven? I felt tears running down my cheeks and knew I was sobbing. Was there nobody able to help me? I desperately wanted to be clean again and have my pain soothed away.

The welcome sound of lapping water fell on my ears. Water! To wash away the dirt and sin and cleanse the sore and tender parts of my tormented body! It sounded close by and I had to find it, stumbling towards it as fast as I could, until suddenly I felt myself falling into space and knew nothing more after my skin touched the wonderful, cold wetness, and the waters closed over my head . . .

Day 15

I had to quickly break off writing yesterday to try to clear my mind of the shame, since having forced myself to endure it once again, and must continue from the point where I sank, ever so thankfully, into the lake. The next thing I remember was coughing and spluttering and trying to suck in air, feeling hard ground under my prone body and short, vigorous thrusts being pushed into my upper back. When my breathing began to ease I was turned over by someone who knelt at my side and, though it was almost dark, I could recognize Robbie's serious face.

'You all right, now? Good thing I come up when I did.'

I stared at him, endeavouring unsuccessfully to work things out, confused and disorientated, not knowing where I was or how I came to be there. 'You're all wet,' I said, at last.

He laughed as he took off his jacket. 'So are you, me old lad. Here, cover yerself wi' this to hide the important bits.'

Startled into semi-alertness my hands began to explore, proving his words and my horrified suspicions, to be correct. Still dazed, I searched for some explanation as to how I came to be lying beside the lake, wet, naked, and with absolutely no idea of the reason why. My head throbbed with a remorseless drumming which beat through my skull, shutting out memory.

161

'My clothes—where are they?' I asked, feeling utterly foolish.

'Can't see 'em nowheres—don't 'ee 'member where 'ee left 'em?' His eyes probed my face as he helped me up on to unexpectedly painful feet, which coincided with such an intense spasm of nausea that I had to clutch hold of him.

'No—no, I don't,' I answered, feeling even more foolish at my inability to recall anything relating to my predicament.

'We'll look for 'em termorrer. Thought you'd go for a swim, eh?'

'I don't know—did I? Did you go in too? Gosh, my feet do hurt.' I was stumbling along beside him as he attempted to hold his wet coat around me.

'I 'ad to go in to pull 'ee out. I hears this splash an' thinks it must be some mighty big fish, then I sees yer floatin' on top, face down. T'wasn' right, that.'

A sense of immense gratitude filled me. 'You saved my life. I'd be dead now if it wasn't for you.' Tears began to course down my already wet cheeks and I know I averted my face, ashamed of my weakness. Why did I feel so weak? What had happened before I went into the lake? I had a faint recollection of menace and hurt and running away from—what?

Robbie interrupted my efforts to clarify these vexing questions. 'Think nothin' to it. 'T'isn' as if I risked me life—jes' waded in an' dragged 'ee on bank.'

We seemed to have been walking for ages, with him supporting me as I limped along, shivering violently, eyes refusing to focus. 'Where are we going? I don't think I can last much longer like this.'

'Back 'ome to Bessie. Keep yer pecker up—we're nearly there. She'll wonder what's 'appened to ye. What're you goin' to tell 'er?'

162

Bessie! Mrs Marsham! What, indeed, was I going to tell her? How could I tell her something I did not even know myself? The question was quite beyond my present ability to fathom out, but Robbie provided an answer.

'I think 'tis best to say you was walkin' back, felt a bit warm an' thought you'd take a dip, so stripped off, jumped in the lake, lost yer footin' an' knocked yerself out on a stone—rather in the same way as George met 'is end. T'were lucky I come by jes' then an' pulled 'ee out, but we couldn' find where you'd left yer things so we 'ad to leave 'em. 'Ow will that do?'

I said it would do as well as anything I could think of, which happened to be nothing, and at that moment I saw lights twinkling through the trees as we reached the garden gate. Robbie guided me along the path but paused at the wash-house door. 'P'raps I'd as well go in first to explain—an' get somethin' ter cover 'ee up—she'll 'ave a bit of a shock else. You stay an' think on what you're a-goin ter say yerself.'

I stood there cold and shaking until he came back with a blanket, put it around me and retrieved his jacket. Rather shamefacedly I followed him through to the kitchen where Bessie stood grim faced, having assumed the guise of the Recording Angel who had descended ready to jot down my various sins of the day. She began to enumerate the first before observing my woebegone appearance.

'What sort o' time do ye call this, Mr Parr? I should've been in me bed long since. Very inconsiderate...' Her voice trailed off as she studied my bare feet and legs, the blanket and then my face, teeth chattering in a lowered, wet head. 'Lord a' mercy!' she ended. 'What on earth have ye been up to? Come by the fire.'

Robbie was fidgeting, anxious to be gone. 'I told 'ee what 'appened, Bessie, don't bother 'im wi' questions now—he'll be right as rain after a night's sleep. Look, I won't say nothin' ter nobody 'bout this, b'lieve me, so g'night, Mr Parr—Bessie.'

She fussed around making a hot drink and filling a hot-water bottle, talking to herself rather than me, for which I was grateful. I found nothing to say apart from 'Thanks,' and 'Goodnight,' as I limped my way unsteadily up to bed on smarting and partially numbed feet, a state which matched my mind. Without lingering to wash, I blew out the candles before gingerly climbing between the sheets, still wrapped in the blanket, and must have blacked out immediately.

Regaining consciousness, as I remember, was not a pleasant experience. I lay still for a time, because every movement left me feeling physically and mentally sick as I gradually became aware that my body had been subjected to excessive misuse. I tried to follow through the chain of events that had led me to this sorry state, though every cell of my being was crying out for me to forget, to sink back into nothingness again. But I had to know—I must remember.

It had begun yesterday when I went to play tennis at Fio's house and drank a few glasses of the refreshment provided. It was after that when everything started to get hazy, when I lost the power to control my welfare—the drink must have been stronger than I realised. I shuddered as I began to experience a faint impression of the events that had overtaken me at the hands of others, an inkling of the aversion and fear that had given me the strength to break away and run, run as from the powers of darkness, and nothing more until I reached the lake and then found myself lying on the bank with Robbie, who had saved my life, beside me.

At that moment I had resented his interference, death seeming preferable. What was he doing there, anyway? Poaching, I supposed, though I had noticed he was not

164

carrying a gun, only the canvas bag he always seemed to have with him. And what had happened to Fio? Was she all right? Had I come by my injuries protecting her? Or been attacked by the men for some other reason? Nothing was clear, and I was left with the disturbing, yet merciful, fact that whatever had taken place had been buried by my amnesia. I heard Bessie moving about downstairs, but had no wish to see her to try to explain the unexplainable, deciding to pull the sheet over my head and stay where I was for days, months—years, if necessary—until everyone had forgotten about me and my indignity and I would then be able to creep away and hide somewhere else for ever.

It seemed a long time after that before I roused myself enough to attempt to glance at my watch, but it was not on my wrist. The curtains were closed, with daylight showing through, and all was quiet downstairs. I put my legs over the edge of the bed and idly studied the grazes and scratches covering them before noticing my feet, which were dirty, torn and streaked with dried blood. I was also finding it difficult to sit with any comfort, so forced myself to stand, swaying as I went painfully to pull open the curtains and regard myself in the wardrobe mirror with manifest disbelief. Bright red patches mottled a face displaying the puffed-up lips of a mouth that felt sore inside as well as out, and the rest of my body was marked and bruised by what could only have been bites, teeth marks surrounding purple blisters, and all my tender parts raw and swollen. It was as if I had been attacked by both a pack of wolves and blood-sucking leeches, making me fearful of how my injuries were caused and evoking the conviction that I should never fully recover, never be quite the same, though in fact it was probably only my self-esteem that had been mortally wounded.

These thoughts made me feel worse than before, creating a need to seek reassurance, to know there was still normality to be found somewhere beyond this room. I put on my dressing gown, relieved to discover it was long enough to conceal most of my legs—not that it mattered, as Bessie must have seen the state of them last night—then slowly made my way barefoot to the kitchen to find it empty. A note on the table stated that she had decided not to disturb me but had gone to church and would be back at the usual time. The clock showed the time to be nearly half past twelve. But church? On a Saturday? It began to dawn on me that I must have slept all the hours around the dial—and more. Saucepans were simmering on the hob and I smelled meat roasting, at which my stomach immediately revolted, prompting a painful retreat to the privy and a bout of the shakes again.

When I returned upstairs I thoroughly washed every portion of myself but, like Lady Macbeth, was unable to wash away the blood of shame inside me. The soiled sheets on the bed I felt were contaminated with the residue of that night, so I tore them off and tossed them in a corner. An air of unreality enfolded me as I clothed myself, hardly knowing that I did, in clean, loose pyjamas and the dressing gown, before turning the armchair with its back towards the door and gently lowering myself into it. Whichever way I put my body it hurt.

I heard Bessie return and knew she had seen my open curtains, because a little later a tentative knock came on my door. I ignored it, but she came in anyway, cup rattling on saucer. 'I've brought you some tea, Mr Parr.'

I looked straight ahead, wanting neither to see nor to talk to her as yet. 'Thanks, put it down, please—and I don't want anything to eat—I'm not hungry.'

'Well—p'raps you'll have something at teatime.' She set the cup down beside me. 'Would ye like for me to call Doctor?'

'No—no, I'm all right,' I insisted, hastily. The only reason

I would have welcomed him would be to ask about his daughter's welfare, but if she had been hurt I was sure that Bessie would have heard via the village grapevine and told me.

'Very well, if you say so.' I heard her gather up the sheets before going out.

I sat there until evening. Bessie was wise enough to leave me alone while I wrestled with my incomprehension and the misery of it all. I shied away from *really* wanting to know what had happened, beyond wondering if it had been by some devilish design on the part of those present in the garden or had occurred by chance. I was more anxious to know about Fio, but would not find that out by introspection.

Physically I was feeling slightly better, my head no longer achingly heavy and the rest of me less tender as I became more accustomed to the soreness; I even began to think about food, so put on socks as the only bearable covering for my feet and carried the cold tea downstairs, hobbling into the kitchen where Bessie, now back from Evensong, looked up enquiringly as I entered. I had no idea of what to say or what her reaction to my obvious fall from grace would be, but something had to be said. I waited for her to speak first.

'Come and sit down, Mr Parr. There's supper on table— you must be hungry by now. I'm glad you've come to keep me comp'ny—I've been worried 'bout ye. Kettle's boiling— you ready for a fresh cup?' She bustled around without a word of reproach or demanding the reason for my having returned late that night in the guise of a half-drowned, skinned and mauled rat—which is exactly how I felt. My heart went out to her in my dejection and loneliness, and I was filled with the warmth of great affection for this kindly soul.

Sat at the table, I managed to swallow sufficient food to

167

take the edge off my appetite but had to make an effort to keep it down. I knew I looked pale, which was enhanced by the sore patches, and the fact that I was unshaven must have added to my unsightly appearance, but Bessie made no comment. When I said I had finished eating she insisted that I relax by the fire while she re-made the bed, and on her return I felt I should make an attempt at a belated apology.

'I really don't know what to say . . .' and that was the truth, what could I say? I had disgraced myself, both in her eyes and my own.

She was emptying the contents of the cold hot-water bottle into a bucket—all water was precious and kept. 'You don't have to say nothin', Mr Parr. Whatever caused this is your business, not mine. As far as I'm concerned, you went off to play tennis an' came back rather late. That's enough. Let's leave it at that, shall us?'

That was not enough for me—I wanted her forgiveness. 'Mrs Marsham—Bessie—I'm truly sorry. I don't exactly know what happened except that it must've been my fault—I had too much to drink.'

She straightened up and turned towards me, her face blank. 'Mebbe so, if that's what ye believes, but don't fret 'bout it upsetting me. Now, you can't go to school tomorrow, the state you're in, so I'll get someone to take a message that you've catched a chill—which is true enough, the way you've bin shiverin'. You'll look an' feel heaps better after another day's rest.'

I saw no point in arguing. I hated letting the school down and was worried about Fio, but had no wish to parade myself before inquisitive eyes as yet.

The following day was washday Monday. Bessie brought my tea later than usual and I was able to lie in bed while assessing my physical and mental condition. The latter produced an overriding sensation of humiliation, the physical more obvious. I felt less swollen and tender but scabs had formed, and my body had stiffened to such an extent that I was barely able to move for a time. When I did manage to get downstairs, still in dressing gown and socks, it was to find a letter from Joyce that detailed the arrangements for our holiday, and which ended by saying how much she was looking forward to seeing me at home next Friday. I wished it were today.

Bessie came in from the wash-house carrying a bundle of clothing. 'See what I've found,' is how she greeted me. 'Put in shed with your watch on top an' the racquet an' bike there, too. Wonder who brought 'em back? Robbie?'

Ignoring her question I, too, wondered who had brought them back as Robbie would not have known where everything was. Could it have been Fio?

A round of toast sufficed for breakfast. As I ate I watched Bessie through the open door using the bellows on the fire under the copper, the steam beginning to rise from the washing that had been soaking overnight. With no desire for solitude, and plagued with the torment of unresolved thoughts, I edged my chair nearer to watch as she dealt with the rinsing baths and buckets of water.

'Would you like the door shut, Mr Parr? I don't want ye to feel cold. I left it open for the draught to flare the fire an' cool the air out here.'

'No, you carry on, Bessie, don't mind me, I'm warm enough. There's nothing else for me to do, so I might as well learn where my clean shirts come from.'

'You can shell the peas then,' she said, putting a basket and colander on a chair beside me, so I sat doing this undemanding, simple task while she slaved at the laundering—and slaving it certainly was in the days before washing machines arrived.

I learned that after the water boiled, the white clothes and linen were lifted out of the suds with the aid of a wooden copper-stick before being dropped in the rinsing baths and swished around with a blue-bag to make them look even whiter. Next, they were squeezed through a mangle, and it was obviously a real effort for her to turn the handle while easing the heavy, wet linen through the wooden rollers. I offered to help but she said I would only get in the way, then after starching various things, like my shirt collars, she carried the weighty basket outside and pegged it all on the line. After a cup of tea she was back at the sink, rubbing the dirt out of the 'coloureds' against a washboard, before repeating the rinsing and mangling. When all was hanging out to dry she started the clearing up, emptying the copper and baths and mopping the stone floor. I felt tired merely observing, but Bessie was busy again preparing midday dinner. After that I stayed for a while to watch her ironing the articles that had dried, the irons heating on the kitchen range, and once that was completed and all was airing on the rack hanging from the ceiling, she sat down for a well-earned rest while I went upstairs to prepare for school tomorrow.

When I came down again for supper, Bessie handed me a small bunch of wild flowers. 'Tom brought these to put in your room. He wanted to see you but I told him no, you're not quite better yet.' She smiled. 'He's a good little chap an' thinks the world o' you. Thought he were lookin' a bit peaky, though. I'd hoped he'd be happier now Robbie's here, but I feel there's something troubling him.' I took the flowers from her, touched by the gesture, and silently vowed to make time at the earliest opportunity to have that delayed talk with him.

The next day, after shaving and dressing, I managed to get my shoes on more or less comfortably. Outwardly I looked much as usual, but riding the bike revived the soreness and pain and the discomfort increased the humiliation I felt. I viewed everyone I passed with suspicion—had they all heard about what had happened to me and were laughing behind my back?

Arrived early at school, I screwed up my courage and knocked on Miss Millard's door. There was no doubting her genuine concern as she welcomed me with my feeble apology. 'These summer chills can be very troublesome. Luckily, as this is the last week of term we don't adhere to a rigid timetable, so your being away yesterday was easily covered by extra games and readings by Miss Macdonald. She was the one I called upon to deal with your absence.'

I studied her face closely to note any scorn or knowing-ness in her expression, but could detect none. All the same, I had the firm impression that those impassive eyes behind the specs were not as guileless as they appeared to be—I suspected she knew I was juggling with the truth.

Fio swept into school a moment behind Tom just as the bell ceased clanging, so I was unable to speak to either before prayers. I was very relieved that she appeared to be totally unscathed and as lovely as ever, and even more sure that I had been the victim of some misadventure after I had left her home of which she knew nothing, stupid, blind fool that I was. She ignored me in assembly, looking the other way, which had me worried about how I had behaved in front of her friends. My anxiety to find out what *had* taken place made it hard for me to concentrate on the children, so I gave them the usual question-and-answer exercises. I had managed to thank Tom for calling to see me as we walked to the classroom, but the moment had been brief and I was conscious of his wan face turned to me in class.

The presence of the other teachers at break prevented any discussion with Fio. I thought that might be as well, it would be better done away from school, so when the bell rang and I saw Tom hanging back I told him I was busy and to go home to dinner. I noticed his look of distress as I tried to hurry, without showing that my feet were uncomfortable, to the bicycle shed, and rode slowly, avoiding any bumps, which gave Fio time to reach her house before me. I was glad to see that Dr Mac's car was not in evidence as I rang the doorbell and waited expectantly for the housemaid to let me in. I stood about in the hall until she came back and ushered me into the dining room where Fio was sitting, wearing an unwelcoming expression.

'I'm having my lunch,' she said, coldly and unnecessarily. I walked around the table towards her but she swiftly arose and moved away, keeping the table between us. 'I'm surprised you have the cheek to come here,' she went on, 'after dashing off the way you did the other night.'

'My darling Fio, that's why I had to come and see you—I want to know what happened. I know I drank too much, but didn't realise the stuff was intoxicating. You don't look as if you were hurt. Was the other girl all right?'

Her eyes widened as if surprised, then narrowed again. 'You don't know what we did, then? Really? Don't you remember anything?' I shook my head. 'What a pity! I'd decided to teach you a few sexual variations that I thought you deserved to be taught, you virtuous prude, and now you tell me you didn't know anything about it! Wasted on you, was it? Well, never mind—we all enjoyed *you*!'

I was aware of myself standing immobile, gaping at her, bewildered not only by her words but by the venom behind them. 'Fio . . .'

'Oh, for goodness' sake! Stop looking like the lovesick fool you are! You must've noticed that I can't stand you near me for more than five minutes. It was fun to start with, you were so ignorant about everything and I found it hard to believe you had really come down in the last shower of rain. Couldn't you see that it takes a man—or men—to satisfy me? A priggish, sanctimonious boy never had a hope! And another thing—how dared you suggest to Dad that I

172

was interested in you? You caused me endless trouble having to explain it away—he was quite put out with me!'

I had been struck dumb by the cruelty of her outburst before a feeling of outrage began to displace my sense of anguish. 'Then why did you pretend you loved me and we'd tell everyone when term was over?' I charged her, angrily.

'I didn't really—you assumed it. I thought I'd keep you dangling in case you might come in useful, and you did last Friday. It made a nice change for us. Usually we go to the Old Manor to have our fun, where nobody disturbs us—I took you there once,' she winked a glittering, green eye, 'but not always, and the tennis ploy worked well to enable us to net you. Pun—see? We had a whale of a time volleying with you—you should've seen your silly self!' She laughed, spitefully. 'And then you had to run off, squealing like a pig with a butcher's knife at its tail! If you'd only waited a moment you'd've been delivered, clothed, at your very door, but as it was I had to send Robbie off to see you didn't do yourself a mischief—which, in fact, you nearly did! That could've caused a nasty scandal and put a stop to our little games!'

Day 16

I stared at her, in a daze. 'Robbie was there? He knew?'

'Not only knew, would-be lover boy, but joined in with gusto—and also took plenty of snapshots—while you ... Well, never mind. We made the most of the little you could offer!'

If I could have reached the knife on her plate I would possibly have plunged it into her, my anger was so intense, but I began to doubt as I considered her words. 'I don't believe you,' I blurted out at last, searching for a way to prove her wrong. 'Robbie was out poaching and chanced to be there to help me. Besides, he's courting Lucy—he'd want to be with her, not with you, and Tom could be out at any hour and might chance to see him and tell her.'

Again that sly smile, eyes shining with malice, hands held out before her, hands with long nails on fingers curved like a bird's claws. She reminded me of a mythological Greek monster, a rapacious Harpy, part woman, part bird.

'Believe what you like, but Robbie dotes on me—always has. George did, too. He was an earthy man, full of a tremendous, fierce strength. I miss him. Wonder who might've killed him? That's if the gossip's true. He could always make Lucy and Tom do as they were told, but Robbie has to make sure they sleep soundly when he's out with me—and taking saucy pictures with his camera! He sells them when he gets back to barracks to make extra money—

174

develops them in the photographic unit where he works. I'll make sure you get some prints. So, dahling, you'll soon be able to run along home to your mumsie and tell her all about how I tried to find a man in her son and failed pitiably. Really, I don't think there's one in you. Now, go away—and mind you keep all this to yourself—not that you'd be believed, anyway!'

She stood staring me out as I gathered my scattered wits and blundered blindly outside. I left the bike leaning against the wall and walked back to school. There was no time left to go home for dinner—not that I could have swallowed it.

Finding the playground deserted, I sat on the seat beneath the sycamore tree as much out of sight as possible, feeling too badly hurt for further thought concerning that dreadful encounter to be an option, so tried to concentrate on ordinary things like the winged seeds forming among the leaves. Most of the saplings had been cut to make the ever-popular whistles, which led me to thinking about Tom.

Tom . . . and Robbie who had saved my life, but who had also seemingly been an instigator in my nearly losing it while having taken a part in, and contributed to, my humiliation by taking photographs! I cringed at the thought. And George . . . How could she have . . . ? No wonder he had sneered at me. I had to face the fact that I had been an infatuated, gullible idiot, manipulated at the whim of a— what? Even now it was difficult for me to accept that she was as cruel and wanton as she appeared. Her beauty had bewitched me. Bewitched. Was that it? Had I been a victim of the witches and warlocks I had read about, with Fiona— her pet name already erased from my mind—as head of a coven? Calling up ghosts and spirits—and even the Evil One himself? The more I thought about it the more feasible it became, absolving me from the blame of being over-powered by lust and desire. After all, who could resist the

175

potions, wiles and machinations of a proficient witch? Is that what she had meant by saying that Robbie made sure that Lucy and Tom slept soundly? Did she help him to cast spells on them?

I now realise that my brain was so confused by inward grief that it was accepting any solution that gave it ease. My love had been transformed into hatred, which was as nothing compared to the loathing I felt for myself in being so utterly befooled. Tears of shame pricked behind my closed eyelids before children's noisy voices disturbed my meditation, and another, nearer, brought me to full awareness.

'Sir? Are you all right? Can I talk to you now? I really do need to.'

I turned my head and gazed into Tom's pleading eyes. Full of pity as I was for myself, I could spare none for him. I looked at my watch. ' 'Fraid it'll have to wait again, Tom,' I said, dismissively. 'It's nearly time for the bell.'

I saw his crestfallen face and almost relented, until a wave of recollection about that awful night swept over me again. I stood up and began to move towards the entrance as he moved beside me. 'I think me mam's goin' to wed me uncle,' he persisted, no joy in his tone.

Was he aware of Robbie's duplicity? For that matter, was the man really involved with Fiona or was that another lie? I was beginning to think there was nothing, no single, sinful action she was incapable of attempting. However much I disliked the idea of facing Robbie again, I would still need to thank him properly for pulling me out of the water, whatever his reason, and try to discover whether there was any truth to be found in Fiona's allegations.

'I'd like a word with your uncle, Tom. I'll walk you back after school.'

He shook his head. 'His leave was up an' he's gone back to barracks—to buy hisself out 'e said.'

So that was that. I would not see him again and maybe it was for the best. The sooner I got away and put all thoughts of this place out of my mind the less troubled I would be. I did not belong there, and right then I wanted to be left alone.

The small voice coming from the boy beside me was continuing. 'They're sayin' someone killed me dad. D'you know who 'tis?'

The bell began its clamour, banging noisily around in my aching head. I know I should have stopped and listened to him, taking heed of the appeal in his voice, but only felt irritated, selfishly intent upon isolating myself, too upset to want to indulge in any conjectural thinking. We were walking at a tangent towards the building and meeting up with the other children, Frank among them, his face wearing the insolent expression that reminded me of George. I felt threatened, as if they were both taunting me—which shows how badly my mental stability had been affected—and so I spoke loudly, testily, and without due care.

'Don't be so silly, Tom, it doesn't matter what anyone says—the coroner said it was an accident and that's the end of it! You should be glad he's dead and gone—I'm sure your mother is! It's pretty obvious you're both better off without him!'

Once said, there was no way I could prevent those words from ringing into every ear within hearing. A hush quietened the chatter as Tom, head lowered and with burning cheeks, pushed through the children in front of him, and I saw Fiona approaching the door just ahead of me.

'Well done, Mr Parr,' she observed, clearly and contemptuously.

I have no remembrance of what I taught or how I conducted myself for the remainder of the afternoon. When it was over I tried to intercept Tom before he left but he was too quick for me, though what would I have said? What

177

could I have said? What he might have said would have been a different matter. I walked dejectedly back to the cottage, watching my feet kick at stones along the dusty roadside.

Bessie stared at me for a long moment when I went in. She put down her sewing and got up to pour water on the tea leaves in the pot. 'S'pose you were delayed in school dinnertime,' she said in a quiet voice. 'Returned the bike already, have ye? Bit soon, weren't it?' She hardly paused for an answer. 'I saved your dinner.'

'Thanks. I'll have it after I've washed,' I replied, thankful that she had made explanations unnecessary. I managed small talk as I ate, congratulating myself on keeping my chaotic feelings hidden, and afterwards we cleared the dishes away.

'You must be pleased term's nearly over an' you can leave here.' Bessie was hanging up the tea towel to dry as she spoke, almost echoing my very thoughts. The pile of plates I was putting away began to rattle like chattering teeth. I saw her glance at my reddening face, but her look was kind.

'I'm not gifted wi' second sight, but I'm wise enough to know how many beans make five,' she said.

'What's that?' I asked, perplexed.

'How many beans make five. You know—one and a half, two and a half and a whole one. Good, I'm pleased to see you can still smile. You'll worry yourself into an early grave the way you're going on, an' nothing's worth that. A change of scene is what you need, an' 'tis proper you'll soon have it.'

'You're right, Bessie.' I was grateful for her good sense and apparent concern for my welfare, but it still failed to dispel the uncleanness that lurked within and my heart beat faster as she continued.

'I hear Robbie's also gone for a change of scenery. Buying hisself out, is he? Old Tom must've left some money somewheres, then, because he's never had two ha'pennies to rub together that he didn't gamble away, an' George never earned much but allus had plenty. Good luck to him, I say, if he's on to a good thing wi' Lucy.'

Or making his fortune by selling photographs of me, I was thinking, but I wanted no further talk about him. 'A walk might do me good,' I suggested.

As I wandered through the trees I debated on whether I should go to the farm and try to make my peace with Tom, but the memories that were summoned up when I reached the lake tended to swamp everything else but my own wretched misery, so after a short time I returned, seeking an early bed with the excuse of sorting out my things ready for packing.

I closed the bedroom door with a sigh of relief and put my back against it, still full of the sickness of anger, and my eyes looked into those of the girl in the picture, imagining them to be filled with sympathy for me. She, also, had suffered the pain of betrayal, her love destroyed, to leave a similar bleeding wound deep inside her. I found it difficult to believe that mine was not visible for all to see or that it could ever heal, so applied a poultice of bitterness and hatred in an effort to doctor it, knowing now that the scar remains to this day. Maybe it had been worse for Lucy, who had the added suffering of being married to George, and I was reflecting on how she had managed to endure it for so long when another thought broke in. Had Tom told her about the painting? If so, that might have aroused her memories, and she could have unthinkingly exposed the depth of her misery and unhappiness to him.

Lucy. Did Tom want to tell me that he had a suspicion of her involvement in George's death? He would desperately need to share his fears with someone and hope to be reassured—they would be too much of a burden for him to carry alone. Then who better than someone who was not a part of the village and would soon be gone from it? How cruelly had I ignored him!

I sat down in the armchair while considering this new supposition. Could Lucy have reached the end of her tether and decided to free herself and her son from George's tyranny? It was the injury to his head that allowed equivocal doubts to arise in my mind, though at the inquest it had been glossed over—it was as if everyone was saying good riddance to a bad lot. Now, I was thinking it could have been the result of a blow from a stick or stone, enough to stun but not kill—the water did that. Might she have planned it that way? I doubted it—she would be scared to get close enough to hit him in case he caught her, drunk as he was. No, I could not accept the idea of her involvement; it might as easily have been Kate Acaster in retaliation for the attack on her son, although the same doubts applied to her. A more plausible idea of an assailant would be either Frank or Tom with their catapults, Frank still smarting from his beating or Tom from his constant ill-treatment. And what about Wills? Had he betrayed his feelings for George by that glance of utter contempt? Hardly sufficient for murder, though, unless there was more to it than I knew. Fiona would be the one most capable of killing but she had the least reason, from what she had said. The more I searched for likely murderers the more unlikely each proved to be. I let my thoughts run riot to prevent them returning to the horrendous disclosures that had disrupted my day, and finally went to bed in a state of mental exhaustion.

My time next morning, after assembly, was taken up with finishing the written reports while Fiona took the girls for games and Mr Richards supervised the boys playing cricket, so I did not see Tom again until prizegiving in the afternoon as I sat on the platform with the rest of the staff. I felt disappointed that the boy had not done as well as expected after his excellent start in the first half of term. His interest in learning seemed to have lessened after George's demise, when the reverse might have been anticipated. He had come sixth in class when he should have been top, with Frank coming much lower. It was the girls, with their openly ardent looks in my direction, who swept the board, having apparently been following my every word!

After the prizes of books and cups had been handed out to the worthy ones who sat cross-legged on the floor below the platform, Miss Millard tapped on the almost empty table and called for order. 'Please be quiet for a few more minutes,' she said, briskly. 'There is one more duty I have to perform before you can go. I want to thank Mr Parr for coming to us at such short notice and fitting in so splendidly. He has added considerably to your progress, which I hope will continue without him in the future.' She turned to me. 'We all wish you well when you take up your new position and, to mark our appreciation, we would like you to accept this small gift to remind you of your brief stay here.'

Everyone clapped as I stood up, blushing with embarrassment, as she handed me a small, tissue-wrapped packet and sat down, leaving me to reply. Whatever other harm Fiona had wreaked she had surely undermined my confidence, temporarily at least. The sea of faces swam before me as I licked dry lips.

'Thank you—everybody,' I began. 'I think I've probably learned as much from you, in different ways, as you have from me, and I look forward to coming back to see you all sometime in the future. Thank you once more.'

'Liar, liar,' resounded in my brain, I would *never* come back here again! Then I noticed those with me on the platform hovering, glancing expectantly at the gift I held, wanting obviously to appraise my reaction to it. I quickly tore away the tissue paper to reveal a silver paper knife in the shape of a dagger, its point sharp enough to at once stick into my thumb and produce a spot of blood, which I quickly concealed.

'This will be very useful,' I said, bleakly.

'Oh, we do hope so,' put in Mrs Richards, all of a flutter. 'Miss Macdonald insisted on buying it for us in town.'

'It's very kind, although I doubt I shall be able to forget any one of you.' I could find nothing better to say.

We began to disperse, the children heading for home, and I found I had missed Tom yet again. As I was tidying my desk a sound made me glance towards the door, and there was Fiona leaning against the frame in the very same attitude as when I first saw her, smiling that same wicked smile. She spoke in a loud whisper.

'Hope you like your keepsake, Lover Boy. I chose it for you especially. Every so often it'll draw your blood and you'll think of me. I must be the only one who's not sorry you're going—you've outlived your usefulness as far as I'm concerned. No need to worry, there'll be plenty more waiting for *their* first lessons in love in the woods—the boys are forever growing up. Tom'll be ready soon. 'Bye.'

She vanished from my sight, and I hoped it was for always as I gripped the edge of the desk in an endeavour to hold back the fury that filled me. What could I do to stop this evil creature? Denounce her to Miss Millard? Constable Wills? Who would believe me? She was the child of the respected Dr Mac and had been very clever in hiding her activities. Nobody had breathed a hint of anything amiss to me, not even Bessie, and where was my proof? Any accusation I made would involve my own foolish conduct and accomplish nothing. It would be said that I was retaliating for being rejected by the object of my affection, making me a laughing-stock, and though I would soon be too far away for it to affect me, I wanted to be remembered with dignity by the children and good people of the village.

As I stood staring helplessly at the empty doorway I saw Miss Hope come out of the room opposite. The door had been ajar, but could Fiona's whispered words have carried that far? I probed the elderly teacher's solemn, lined face for a clue, hoping she might look concerned and ask the meaning of what she had overheard, but she merely went along the corridor without a glance in my direction. Perhaps, unjustly, I felt relief, for how would I have answered her?

Unable to cope with this further complexity, I obeyed a sudden impulse and hurried out of the school and along to the shops to ask Mr Hillman the times of trains, then went to the post office and filled out a form. When I was satisfied with the message, I took it to the counter where the prim postmistress waited.

'I want you to send this telegram, please,' I said.

She read it through, counted the words, and I passed over the money requested. 'I thought you were going home on Friday, Mr Parr. Why are you leaving tomorrow? Is there something wrong?'

'Er—no—nothing at all—it's only that my mother is missing me.' I said the first thing that came into my head, giving her a bright smile with my lame excuse, while inside my head I was again repeating 'liar, liar'. I felt a little better then, as one usually does when a decision has been made, and continued my journey with a lighter step as I made for the garage. Jim Carter came out, wiping his oily hands.

'Can you take me to the Halt tomorrow, about one thirty?' I asked. 'There's a train that comes through at two.'

'Leavin' so soon? Be at the inn this even' then?'

'Maybe—I expect so.'

We had finished our meal before I could bring myself to acquaint Bessie with my news. 'I hope you won't take this the wrong way,' I began, 'but I think it would be best if I catch a train home tomorrow.'

She gave me a sharp look. 'A bit unexpected like, isn't it? I thought you'd planned to spend the afternoon saying your goodbyes after school closed. You'll have to hurry to get them all in now.'

'Well, there aren't so many really,' I said weakly. 'I suppose, as breaking up is so near, I've come to realise I must've been feeling homesick and there's a train at two that will get me back in good time. I've sent a telegram and arranged it all.'

Her expression softened. 'No use my trying to talk you out of it then, is there? Of course, there's no sense in hanging around if you don't have to. I'm being selfish 'cos I'll be sorry to see you go—I've enjoyed you being here.' Her gaze remained unwavering. 'Wonder if you can say the same?'

I knew I was colouring up. 'Of course I can!' My words were over-emphasised before I quickly subdued them, putting an arm around the plump shoulders. 'Bessie, I could not have wished for a nicer landlady—there's no kinder person anywhere. It's a pity everyone isn't the same.'

She gave an embarrassed cough. 'Thank ye, Mr Parr. I understand yer meaning perfectly. Now, you'd better get along to the inn for a farewell drink—but not too many!'

All the regulars were there when I arrived, already made aware of my imminent departure, and I was truly sorry to be saying goodbye to the people who had accepted and welcomed this newcomer so warmly. The ale flowed freely and I had to be firm in refusal. Dr Mac came in near to closing time and my stomach tightened, but he was friendly, expressing regret at my going.

'I hear you've done well by the children,' he said, his bearded face close to mine. 'I would've liked you as a son-in-law, but it seems it was not to be.'

I stared hard at him, wondering how much he knew and how he could have fathered the creature who was his

184

daughter, then remembered what Bessie had said about the mother, how she had left because she had found life here too dull. Well, Fiona had surely found ways of livening it up! Did he know? If his wife had been of the same disposition he might suspect, but I was not going to be the one to make suspicion a certainty. At closing time I rolled home, only mildly the worse for wear.

The next morning was mainly taken up with tidying the classroom and making sure the frogs and newts, fish and other livestock would be taken home to be cared for during the holiday. While handing out reports and holiday tasks I had a word with each of my pupils about their work, urging Frank, in particular, to try harder and read more poetry. Tom was cocooned in an invisible shield of unconcern, remote, which increased my regret at not having made more of an effort to find out what had been troubling him. I drew him to one side.

'Tom,' I said, gently. 'I'm sorry we haven't had that talk, but I think, now things are easier at home, that you should let any worries you have take care of themselves while you concentrate on learning. You've a good brain and can do well, better than you have recently. Do you understand?'

His response was wooden as he avoided my eye. 'Yessir. This is for you.' He put a small box in my hand as the bell rang. 'Better go now, sir.'

He disappeared into the throng of children surrounding my desk, mostly girls pressing bags of sticky sweets on me as they said goodbye, tears in their eyes. I hastily thrust everything into my pockets, and when I managed to extricate myself there was no sign of Tom and no time left to search for him. School had finished early before dinnertime and I successfully avoided any contact with Fiona. Miss Millard's door stood open as I went to say goodbye.

'Come in, come in,' she said, warmly, brushing aside the pile of papers on her desk. 'Sit down for a moment. We're really sorry you are leaving us, but grateful that you came at all. I've taken note of various improvements we intend to make that are entirely attributable to you.' Her eyes were guarded. 'One is never too old—or too young—to learn, you know.'

I was in too much of a hurry to pick up her meaning. 'Miss Millard, I'm afraid you must excuse my dashing off as I've decided to leave by the two o'clock train. I just wanted to thank you before I went.'

In that manner I hurriedly parted from her, the others, and my responsibilities. Then it was farewell to 'Girl in a Yellow Dress' and Bessie, who pressed my hand sadly as I got into the cab, promising to keep in touch, and waved us on our way. I boarded the train at the Halt with Jim's help, metaphorically wiping the dust of West Halsey from my feet, and sat back with enormous relief. Sometime later, I put my hand in a pocket to rid it of the bags of sticky sweet offerings and came upon Tom's small box. I cautiously lifted the lid—and my heart thumped with a surge of regret at my inability to have soothed his fears and afford him peace. Inside, spread out on cotton wool, was a perfect likeness of a kestrel in flight, beautifully modelled in plasticine.

Day 17

Once settled in at home, I began to regard those last days as akin to living through a nightmare and waited for the horrible dream to fade, but it was not to be as easily disposed of as the silver dagger which was immediately consigned to the dustbin. There would be unwary moments when I was lulled into recalling the sensual bliss that had preceded them, which would hastily be replaced by the horror I felt at having been seduced by a temptress instructed by the Devil. What mostly lay heavily on my conscience was the fact that I had run away to protect myself, abandoning those others as yet blissfully unaware, who would eventually come within her sphere of activity, leaving them vulnerable without unmasking her devilry. I had turned away from them, and as there was nothing I could do about it now somehow managed to convince my cowardly self that it was best put behind me.

The money I had accumulated was lying idle in the bank and your Auntie Joyce was nagging me to begin my search for a car. I looked for the cheapest available, settling on an Austin Seven Tourer at £125. It would have been £10 more for the saloon. I walked into a showroom, signed papers, bought a licence and chugged home—as easy as that in those days! Oh, I still recall the joy I felt while showing it to Mother and Joyce! For the first time in months I felt at ease.

Joyce was full of plans for our stay at the beach house with her boyfriend, Stephen, and Babs, the girl I had met at Easter. Though having been made even more wary of females, I was remembering her as serene, not at all forward, undemanding and easy to get along with, so hoped to endure the holiday by remaining reserved and taciturn. She came to stay overnight the day before we set off, and I was pleased to note that the reason I had forgotten how she looked was because her appearance had nothing outstanding about it. She had a lissom body with shapely legs, short, honey-coloured hair and a pleasant, unremarkable face, the exception being an attractive full-lipped mouth and large, alert brown eyes. There would be no danger of my falling under her spell, though I doubted she had one, I thought thankfully, as I got the car filled up for our journey the next day.

If you have ever seen an Austin Seven Tourer at a vintage car rally, Paul, you will find it difficult to imagine how four people and luggage could squash into one and actually enjoy being sardines, but it was less cramped than you would think, because it was aided to a great extent by the use of a borrowed trailer attached to the rear of the car to carry the baggage. We set off in fine style for our month by the sea, finding the house in a delightful setting, with the added advantage of having someone to come in daily to clean and cook meals if required. Two good-sized bedrooms sufficed, with girls in one and us boys in the other, no other arrangement being contemplated in those far-off days of moral correctness, and it certainly suited me. I got on well with your Uncle Stephen who was, and still is, a quiet, stolid fellow with a wry sense of humour, very much suited to your volatile Auntie Joyce.

We swam every day, the exercise and freshness of the sea air beginning to strengthen and cleanse my whole being, so that at last the nightmares began to fade. Babs helped, too.

188

We walked daily along the seashore without much conversation as there seemed little need for it, and after a time I could feel the glow of inner health returning and laughter replacing my dark musing. Babs blended into my every mood.

'I'd rather you didn't call me Babs,' she said one day.

'Why? I thought that was your name.'

'It's just a nickname. I was teased horribly at school about being a baby, so I grew to hate it. Joyce knew me then, and still can't remember to call me Barbara.'

'Then I shall beat her with my newspaper until she does and that name shall never pass our lips again!' And it never did, which is why your mother was always called Barbara, Paul.

The time flew by as quickly as it had latterly dragged at West Halsey. Joyce did ask me some questions about the school, but my non-committal answers bored her sufficiently to avoid further pursuit of the subject. Barbara was more perceptive and, while not openly mentioning it, managed to convey that she realised it had not been a happy time for me. I told her about Miss Millard, Bessie, Tom, the Pipers, and how George had lived and died, and that seemed to satisfy whatever curiosity she had, accepting that I did not wish to dwell on a part of my life that was over and done with.

Then, as with all good things, the stay at the seaside came to an end and we reluctantly re-packed our luggage and ourselves into the car, the four of us now firmly bonded in lifelong friendship and affection. I saw myself as more mature, wiser, and certainly happier, taking refuge in the belief that my recent experiences must be the worst that Life could ever throw at me and I could now look forward to a placid future presenting only minor aggravations. Wiser, was I? Life had barely lifted the lid off her box of tricks.

189

We arrived home without mishap, full of sun, sea air and exuberance to entertain my mother with stories of the trip. Stephen went straight home, as he lived nearby, but Barbara stayed on for a few days until I was to drive her home, about thirty miles away. Mother was delighted with the way we two were getting on, confessing to having been worried about me when I returned from West Halsey. Now my psyche had happily been restored, apart from suffering the brief pangs of recall which caused me to squirm inwardly, and I was eagerly looking forward to each new day—that is, until the telegram arrived.

'PLEASE TELEPHONE URGENTLY,' it said, and was signed MILLARD.

I regarded it with disbelief. What on earth could she want? Various impossibilities flashed through my head, discarded on the instant but with nothing better with which to replace them. I had been transported with the speed of light back to that tennis court in the garden, and felt physically sick. I decided to have nothing to do with whatever she wanted, but as there was no point in deferring the vexatious task, however much I wished to ignore it, I went out to phone her.

With some trepidation I heard her clear, precise voice. 'Oh, Mr Parr, thank you for ringing so promptly. I'm at my wits' end to know what to do, with the new term beginning next week. You see, Miss Hope has badly sprained an ankle and will need a week or two before being able to put any weight on it. She should be able to hobble about the school by then, but for the moment . . .'

'I'm so sorry,' I interrupted, relieved to know her purpose in contacting me and aware of what could be coming next. 'I expect she's in a lot of pain.'

'She's bearing up well. Now, Mrs Phillips, for whom you stood in, is ready to resume her duties and I have a new teacher starting but neither can fill Miss Hope's position, so

190

I'm asking if you can possibly come back for just two weeks? I know the term at your new school begins later than ours— I'd be very grateful . . .'

Never! Drawing a deep breath I prepared to refuse as politely as I could and, if she should argue, then downright forcefully, but before I could speak she continued, 'Miss Macdonald will not be rejoining us, you see.' She paused. 'As I understand it, she has no intention of returning to the village at all, and her father is very upset.'

As I digested this unexpected news, the words of my refusal were suspended in my mouth. Why had she so specifically mentioned that fact? Was it merely to stress the difficulty she found herself in, or had she become aware of the darker things that had been enacted under her very nose? But, either way, it made no difference to me.

'I'm very sorry, Miss Millard. I'd like to help but I've too much swotting up to do before I begin at my new school.'

'In that case, I apologise for having bothered you.'

I could sense her disappointment, then realised that she would not have invited me back had she been disapproving of my behaviour. However, better let the past lie buried, and that would have been that had she not persisted.

'Mr Parr,' she went on, hesitantly. 'I feel I must say that I'm very worried about Tom Piper. You got on well with him, I know, so may I ask if he confided anything to you before you left?'

Conscience smote me hard. When the boy had obviously wanted to do just that I had brushed him aside, leaving him to shut his worries away within himself. I thought of the model kestrel still lying in its box, carelessly tossed aside when I arrived home, and again regretted having failed him.

'No, he didn't—but I know something was troubling him. Why?'

'There's nothing specific, but when I spoke to him

191

recently I noticed he's become very low in spirits, and thinner. I had a word with his mother who said he seems all right to her, but I fear she's too taken up with thoughts of her marriage. She weds Robbie in two weeks' time.'

Robbie, who had saved my life, no matter what other evil things he had done. Perhaps I ought to go and hear his version of what happened that night and put things right for Tom if I could. I surely owed him that. Tomorrow would be Sunday, when I was taking Barbara home, so I could drive straight on from there, taking my books with me to study. In such ways do well-meaning persons fall into traps of their own making, but in this case I have no idea whether it was God or the Devil that prompted my decision.

'On second thoughts, Miss Millard, perhaps I could manage to come and do my studying while I'm with you, so I'll arrive tomorrow evening by car.' Show off!

'Oh, Mr Parr—you don't know how pleased I am! Mrs Marsham was delighted to think you might come. I'll tell her to expect you, then.'

I hung up the receiver with a click that sounded like the crack of doom. I had allowed myself to be talked into returning to soil I had vowed would nevermore lie under my feet, then thought of Bessie and Tom—it would be good to see them again.

I set off with Barbara early the next morning and we parted with mutual regret, promising to write and meet again when we broke up for the Christmas holidays. I ventured to kiss her on the cheek, the first, and could see by the light in her eyes that it was not unwelcome. I sped gaily on my way in my new toy and made good time to West Halsey, arriving before dusk. Bessie greeted me cordially and, after admiring the car, sat me down to a hot meal before topping up the teapot ready for a chat, then knitted while I told her about my holiday and how well I was getting on with Barbara.

192

'I'm glad you've found a nice young lady,' she said. ' 'Tis fine being on your own 'til you find that sharing wi' the right person makes a world o' difference.'

We continued in that vein for a time with no mention of Fiona; I had made up my mind to say nothing about her unless Bessie broached the subject.

After a silence, she queried, 'You know 'bout the wedding?'

'Yes. When is it?'

'Sat'day week. Robbie's come home, though his discharge isn't through yet an' they still have the man from East Halsey workin' the farm. He's finished harvesting, so I s'pose they'll let him go now Robbie can take over. Must've cost Lucy some lot o' money in wages. George prob'ly left more'n anyone guessed—or it could've been old Tom—we never knew 'bout that, did us? George didn't make no will, neither.'

'It'll be so much better for Tom to have a settled home life,' I observed. 'Miss Millard was saying that he's changed, lost weight and seems unhappy.'

'I've only seen him running past once or twice and not to talk to, so can't really say how 'e is. Lucy seems happy enough—spoke to me quite friendly t'other day. I would like for us to be the way we were, an' once we gets down to having a chat I'll be able to tell her 'bout the Captain an' she can take the picture off me 'ands. Shouldn't think Robbie 'ud mind—not like George would've done.' She glanced up from her knitting and caught my eye. 'Someone's started that rumour again.'

I had forgotten. 'What rumour?'

' 'Bout George having bin murdered. That's the word used an' 'tis gaining ground, though no partic'lar name's been picked on.'

'That's because it's not true. It's just making mischief for the sake of it. Why can't they let the fellow rest in peace, wicked though he was?'

193

Bessie gave a knowing look. 'That could be why—'e's not able to rest.' She went on clicking the needles, then, 'He weren't the only wicked one, be all accounts. We'll be very sorry to lose Dr Mac. S'pose you've heard?'

Clenching my fists, I said I had.

'There'd been gossip of what went on up at surgery an' elsewhere for the past year or so, the wild parties an' such. Kate Acaster knows—she had to clean up after 'em—but she couldn't talk openly in case she lost 'er job. Fiona were following in her mother's footsteps—they're two of a kind. There was allus the chance you might avoid gettin' mixed up in it, but t'were too much to hope for, you being such an innocent lamb all ready to be slaughtered—if you'll forgive me for saying so—an' too much of a decent gent to put blame where it belonged. You'll be glad to know I've not heard your name mentioned by the gossips, but I could hardly miss the signs, could I? Us bein' so close.'

I gazed at her, open-mouthed. 'Why didn't you warn me, then?'

'Would you have taken notice if I had? You'd have called me an interfering old busybody, wouldn't you? An' you'd have been right.'

I had to admit the truth of that. My imagined love for Fiona would have swept away any criticism and I would still have gone blindly into the Harpy's nest.

Driving to school next day, I stopped at the garage to fill up with petrol. Jim Carter seemed pleased to see me, examining the car while making clucking noises of sincere appreciation.

'She's 'an'some—you won't 'ave any trouble with 'er. Got a starter motor, too. Better'n crankin' the 'andle.'

After a few more of his observations, we agreed to meet in 'The Guiding Light' and I went on my way. School was closed until tomorrow, Tuesday, but I went in to report my arrival to the headmistress, met a rather hearty Mrs Phillips,

194

happily fully recovered, and discussed the level of work I had achieved with her class. The new teacher, taking Fiona's place, hardly gave me a second glance. She was young and enthusiastic, barely more than a schoolgirl herself, but sensible and capable, her mind directed entirely towards her work. I was pleased—and relieved.

Later, I went to the shops and bought flowers for Miss Hope before calling to commiserate with her. She was pale, her normal sharpness blunted by the pain of her heavily bound ankle, but she managed a welcoming smile.

'You're looking very well—more contented, too,' she said, 'and happily seeming unaffected by any iniquitous encounter in school last term. I'm very glad.'

I scanned her colourless but benign smiling face. So, it would appear that she *had* overheard Fiona's remarks to me and interpreted them correctly. Could that be the reason for the Harpy's sudden departure? Or had she left for her own private reasons? It no longer mattered, whichever way it was, but what did matter was that no one was looking askance at me, which boosted my confidence further.

The afternoon was free, so after writing letters to my mother and Barbara I strolled along to post them, being warmly greeted by everyone I met. I felt recovered enough from the events that had taken place at the end of the summer term to walk in the woods again, so took the footpath alongside the stream and crossed it by the little wooden bridge. I could hear voices in the distance, children laughing and shrieking, making the most of their last day of freedom. The summer was continuing on into autumn and the sun remained hot by day, though the evenings were beginning to draw in with a slight chill, causing mists to rise and hang about the valley.

As I walked I listened for the sound of Robbie's gun or a sycamore whistle, but heard nothing more than the occasional whirring of unseen birds' wings, and the quick scampering of squirrels searching for nuts to hide against winter's famine, as Tom had told me they would. I tried to imagine what could be troubling him—was it jealousy that his mother loved someone else? His skinniness could be due to sudden growth. I thought back to when I began to shoot up tall and lanky—outgrowing my strength they called it. Before I reached the lake I had made up my mind to call at the farm and find out for myself, so turned and cut through the trees.

Coming out above the farm, I was faced by the hedge separating it from the buildings and stepped through a gap. I could hear the horse stamping its hooves but the only other signs of life were the chickens scratching about in the dust. I carefully skirted the kennel, expecting the appearance of a furiously barking dog that failed to emerge, and called out when I reached the open front door. Getting no reply, I went along the side of the house and rested my hand against the walnut tree, peering up through branches full of small green, oval globes, the forming walnuts, to the window of Tom's room. I called again, which brought Lucy running around the corner of the house with pegs in her mouth and sheets in her arms. Seeing me, she gestured for me to wait while she rid herself of her burden and in a moment was back, a vivacious woman in a pretty frock, so changed from the previously sad, graceless person.

'Why, Mr Parr! I'm glad to see ye back again—thought ee'd gone fer good. Tom'll be so pleased.'

'I'm only helping out for a couple of weeks,' I hastened to say, 'until Miss Hope feels able to take over again.'

'Oh, ay, the poor soul.' Lucy was all concern. 'I were told 'bout her ankle. How is she?'

'Coming along nicely, she says. Er, I believe I have to congratulate you.'

She coloured up. 'Thank 'ee, Mr Parr. Now, if you're

come to see Tom, I'm 'fraid he's out playing somewheres, an' Robbie's gone to town on his bike. He's very keen on horse racin' an' goes there to put his bets on.'

'I'll probably find him in the inn this evening, but it was Tom I wanted to see. Has he taken the dog for a walk?'

'The dog? Naw, it turned savage. Robbie got rid of it.'

'I see. How is Tom, by the way?'

She seemed surprised by the question. 'Well 'nough. Why do 'ee ask?'

'Because I heard he was looking a bit under the weather.'

She laughed. 'S'pect he were in one of his moods—you knows what boys are like at his age. He's all right. You'll see 'im in school tomorrer.'

Was I to believe Miss Millard or Lucy? I decided that a mother should know her own son best and said goodbye.

That evening I drove to the inn and parked the car outside to show it off. It caused some comment among the regulars, but there was never a hint of envy. Bill Angove was his old, friendly self and entertained me with snippets of local news, before reaching the main item of interest.

'The school's lost Fiona Macdonald, I hear. It'll upset the boys more than the girls. Have you met her replacement?'

'Only briefly,' I answered. 'Seems an excellent choice, a pleasant girl who appears to be more keen on teaching than anything else.'

'Unlike the last one, who set her cap at all and sundry, eh? Oh, you needn't raise your eyebrows—word gets around. Thought you'd been taken in at one time, but luckily you managed to avoid it. Just like her mother, 'tis said, and has upped and left in the same way. We're all sorry for the Doc—did his best by her. He's thinking of selling up and going back to Scotland, I hear. Be a great loss to us, I can tell you.'

He went to serve another customer as I mulled over his

197

words and took myself to the Snug. Robbie was standing at the end of the bar regarding me. I took a deep breath and smiled, and his own face creased into a grin.

'Luce said you'd be 'ere. We didn't expect 'ee back.'

'I'm glad I was able to come,' I replied. 'I wanted to thank you again.'

He waved a hand of dismissal as he lit a cigarette, his eyes hooded. 'I 'opes I won't hear mention of it no more—'tis over an' past.'

'I wanted to ask you what happened that night,' I went on, carefully. 'Fiona told me you took a part in what was done.'

He looked away. 'You don' want to believe everythin' she said—she made things up. Ferget it. Who'd a' thought she'd leave 'ere like that, though?' He shook his head. ''Ow long are you stayin'?'

'Not long enough to see you tie the knot, I'm afraid. I'll have to leave the day before to be in time to start at my new school, but I do wish you good luck.'

'I've waited a long time fer that,' he said, slowly, 'but 'tis all comin' together now. Everythin' comes to them as waits, they says. I've 'ad a good day wi' the 'osses, too.' He gave a wink, gulped down his ale, saluted, and left straightaway.

I arrived at school bright and early next day and put my things in Miss Hope's classroom. I already knew most of the children in her form, so names did not present a problem. I picked out Frank at assembly, browner and bigger but otherwise much the same, and then Tom. He did not glance my way but gazed straight ahead, his attitude stiff and unnatural. I could see an obvious change in him, an air of seeming anxiety, and there was plainly less flesh on his bones. Gone was the healthy glow of a golden skin—even his fair hair lacked sheen. I supposed Lucy was too taken up with her own affairs to have noticed, and I was aware

198

how easy it can be to miss gradual changes in a person you see daily. I would have to call on her again.

When break came, I was delayed by a query, but before I left the room I looked out of the window at the various groups of children at play to see Frank and his cronies performing 'The Ballad of Halsey Manor', with Tom again as the hapless victim. He was taking more punishment than usual and jumped on the seat surrounding the sycamore tree, putting his back defensively against it. Then the others dispersed, chasing a ball, but Frank stood his ground, shouting, as if taunting him. I opened the window and clearly heard him chanting a nursery rhyme, only it was not quite as I remembered it:

'Tom, Tom, old Piper's son,
Killed 'is dad an' away he run,
He told some tale, an' he did wail,
But they still strung 'im up in the nearest gaol!'

Hardly believing I had heard aright, I shouted, 'Frank—Tom—you two boys come in here at once!' and waited until they did. Tom stood like a woebegone waif, but Frank exhibited an obvious bravado as if uncaring of anything I might say or do.

'Would you care to explain what you were doing?' I enquired of the latter.

'Just 'avin' a game, sir.'

'Still fancying yourself as some kind of poet, are you?'

'Don' know what you mean. Nice car you got, sir.'

'Kindly repeat what you were saying outside,' I ordered, full of a cold anger.

'Cert'nly—sir. "Tom, Tom, the piper's son, stole a pig an' away he run . . ."'

'It didn't sound like that to me,' I interrupted.

'Mebbe you was too far off to 'ear prop'ly. Tom knows—don'cha, Tom?'

The boy thus addressed raised his drooping chin without meeting my eye. 'Ay—yes, that's what he said, sir.'

Faced with that deliberate denial there was nothing more I could do, but felt deeply shocked and uneasy. I was reluctant to bring this unresolved problem to Miss Millard as yet, so had to leave the matter there for the time being. At the end of the day I drove back to Bessie, finding myself unable to discuss the matter even with her. However much I endeavoured to ignore it, the ugly thought would not be dispersed. What if it were true? It would certainly explain the change in Tom.

Day 18

That evening I tried to study for my coming term, but concentration was nil as my mind kept straying to the chilling tableau of the two boys in the playground. Had I misheard? It was possible, but I doubted it—Frank's voice had registered clearly enough. I felt I should take some action, though if both boys persisted in denying it, what *could* I do? Tom appeared to be suffering a form of torment, enough to have changed him in body and spirit, and although that was consistent with guilt feelings I could not bring myself to believe that he had deliberately . . .

Lucy had had the most to gain, so was he suspicious of *her* involvement? With childish logic he would stage her in an imaginary murder scene, one that would become reality the more he thought about it, and then he would live in fear of all being revealed and the constable come to take his mother away for ever. Was that it?

Miss Millard, similarly concerned about the boy, tackled me next day. 'Have you had a word with Tom yet?'

'Not with any relevance—he seems reluctant to confide in me again. I did go to see his mother but she finds nothing wrong with him. I'm wondering, though, if Frank Acaster could be intimidating him in some way. I'll do my best to find out.'

'And so will I, Mr Parr. By the way, you might not have heard that there is a rumour that George Piper was murdered. According to Wills, that idea is entirely without foundation, but it could be having an effect on the boy. Folk can say such damaging things without realising it.'

With Frank in mind I had to agree with her, and despite my resolve to ask Mrs Phillips to keep both boys back at dinnertime so I could question them, I delayed, feeling uncertain as to how I could safely broach the subject.

The afternoon being sunny, but not too warm, I had walked back to school and after lessons were over began on the return journey. As I reached the humpback bridge I could see the lower half of a boy leaning over the parapet, legs stuck out of short trousers, boots kicking the stonework. I peered over in my turn to see Tom running across the stepping stones, and heard Frank's voice chanting,

'Tom, Tom, old Piper's son,
Killed 'is dad an' away he run . . .'

There was no mistaking it this time. I caught the boy by the back of his collar and jerked him on his feet, tempted to shake him like the little rat I was thinking he was. He screwed his head around to see who was holding him, eyes popping wide with surprise and fright. There was nobody near and no traffic in sight as I relaxed my grip and pushed him against the wall, keeping my anger in check with difficulty.

'How dare you make an accusation like that! I intend to take you straight to Constable Wills and see what he'll have to say, but before I do, please explain yourself to me. What right have you to suggest that Tom did such a terrible thing?'

I had expected him to crumple up, looking shamefaced, but he stood firm while shrinking back as if expecting me to hit him. ' 'Cos 'tis true—'e did kill 'im!' His voice was low, but defiant.

I was taken aback. 'What makes you think that?'

'I don't think—I saw 'im do it.'

'You saw him do it,' I repeated, idiotically, the bluster inside me instantly deflated and blown away.

'That's right.'

I desperately tried to grasp one of my whirling thoughts. 'Then why didn't you tell someone?'

'I did—I told me mam.'

'And what did she do?'

'Nothin'—only said she'd stop me penny a week if I told anyone else, an' then she'd give me a good 'iding fer tellin' lies.'

'And were you?'

'Naw—an' I did start by keepin' me mouth shut. Then I didn' see why that swanky little goody-goody should git away wi' it.' He scowled, full of enmity.

'Was it you who started the rumour about murder?'

'Mebbe.'

I found myself in a quandary, unable to believe and yet being forced to accept it. 'What did you see him do?'

'Drop 'is dad's 'ead down under water an' then run away.'

'And where were you at the time?'

'Among the bushes, comin' down the far bank o' the stream.'

'At that time of night? What were you doing there?'

He looked even more uncomfortable, shuffling his feet, his voice so low I could barely hear it. 'Gettin' veggies for Sunday dinner as usual.'

'Stealing them, you mean. From the Pipers'?' He nodded. 'Whatever did your mother think you were doing out so late? And didn't she wonder where you got these things you brought home?'

'I do same ev'ry Sat'day. I tells 'er I do odd jobs around while she washes up at the whist drive an' she thinks I gets paid with 'em. She's grateful, too, 'cos we're poor. I gets 'ome first so she don't know I've bin out late.'

I drew a deep breath. It sounded plausible but I knew I was dealing with a particularly slithery little snake in the grass. He could have killed George himself—he had reason enough to hate him—by first knocking him down with a stone from his catapult. Of course, the same theory applied to Tom. 'Let's go and find your mother,' I said, wondering what else I could do.

A flash of panic replaced the animosity in his eyes. 'Naw, I won't go with 'ee! She said I weren't to tell nobody! I'll say I made it up an' never saw nothin'! P'raps I didn'. If you goes spreadin' it about, me mam'll lose all 'er work an' we'll 'ave no money, nowhere to live an' nothin' to eat!'

Which is doubtless the way in which she had threatened him. As I regarded him now, trembling with passion—or was it fear?—I felt inadequate as to how to deal with this crisis I had unwittingly brought about, so tried to back away from it.

I put a hand on his shoulder. 'Frank—go home to your tea while I give this some thought. I know that if you've told me the whole truth then nothing will happen to either you or your mother. She won't lose anything by it as no blame attaches to her.' Unless she killed him herself, my inward voice said. Then, 'Off you go, I'll speak to you tomorrow,' I finished hastily.

I refrained from mentioning it to Bessie at teatime, remaining hesitant as to what to believe myself—unable to separate fact from what might be fantasy in Frank's horror story. The idea of my golden boy deliberately setting out to kill was something I was finding hard to accept—he had said he hated killing. Then the memory of the day when George had threatened Methy came to mind and I knew there could be a possibility, but as I was getting nowhere by making unconfirmed assumptions I set off for a walk to clear my head.

It was early evening when I reached the lake. The sun still shone through the trees, highlighting the water with a sparkling brightness that contrasted sharply with the black, shadowy patches, stirring up thoughts of the night of Robbie's timely arrival here. I contemplated my rescue with thankfulness, no matter what else he was supposed to have done, thinking how fortunate I was to have escaped a watery death among the fishes—and also lucky to have escaped the witch's coven—if such it was. Then familiar whistled notes cut in on my musing, and I saw Tom sitting with his back against a tree in the same manner as when we first met there, but how changed he had become. No longer the carefree lad who happily imparted his knowledge of nature to me, but morose, withdrawn. I went and sat beside him.

'I heard you comin',' he said, his eyes fixed on the lake.

'I'm glad you're here, Tom. You wanted to talk to me before and I'm sorry I wasn't able to listen then. Like to tell me now?'

'Don't think so.'

'But I need to know what's wrong. What's worrying you?'

'Nothin'.'

'Has Frank been annoying you?'

'No more'n usual. He don't bother me.'

I tried another tack. 'Your work seemed to suffer at the end of last term—any idea why that was?'

'No, sir.'

How could I pierce his armour of indifference? 'Were you—and your mother—very upset by your father's death?'

'Not pertickly. I 'oped things'd be better then, but it only brought more trouble.'

I felt he was relaxing his guard. 'What kind of trouble?'

'Just more o' the same.'

205

'But life for you and your mother must be easier,' I insisted, 'you've got Uncle Robbie to look after you both. You don't mind him marrying her, do you?'

He looked down, cheeks flushed, ignoring the question. ''E shot the dog.'

'Your mother told me he had to, because it turned savage.'

He swung his head sharply to regard me. 'Only 'cos 'e kicked at 'im ev'ry time 'e went past! 'E's jest as bad as me dad were, an' *he* surely deserved what 'e got! Frank's sayin' I killed 'im. What do 'e know? Was 'e there?' He waited for me to answer, and when I kept silent he went on, 'Well, then, p'raps 'e did it hisself!' He got up. 'D'*you* b'lieve 'im? How would you prove it if I said it were 'im, or anybody else, had done it? How would you know 'less they owned up? An' nobody's a-goin' to do that now, 'owever much you pesters 'em, are they? Why should they? Why don't you leave me alone? I hates yer—I hates all o' yer!'

He had begun crying long before he ended his outburst, and suddenly made off with the speed of a hare. I wryly congratulated myself upon handling a difficult matter with granite gloves and slunk back to Clover Cottage, my self-regard badly dented yet again. There was no doubt that tomorrow I would have to hand over the responsibility for this anguished boy to someone more capable of dealing with it. Miss Millard? Constable Wills? Dr Mac? I wrote a letter to Barbara outlining my dilemma, then stuck my head in my books and tried to put everything else out of it.

I tossed and turned all night with occasional nightmares that were interrelated—one where Tom, or was it Frank—or maybe a composite of both?—anyway, a boy was slinging stones at George with a catapult. And then another dream, where Lucy and Kate Acaster were attacking him with heavy sticks. I applauded as I saw him fall, but he got up again

206

and staggered forward as I realised with mounting horror that he was coming for me! I could see his ugly, twisted face getting nearer and nearer, and I found my feet so firmly stuck in the ground that I had no chance of escaping his bony hands as they reached out for me ... I awoke in a cold sweat, too nervous of risking a recurrence to try to sleep again, and by daybreak had decided to tell all I knew to Miss Millard as being the most able to influence the welfare of the two boys.

I found her in her room before school. She listened gravely and thanked me.

'I will have to question them,' she said, 'but I still think it was an accidental death, and I believe Tom's problem now to be that his mother loves someone other than him. Frank, I think, is being deliberately malicious. You say he will deny everything if pressed?' I nodded. 'That's just what I'd expect. I'm sure he made the whole thing up just to get back at Tom—he's been jealous of him all his life. It isn't often I have to resort to the cane, but this time ...'

'Headmistress, could there be the barest possibility that he's telling the truth? I was inclined to believe him.'

She paused, as if considering it, but her eyes were saying how surprised she was to hear my question. 'Mr Parr,' she said at last, 'I have known Tom Piper since he was a baby, and I'm rarely wrong in my assessment of a child. Let me ask if you can imagine someone, who is so obviously of a virtuous disposition, indulging in such a heinous act, however much tempted to do so?'

I did not care to argue, but thought it a dangerous supposition to make, believing that it would be conceivable if enough compelling pressure were applied. She was relying on her instinct and instinct is a notoriously unreliable way to presume a truth. However, I had handed over my responsibility so now it was up to her, and I left to have that promised word with Frank, informing him that I had told Miss Millard everything and to expect to be summoned to her room.

He seemed, understandably, shifty and uneasy, probably full of anger at what he would consider my treachery, but I felt it to be the end of the matter as far as I was concerned—that is, until school was over and I was halfway through tea. Bessie was relating the day's gossip she had garnered, while I listened with wandering attention until it was alerted by something I thought I had heard.

'What was that?' I asked. 'What did you say just then?'

'Oh, was it the bit about old Mr Magor? You know, he's the local pig farmer. Well, he were celebrating the birth of his first grandson at the inn last even' an' had too much to drink too quick, an' though t'were early, barely dusk, his son, John, thought he'd better get his dad home while he could still stand. He went to fetch horse an' cart from along the road, leaving old Magor sitting on a seat outside in the fresh air to bring 'im round a bit, an' today Magor's full of a tale 'bout seeing a flickering glow moving up alongside a field on t'other side o' stream. Then, while he were a-lookin', back comes John wi' the cart an' wouldn't take notice of 'is dad's rambling, nor the time to take a look for himself, so just put him on cart an' drove off. The old man won't stop talkin' 'bout it today, though, saying he saw the "guiding light". 'Tis Gospel truth, Mr Parr, that alcohol fumes in the head lead to will-o'-the-wisps in the eyes—as you've prob'ly found out for yourself!' She smiled knowingly.

I sheepishly agreed, burying my head in my books again while she went off to see the weekly Wednesday film, and it seemed that no time had passed before I heard her say goodnight to our neighbours and come inside to warm her hands at the fire.

208

' 'Tis a bit chilly outside. S'pose you notice it more when the days keep warm. There's been a patchy mist about, too.'

'Did you see any ghostly lights on the way home?' I asked, facetiously.

'No, I didn't, but there's talk of some saying they did earlier, going up alongside the hedge over the stream but were too scared to go an' find out what it really was, the silly softies. Lot o' nonsense, if you ask me. It only takes one chap who's had a drop too much and imagine he's seen something odd, for everyone to start seeing it. Could frighten the life out o' the Pipers if they hears of it coming up near them. Pity some folk haven't got better things to do!' End of conversation.

When I went to bed I found that, though it was not cold, I felt shivery as I put my head on the pillow and prayed that George would not, should he yet suffer restlessness, be on the prowl in my bed again so soon after last night, but all was well.

Thursday dawned sunny and bright, driving away any lingering dark shadows. We were having a real Indian summer, as Bessie remarked, and a letter from Barbara ensured that all was right with my world. I drove to school full of happiness, prepared, so I thought, for anything. During break I read my newspaper while the others chatted about the spooky light appearing near the Pipers' place and, hearing Tom's name mentioned, I asked about him.

'He's not turned up today,' Mrs Phillips explained. 'Looked a bit pale yesterday, so perhaps he's ill—or maybe scared of the ghost!'

I felt vaguely disturbed, Frank's words at the back of my mind. 'I hope not. If he's not here this afternoon, I'll call after school and find out why.'

As nothing had been seen or heard of him by the final bell I drove straight to the farm, jolting along the rutted lane. As I switched off the engine, Robbie came out of the house wearing his khaki uniform and carrying a battered suitcase, kitbag and greatcoat slung over a shoulder. Lucy followed close behind.

''Allo, there,' he said, cheerily. 'Thought I 'eard the sound o' yer motor.'

'I've come about Tom. Is he not well?'

'Seems all right to me.' Lucy appeared unworried, hanging on to Robbie's arm. 'Why? What's the matter?'

'We've been wondering why he wasn't in school today.'

Robbie lowered the suitcase. 'He's been there all day—far as we knew. Did you 'ear that, Luce? The little so an' so turned up 'ere on time for 'is dinner, didn't 'e? Playin' truant, now. I told ye, Luce, he's been gettin' out of 'and lately, turning bolshie all of a sudden. I'll 'ave to see to 'im proper when I gets back—give 'im a beltin'. Don't tell 'im I've gone away—he might be'ave better if 'e thinks I'm still 'ere. Oh, yer don't know, do 'ee Mr Parr? This telegram come not an hour back.' He held up the plainly printed, familiar buff form, at arm's length for me to read: 'RETURN TO BARRACKS IMMEDIATELY FOR DISCHARGE', and was signed, ADJUTANT, then he put it back in his pocket.

'Good, in't it? It'll be all over an' done with an' I'll be back in time fer you to change yer name afore you knows it, Luce,' he went on, squeezing her waist and kissing her cheek. 'Only, you won't be, will yer? It'll be the same.' He laughed and turned to me. 'Now, I were just off to get Jim Carter to take me to catch the five-ten, 'cos I can't ride me bike carryin' all these. Could *you* give us a lift?'

'Of course, it's the least I can do,' I said.

'Thank 'ee, Mr Parr, we don't 'ave to 'urry, then. Time for another cuppa.'

He ushered me through into a kitchen that was clean

and tidy but not nearly as cosy as Bessie's. I sat by the table as Lucy re-filled a teapot from a boiling kettle.

'I'd like to know what Tom's been up to,' she said. 'He don't talk to me like he used. S'pose he's getting that much older.'

'Or too wayward, I reckon, on'y you can't see it.'

'He's never been any trouble 'til now, Rob. I'll make sure he's in school Monday, Mr Parr.' She stirred the pot and began to pour. 'Sugar?'

'One, please.'

She pushed a sugar bowl towards me, but Robbie intervened. 'Can't give 'im that, Luce, it's been standin' on table gatherin' dust. Here, 'ave some o' this.' He took a new packet from a cupboard and opened it. 'Nothin' but the best fer you—stick yer spoon in. Sugar feels rough to touch but goes smooth when wet, like makin' your choice for service with a tennis racquet, eh? Let me pour you another, Luce.'

I gave him a quick glance, wondering if his words were derisive, but his eyes were lowered as he put several spoons of sugar from the bowl into Lucy's cup, remarking about her sweet tooth like her son's and having to build up her strength for the big day. He obviously thought the dust would do her no harm. I drank my tea, looked at my watch, and said we ought to leave.

He lighted a cigarette as I drove, giving me an oblique glance. 'Any idea where Fiona is now?'

I kept my eyes on the road. 'No idea at all.'

'I 'ope she comes back sometime—she were a lot o' fun. On'y thing were, she liked to be looked at—to 'ave people watchin'—know what I mean? Seems it got 'er goin', actin' like she were on a stage, givin' a show. She'd plan for one or two to be there when she got what she called a novice— an' prefer'bly 'ave pictures taken. I've got some if your

211

int'rested.' I sensed his sly smile. 'You can't deny you enjoyed 'er. We all did, for that matter—George in pertic'lar.'

Feeling increasingly hot under the collar and keeping my temper in check, I said nothing as we drew up at the Halt and sat in the car listening for the train's warning whistle. After all, I would not be seeing him again. Trying to think of a more acceptable topic of conversation to pass the time, I noticed the derelict driveway on the other side of the road and was reminded of its previous history.

'I didn't want to say anything in front of Lucy, but have you heard about the mysterious moving light people say they've seen?'

'Oh, that, ay. I were at the inn when Magor got tipsy, but it weren't spoken of that night an' I only 'eard 'is story yest'day. S'prised 'e didn't see some fairies, too!'

'Well, bearing in mind the tale about the Old Manor at the end of the drive over there, shouldn't you feel some concern?'

He stared at me, open-mouthed for a moment, before bursting out laughing. 'Oh, golly! You don't really b'lieve that rubbish, do 'ee? I took ye to be a fully 'sperienced man o' the world—but I were wrong 'bout that once before, o' course.'

Conversation became stilted again following his pointed remark, and I was relieved to hear the whistle of the approaching train. I got out of the car. 'I'll help you with the case.'

'No need, I c'n manage—not much in it. It's just to collect me things in barracks. No need fer you to stay now.'

But I'd quickly lifted it from the back seat to hasten his departure, wanting him gone, and hurried in front of him on to the near platform as the train came in sight. Robbie caught up with me and stood waving it down until it stopped, then he jumped in and I handed up the case.

'Ta,' he said, unsmiling, with a seeming ill grace.

'I'm just thanking you for what you did for me.'

Again that cool look. 'As I said before—ferget it.'

The guard blew his whistle and I watched the train steam away, still smarting uncomfortably at being reminded of both Fiona and my humiliation. Anyway, I would soon be gone and it would all be forgotten again.

Back at Clover Cottage I noticed Bessie limping. 'Fell over the mat and hurt me knee,' she informed me. ''Tis swollen up but will soon be right as rain if I rests it, so I'd be grateful for a lift to choir practice this even'.'

'Delighted to take you,' I assured her. 'I'll have a drink at the inn and wait to drive you back.' It would also give me the chance to investigate the mysterious light, should it reappear.

After helping Bessie into church I parked outside the inn. It seemed that most of the men in the village shared the same idea as myself, for the place was filled with more customers than was usual at this early hour, all crowded into the public bar. The chatter was mainly about whether the reports were true, and, if so, what did it mean? Jim Carter, bowler hat on the back of his head as always, had no doubts.

'If it come ternight for the third time, we'll know 'tis George Piper huntin' fer the one wot put 'im under, an' I fer one wouldn't go nowheres near'—a sentiment endorsed by the rest of the assembled company, judging by the mumbled sounds of agreement, though there was no specu- lation as to whom 'the one' might be.

Dr Mac put in a surprise appearance a short time later, surprising because I understood that he had avoided the inn since the news of his daughter's permanent departure had become public knowledge. The last time I had seen him had been at the end of term and I found he had visibly aged, his shoulders bowed in a tired manner. I felt sympathy

213

for the man in his deep disappointment, his high hopes for his daughter fallen so short, and when he saw me he came over.

'Hello, Eddie, I'd heard you were back temporarily. It was decent of you to help Miss Millard out after what must've been a trying time for you, as a little bird told me. I didn't know, or rather, wouldn't let myself know. You see, I'd hoped—anyway, I'm sorry if I gave you too much encouragement—you'd have been just what the doctor ordered!' He grimaced at his attempt to joke and changed the subject. 'We've got a full house for tonight—there'll be great discontent if the curtain doesn't go up on another showing! It'll be something of an anticlimax if nothing happens soon—the sun's over the hill already.'

Constable Wills, in uniform, had arrived in the last few minutes, refusing all offers of a drink. 'Have one later, thank ye, when I'm off duty. Thought I'd better come along to keep an eye on things. Wonder if some misguided idjit could be out there playin' tricks to liven us up?'

'It would have to be someone with a spiteful sense of humour,' I answered, 'since it seems to be aimed at the Pipers. It's a pity Robbie's not home to look out for whoever it might be.'

'Not home? Where is he then?' asked Wills, one amid a sea of curious faces.

'He had a telegram this afternoon ordering him back to barracks—I put him on the train . . .' I stopped speaking as a man began calling excitedly from outside.

'There 'tis—over there! Can't 'ee see that strange-lookin' glow through the mist just below hedge on t'other side o' stream? 'Tis movin' slow up towards farm!'

We all made a concerted move to the door to see it with our own eyes, jostling our way outside. The two cars, Dr Mac's and mine, were back to back, facing in our homeward directions, but everybody was looking beyond them. A thin mist already lay over the fields in the gathering half-light now the sun had slipped behind the hill, yet, plainly visible, an eerie glow was moving slowly, but resolutely, along the path between the stubble left by the harvested corn and the near side of the hedge below Walnut Tree Farm. The effect was enough to reduce the 'ooh's' to silence, a weird hush, accentuated by the muted sound of the choir singing a harvest hymn, settling over the village.

For a moment I thought I could detect two lights, one ahead of the other, but put it down to visual distortion occasioned by the mist, and at the same time imagined I heard faint whistled notes. No doubt we were all wrestling with our various beliefs and superstitions, anxious to find a rational explanation, and I, for one, finding none.

I felt the hairs on the back of my neck rise like those of an animal when it senses danger and was reminded of Fiona's witchery, but she could have no involvement in this—she had gone, thankfully, and taken her evil magic with her.

No one spoke until one man crossed himself, whispering: 'May God in 'is 'eaven protect us. Why in't Vicar 'ere?'

The spell was broken but still no one moved, staring in awe at the glow in the mist. ''Tis the "guidin' light"', said another voice. 'George Piper's out ter get 'is revenge. I allus said 'e'd been murdered. You won't ketch me a-goin' up there. There's nowt *you* c'n do 'bout a ghost neither, Wills.'

We all cast our eyes on the constable, who appeared to be uncertain as to how to proceed. 'Don't see as how I can arrest a sperit,' he said, thoughtfully, seeming in no way motivated to leap into action. ''Tis'n breakin' no law.'

'Well, man, at least you can go and find out exactly what it is!' the doctor exclaimed loudly and impatiently.

'You c'n be sure 'tis up to no good,' was Jim Carter's sepulchral aside. 'Like it were all them years ago. Look at wot it did then! 'Oo's it lookin' for now, do'ee s'pose?'

215

After another brief, uncomfortable silence, Mr Hillman remarked, albeit reluctantly, 'I think I 'eard young Tom's name mentioned . . . I b'lieve Frank Acaster says 'e saw 'im do it . . .'

Day 19

' . . . and three times led,
Hangs him high on a tree . . .'

As the words of the rhyme filtered into my brain I
became the first man galvanized into action, inciting the
others to follow me without taking the time to rationalize
why.

'Come on!' I shouted, and seeing the constable making
for his bike, 'No time for that—get in my car!'

Being a big man he hesitated, seeming to wonder
whether it would contain his bulk, and others pushed inside
until he climbed on the running-board, putting an arm
through the window and clutching at whatever he could
grip. Jim was doing likewise on the other side and both
hung on like grim death as the car shot forward. As I was
facing in the right direction I got away first, with Dr Mac
only just beginning to turn.

'Where're we goin', Mr Parr?' came Jim's quavering tone.
'We'll not be gettin' nowheres near it, will us?'

I put the headlights on as we passed the shops, speeding
as swiftly as I could persuade the engine to oblige, impelled
by a sudden sense of urgency, responding to an unthinking
reaction. We turned at last up Walnut Tree Lane and I put
my foot on the brake when we reached the barns. The men
leapt out, then stood shifting their feet looking a bit foolish,

the ghostly light lost to view. The silence was profound, the house dark, the door closed, and no sign of life.

'Whadda we do now?' someone whispered.

I was unable to supply an answer at first, then a sixth sense, intuition—call it what you will—came to my rescue. 'This way!' I cried, moving around to the side of the house, while tentatively avoiding unknown shadows in the gloom.

As I passed beneath the spread branches of the walnut tree in the deeper shadows, something hit my forehead and swung away. I ducked instinctively as it swung back and hit me again before I realised what it was. Then, panic-stricken, I reached up to grasp two feet, holding and supporting the legs as well as I could to take the weight of the body as I called for help. Wills ran up and flashed his lamp on us as I heard the shocked, indrawn breaths of the men.

'Quick—cut the rope!' I yelled, and saw a couple of the heftier men lift Jim, holding an open pocket knife in his hand, the blade flashing as it caught the light, and in a few seconds the rope was severed. The sudden release of the weight knocked me down with the body on top of me. I got to my knees and tore at the noose around Tom's neck to reveal a livid weal marking his throat. His face was scarlet, eyes half-lidded, showing white behind them, mouth open, tongue protruding with saliva dribbled down his chin. I feel sick now, remembering, just as I did then.

I cradled the frail form in my arms, suffering such agony of mind as I cannot rightly describe, but as I opened my own mouth to protest at the sheer waste of a life, a sound came from his damaged throat and his eyelids flickered. Hope surged through me as I called for Dr Mac, aware of having heard his car arrive, and then he was beside us, taking over and working on the boy, issuing orders for warm coverings and his bag to be brought.

He asked me to turn on my headlamps to help light the scene so I left, rather unwillingly, and was trembling as I got in the car, everything exhibiting a dream-like quality with sounds perceived as coming from afar. I slowly came to realise that this must be the shock of knowing that this child had killed George and, faced by the mysterious light and unable to endure his guilt, had decided to end his young life.

I stepped out of the car to find Wills standing there. ''Tis tragic,' he said. 'Where can Lucy be? She must've heard the ruckus if she's inside. I'll take a look.'

I found Dr Mac still working on the inert little body. 'There's a bump on his head—must've hit the tree when he dropped—so he's concussed as well,' he said.

I know I fell on my knees, closed my eyes and prayed to God for him to recover, and when I opened them again the oil lamps were alight in the house and Wills was saying that Lucy was in her bed. 'She's so sound asleep that Tom must've drugged her somehow so she couldn't stop 'im doin' what he'd planned,' he told me. 'He must've bin right out of his young mind, either from guilt of what 'e'd done or fear of the light guidin' George's ghost to kill 'im.'

I know I was surprised enough to cast a glance at the big, powerful man, suspecting that he, too, was afraid of the so-called 'guiding light', then realised how he, together with all the others who had been familiar with the ballad from childhood, would have become inured into believing it. Having thus been reminded of the eerie glow, I myself threw a fearful glance at the hedge and saw a glimmer showing through. Sanity took flight as I gazed, still on my knees, transfixed with the dread of seeing George again as the flickering light came inexorably closer to an open gap.

'Mind out! Let's get away—'tis 'ere!' someone began in a hushed voice, which ended nearer a shriek amid the gasped imprecations of others. 'May the good Lord 'ave mercy on us all!'

I cringed, unable to avert my eyes, expecting to see—

what? George's ghost following behind its 'guide'? In the final moments of waiting, in those last, long seconds, I think Dr Mac was alone in attending solely to what he was doing as we others watched in disbelief. The 'guiding light' had come into full view—a flickering nightlight in a small glass jar, firmly fixed by plasticine to the top of Methy's shell. Methy . . . who was now making his ponderous way towards the open barn door.

The effect of this anticlimax had everyone bursting into the foolish laughter of relief, with assertions of, 'I allus knowed t'were somethin' like that!' and, 'Never b'lieved in anythin' spooky!' as I furtively wiped my wet forehead and turned my attention back to Tom. I heard Dr Mac saying that the boy's life had apparently been saved in the nick of time, but his injuries had to be assessed and we must get him to hospital as soon as possible.

He nodded to me. 'Carry him to my car while I have a look at Lucy, to make sure she's all right. Won't be long.'

I picked up the inert bundle. He had been wrapped in a blanket taken from the house, and his ashen white, tear-stained face with closed eyes was held close to mine, his breath coming in painful gasps. I was filled with sadness. I had failed the boy when he needed me. There would have been no need for this suicide attempt had I listened to him when he first wanted to talk to me about his underlying despair, and persuaded him to confess and share the burden of his guilt.

I carried the limp body towards the car, telling myself how clever he had been in using Methy to provide the three 'guiding lights' in the ballad to alert the villagers of possible trouble up at the farm, so that after he was dead his mother would have people come up there to find and look after her. I stood holding him, staring past the barns and into the depths of the wood, unseeing—until something caused me to focus properly. What was it? Another faint glow—or was it two? After I had managed to concentrate all my attention I could see only blackness. And yet . . .

Dr Mac hurried up. 'Lucy will be fine in the morning—I've asked one of the men to fetch his wife to stay with her. Now, it's getting on for twenty minutes since the boy did this and he needs urgent treatment, so get in my car, man!' he ordered, but the sudden, far-off whistle of a train was penetrating my thoughts and I remained unmoving. I had a strong image of a stunted walnut tree moving fast in the entangled, bedevilled wood of this enigma, and was sufficiently startled by it to lay Tom in the arms of a man beside me and urge him to get the boy into the doctor's car instead.

I grasped Wills' shoulder. 'You come with me!'

My tone must have been compelling enough for him not to risk refusal, so he squeezed in beside me as I parried his questioning, turning my car as fast as I could to chase behind the doctor's car now bumping down to the end of the lane.

'What d'you think you're about, Mr Parr?' Wills enquired, with some asperity, as I turned to the right, away from Dr Mac's speeding vehicle and the hospital. 'I should stay wi' the boy, be rights, to take 'is statement soon as he's able to tell us why he did this tur'ble thing. Where're we going?'

'Bear with me, Wills. I'm not sure if I've guessed aright—I haven't had time to think things out clearly—but I've a feeling there may be no time to lose!'

It was very dark now, the headlights revealing the road ahead as we passed Clover Cottage and approached the Halt. As we neared, a lumpy shaped figure ran across the road towards the station just out of reach of my lights, and as I drew up and switched off the engine I heard a train approaching.

'Hurry up, Wills!' I called, getting out as fast as I could and making for the platform, but it was taking him longer to disengage himself.

The figure moved quickly ahead of me, shining a lamp on the ground before it, but how did the beam show behind as well as in front? I followed as rapidly as I could, a rising watery moon doing little to help me on my way, and then the train was coming round a bend, puffing out smoke and sparks from its stack while blowing a warning blast on the whistle as I caught up with the running man. I saw he was waving a bicycle lamp as I managed to grasp his flapping greatcoat and swing him around, causing the kitbag hanging round his neck to thump on his chest. Robbie had not heard me coming above the noise of the engine, and his startled expression betrayed a mixture of rage and chagrin as he faced me, dropping the suitcase from under his arm.

'It was you, wasn't it?' I shouted the words at him. 'You killed your brother, and when you found out that Tom knew it, you tried to kill him, too!' His look changed to disbelief as I spoke. 'Oh, yes, he's alive, and able to tell us the truth!'

'Yer lyin'!' he snarled, but his eyes were fearful.

I was conscious of Wills hurrying along the platform towards us as Robbie endeavoured to tear his coat out of my grasp while continuing to wave the lamp to stop the train, still sending mouthfuls of invective in my direction. The powerful engine began to loom up, steaming into the Halt. I could see the driver leaning out of his cabin, peering down at us, the glare from the firebox lighting his surprised, coal-dust-smeared face, as he observed the scuffle that was taking place below him.

I began to make incredulous sense of Robbie's vicious tirade. 'I should've let 'ee drown in lake after I chased yer in. I on'y pulled 'ee out for 'er sake!'

He was looking at me with such an evil expression that

for a moment I thought I could see Fiona's execrable witch-face superimposed there, and became engulfed by an over-powering loathing, a fervent desire to destroy both of them and my shame forever. I was finding it increasingly difficult to hold on to the coat, the strong, wiry body inside it twisting and tugging, then Robbie swung a fist, catching me just above the mouth, and I felt blood spurt from my nose and tasted it on my tongue. My cry of pain rang in my ears as he moved towards the slowing train, dragging me behind him, my fingers still entwined in the cloth. He turned and grabbed me, forcing me to let go by flinging me to the edge of the platform but, by some miracle, I got a foot behind his leg which stopped me going over. I threw myself on him again, so full of fury that I was intent on strangling him if I could only get my hands around his ugly neck, and my impetus was forceful enough to send him staggering to the edge in his turn, the bulky kitbag, probably containing his camera, tending to overbalance him, one of his legs dangling in mid air over the track as I regained a firmer hold on the coat.

The engine was slowing, wheels screeching on the rails, sparks flying from metal biting into metal as the brakes were applied and the train began to grind to a halt. Robbie managed to half turn towards me in an effort to get his foot back on the platform, then I saw his angry expression change to horror as he stared at something that was hovering at his side. I, too, had a fleeting impression of a translucent shape, a phantasm bearing George's grinning, malevolent, hated face . . .

I have never been quite sure what happened next—not that I have tried very hard to work it out. It has been easier to block out the whole, hideous memory. Whether I would have had the strength to pull Robbie back on the platform I have no idea, but I do know that was my intention as my hand still gripped the coat that stopped the wretch from falling. That is, until I saw the phantasm's insubstantial shape form a hand and place it over mine as I recoiled in terror from George's touch, though I felt nothing, and I fell heavily backwards on to the platform—to find my hand open and empty.

There came a hideous scream as the engine came to rest beside me, leaving in its wake a more ghastly silence by contrast, as if it had rent a hole in the fabric of the night that could never be refilled. Once, I could successfully block it out, but now I wake up hearing it repeated and wipe the sweat from my face, just as I wiped the blood from it when lying on my back, the blurred figure of the constable above me.

'You all right, sir? I saw you tryin' to save 'im, but 'e still managed to throw hisself over. Let me help you up.'

I got to my feet, my eyes drawn to the track below. Robbie's body was upright against the front of the engine, his mangled legs caught beneath the wheels, his contorted face, with terrified, bulging eyes, staring up at me. He was being held there, head at an unnatural angle, by the sturdy canvas strap of the kitbag that had inexplicably caught over one of the buffers, effectively hanging him.

I was shaking so much that I was put into an empty first-class compartment while officials arrived to go through the usual formalities and take my statement, after which Wills brought mugs of tea and sat down for a talk to help me blot out 'that awful sight', he said. He was not to know that it was another awful sight I needed to blot out more, that ghostly hand over mine.

'Feeling better?' He removed his helmet and mopped his brow. 'Won't be long afore a relief engine comes. You've 'ad some shocks today, what wi' finding Tom an' now this. I'm not sure I heard proper what you said to Robbie afore 'e . . . somethin' 'bout killing his brother an' then trying to kill the boy, weren't it? I'm a-wondering how you come by all this information.'

I sat gazing at the white linen on the headrest in front of me, trying to concentrate on something other than the last hour or so and wondering precisely the same thing, harking back to my favourite detective tales and trying to reason out how Sherlock Holmes would have interpreted the facts. When had I first become aware of any danger to Tom? It must have been, as I explained to Wills, when we were outside the inn watching that eerie light, when someone mentioned that Frank had seen Tom kill his father. If he had really done so he would now be terrified, hiding away or scared enough to emulate that son of long ago who might have hanged himself in fear and remorse. Had those few whistled notes I thought I heard been his goodbye? That was when I knew I must find him before it was too late.

'I'd already been worried about Tom, Wills. His work had slackened off and it was obvious he had something on his mind. I should've taken more care to find out exactly what it was—that he was aware of Robbie being the murderer.'

'I felt the same, saw him fretting, but thought reason t'were Robbie a-courtin' Lucy. I really b'lieved George's death to be an accident, an' how could Robbie 'ave killed him since he weren't here? An' why? 'Cept he allus had gamblin' debts an' they might've got out of 'and. Nobody beats the bookies. I had wondered, when George seemed so flush wi' money, whether old Tom had hidden some away an' he'd found it. In which case, Lucy would inherit everything an' Robbie stood to gain the lot. But *how* could he have done it? I thought 'e were in barracks at the time.'

'I imagine he must've done the same as he did today. You see, he showed me a telegram that ordered him back to be discharged—Lucy told me he'd cycled to town this

morning so he could have sent it to himself from there—
you'll be able to verify that—then I drove him to the Halt
and watched him board the five-ten.' I gave a rueful laugh.
'I wondered why he resisted my seeing him off—he probably had no intention of leaving and must've been furious
at my forcing him to go and then have to catch a train back.
He'd have wanted to wait 'til I'd left, go up the deserted
drive after hiding his coat and bags on the way, then on
through the woods to the farm, arriving before dusk all
ready to dispose of Tom. My actions put him right out.'

The constable nodded. 'Having been delayed, he'd be in
some sweat to get back in time for Tom's return after
carrying Methy down, to leave him alongside the lower
hedge with the mystery light on his shell. The tortoise
would want to come straight back home to him—and his
supper, I expect! That boy has a way wi' animals.'

'Yes,' I agreed. 'Anyway, Robbie obviously did get back in
time to find Lucy asleep as he'd planned—I'm sure I saw
him put a drug in her cup of tea before he left.' I told him
about the sugar bowl being swiftly whisked away from me,
taking time for thought as I finished my mug of tea. The
drug probably came from Dr Mac's medicine cabinet, having previously been stolen by Fiona for Robbie to put Lucy
and Tom to sleep during his meetings with her at night. No
wonder Tom had been drowsy and slow in school! 'And if
Tom had come home for tea,' I went on, 'he might have
taken the drug, too, and Robbie would have to start Methy
on his journey himself, as he'd no doubt seen Tom do it.
Either way it makes no difference.'

I returned to Wills' second question. 'I have a theory
about how George died. I imagine Robbie had been unsuccessfully pestering him for money and, becoming desperate,
decided what he would do. So he came down by train that
evening, hiding in the woods and avoiding the paths near
the farm, then waited under the bridge 'til drunken George

was on his way home and appealed to him one last time. It could have been their voices I heard as I crossed over. Rejected once more, he stunned him with a stick or stone and held his face under the water, quickly returning by the way he had come, up the near path, to cross over the stream by the small wooden bridge and back through the woods to the ruins, leaving by the driveway to come out opposite the Halt in time to catch the eleven-ten back. If murder should not be suspected, no questions would be asked about passengers getting on or off at the Halt, would they? Just as no one would have queried it tonight, had it been accepted that Tom had committed suicide because he'd killed his father or, as some would have insisted, that George's ghost had come back and hanged him.' I licked my dry lips.

'That's true—there wouldn't be any point in seeking further evidence.'

I continued on hastily, trying to concentrate on matters of fact, imagining the scene. 'Tom had climbed out of his room that night and saw Robbie when he attacked George. Frank, as the boy told me himself, was coming from the farm fields along the path on the far bank without seeing Robbie, who was returning behind the bushes along the opposite side of the stream, but he did see Tom, who had just crossed over the stepping stones with the intention of helping George. I suppose the boy lifted his head from the water, thought he was already dead—as well he might have been—so dropped it down again. Frank saw him do that and misunderstood.'

Wills took his pipe out of his pocket and put it, cold, into his mouth. 'Ay, seems a very reasonable assumption, but what I'm not wise to is why Tom didn't just tell somebody before going through all that business of providing a "guiding light" to lead us to Robbie?'

'We'll have to ask him, of course, but it could be that at the time he had mixed feelings about it. He had feared and

227

hated George and hoped things would be better with him gone, so in a way he was glad. Later, when Robbie began to show his true nature, beating him and killing the things he loved, in fact, behaving exactly like his brother, he must have felt it wouldn't be long before his mother would suffer in the same way once they were married. It was too late then for him to speak out, especially to his besotted mother, and Frank had begun to spread the story of his guilt, so who would believe he wasn't trying to shift the blame? I think he'd have told me in the beginning, but I was too full of my own troubles to listen to his.'

'Poor little lad. The rest of us should've done more when we saw the spark going out of 'im. Why did Robbie wait so long afore deciding to kill 'im, though?'

'Because he thought nobody knew—that he hadn't been seen. Then his suspicions must have been aroused, maybe in the way Tom looked at him or something said, which triggered a sense that he knew. When he was told about the first eerie light he would've kept watch for a second, saw Tom send Methy off, and suspected he was using the ballad to indicate his uncle's guilt. That's when Robbie decided he could use it to turn the tables and, on the third night, if Tom wasn't already drugged and had come back to wait for the tortoise, hit him on the head with just enough force to knock him out, carried him up to his room and put the rope, tied to the handy branch, around his neck before carefully lifting him out of the window. If he'd dropped him suddenly the branch might have broken and ruined his plan and perhaps smaller branches hindered his fall, luckily tending for him to be strangled rather than break his neck. However it was, Robbie probably guessed that folk would be too scared to investigate the light until it vanished, and Tom must be dead by then.'

'He were right, there. We was all a bit nervous like.'

I went on talking, anxious to think it through to the end.

228

'He'd be in a rush to get away when he heard the sound of our cars starting up, cycling off right away through the woods he knew so well—while we were waiting to take Tom to hospital I thought I saw a light shining deep amongst the trees. I expect he's left the bike in the bushes at the end of the Old Manor's drive, where he collected the things he'd already hidden, ready to pick it up again when he returned for Tom's funeral! I'm sure you'll find it there if you look.'

I heard the puffing of an engine.

'Here's the relief for the coaches,' said the constable. 'We'd better get out afore we gets taken, too. I'd like to thank ye for that plausible explanation, Mr Parr, but one thing more. What gave 'ee the idea that t'were Robbie who'd tried to hang Tom, an' not the lad hisself?'

'That was when I saw Methy come back. Tom would never have left the tortoise to fend for itself, to face an uncertain future with his murderous uncle. He loves the creature, so he'd have made sure it was safe. Yes, I felt I knew the answer when I saw that glimmer from a bicycle in the woods and heard the faint sound of a train. Robbie was the villain in this piece, I was sure, and I pray to the good Lord that Tom will soon be able to tell his own side of it.'

Which he did, I am glad to say, almost word for word.

Day 20

Talking it through with Wills had kept me from dwelling on the horror, but later, as I lay in bed with candles alight against the menacing dark, I could not resist going through the day's events however much I tried. Had I been so conditioned by the 'Ballad of Halsey Manor' as to accept its possibility? Had I really seen a ghostly glow pursuing Robbie? And in that final, awful moment, had George's shade really been beside us? Or had it been an illusion, solely in my mind, of my own making, a subconsciously invented pretext allowing me to circumvent the law that says 'Thou shalt not kill' and thus permitting me to exact retribution? Wills had only seen the beam from the bicycle lamp that Robbie was carrying at the Halt, and neither 'guiding light' nor ghost, but both had been very apparent to me. Again and again I saw that ghastly hand covering mine and recoiled from it.

I was coming to realise the enormity of what I had done—saving Tom was one thing but killing Robbie quite another. I had let him fall, causing his death. It was either murder or manslaughter, but what is the difference? Before completing any action you have the choice of whether to continue or abandon it, unless it is a moment of madness. Was I shifting the blame on to a fancied spectre, the product of a mind temporarily warped by the fervent desire for Robbie's death for humiliating me? My only consolation was in having saved the hangman a job, but what sort of consolation was that? Robbie deserved to have had that final three weeks' wait for the final drop.

As it was, instead of being branded 'killer', I was feted, praised, and treated as a hero, accepting it with a good grace during the daylight hours. But every night the scene was replayed, and I would see that mangled body and hear the hideous scream, as I did long afterwards whenever relaxing a hold on consciousness, making sleep synonymous with dread.

The inquest the following week was straightforward, no awkward questions being asked. Tom's statement had been taken and tallied in essence with the ideas I had outlined to Wills, who revealed that Robbie's motive had certainly been money. The Army was becoming suspicious that he had been developing his own photographs using government equipment, and so he needed to buy himself out before he was charged. Also, he was heavily in debt to the bookies. Wills told me how Lucy said that old Tom left a hoard of gold sovereigns hidden beneath floorboards which George found and refused to share with his brother, giving rise to resentment. Since then, each brother in his turn had been working their way through the money. I truly hoped there was enough left to provide for Lucy and Tom.

My last week in West Halsey was rapidly slipping away before I went to visit Tom, discharged from hospital but kept at home. I thought the farm presented a deserted appearance as I got out of the car, everything shut up and no one coming to greet me. Hesitating, I knocked, thinking there might be no one at home, but after a short interval Lucy opened the door and I could see that the joyful sparkle, kindled by love and Robbie's attention, was gone. She stood before me red-eyed, drab and hunched, regarding me with an unwelcoming stare, the girl in the picture having now apparently vanished for good. Foolishly, I was surprised, sure she would have been thankful for her son's escape from death, but felt only her animosity searing into me. The loss of her lover, however wicked he had proved himself, had been of a greater consequence to her, masking the rest.

'S'pect you're come to see Tom,' she said, in a flat, expressionless voice. 'You'd better come in, then.'

I went through to the kitchen, where Tom was sitting at the table colouring a drawing. He, at least was welcoming but not too much so, keeping a wary eye on his mother. She was drinking tea, but did not offer me a cup.

'How are you, Tom?' I asked. 'I've brought you these.' I handed over a box of sweets and a book on birds of the world.

His eyes lit up. 'I'm all right. Thank you for these, sir—an' thank you for saving me.'

I was taken aback by the sound of his husky, croaking voice, deploring my stupidity as I noticed the purple weal round his throat showing above the open shirt.

Lucy was throwing a shawl around her shoulders. 'I'm off up field for cabbage,' she informed us, 'so you can chat all you want. You'll be gone by the time I gets back, I'm sure,' she ended with a sharp look, thus making certain that I would.

Left alone with Tom I found it hard to know what to say. I wanted very much for him to understand how ashamed I was that I had ever, even for an instant, thought he could have killed George, but the words somehow flew away before I could assemble them. Instead, embarrassed, I looked at his watercolour.

'What are you painting?' I asked, then quickly prevented him from answering as I realised he found talking difficult. 'No need to tell me—I can see what it is although it's not finished. A kestrel, isn't it?'

He nodded, holding up the paper. There was no mistaking his talent. 'I can't remember if I thanked you properly for the model you made me,' I said. 'I'll keep it on my desk at home and think of you whenever I see it, think of you as the kestrel flying free, swinging high up in the air.'

He grinned, his face still thin and pinched from the torment he had endured.

'Now you get well and work hard at school. I'd like to know how you get on. I may be far away, but one day I hope to pick up a newspaper and read that Tom Piper has been awarded a prize for being the best painter—or sculptor or whatever—and I'll show it to all my friends and say, "I'm proud to tell you that I knew this man years ago when he was a boy and modelled this kestrel for me"!'

We both laughed, and I talked a while more until all of a sudden I felt sad and serious. 'Better go now, I'm off home tomorrow. There's one thing more. Do try to make friends with Frank. Will you do that for me?'

He nodded again. 'He came to see me an' said 'e were—was—sorry he'd made a mistake.' The laboured voice was little more than a whisper. 'He's all right.'

'I'm pleased about that.' I prepared to go, finding it difficult to know how to leave while wishing I could protect him from any more of life's ills, so just ruffled the hair on top of his head, as I used to ruffle yours, Paul, and held out my hand. 'God be with you, Tom, and take care of you.' He gave me a firm handshake, and I left.

The next day I took my leave of Miss Millard and the school once again, before saying goodbye to 'Girl in a Yellow Dress'; I was hoping that her beauty could now be displayed more openly. I carried my case down the stairs to where Bessie, dear, warm Bessie, who had staunchly supported and fussed over me during these last, traumatic days, was waiting at the foot.

'What are you going to do about the picture?' I asked.

She shrugged. 'I've no idea yet—nothing at present,

anyways. I don't think Lucy would be thanking me for reminding her of the other love she lost. I don't want to keep it an' Tom should have it sometime. Mebbe later on.'

'I'm sure that's best, Bessie. Well, better be off.'

Her eyes had misted over. 'I hope you'll be happy in your new job—an' with your new young lady. Barbara, isn't it?'

I felt a rush of pleasure at the thought of seeing my girl again, tempered with anxiety that she might reject my attentions if she thought I was a murderer. I never have been able to come to an acceptable conclusion about that, which is probably why I was unable ever to reveal my part in Robbie's death to her.

Bessie was saying, as I climbed into the car, 'I'll send you a Christmas card with all the news. Have a good journey, Mr Parr, an' good luck . . .'

I went on my way, as I had once before, with the firm intention of never returning to resurrect all those painful memories. A new start and a new life was my objective and I found it worked for most of the time. I was too taken up with thoughts of your mother, too busy and shielded by my changed teaching environment for demons to creep out and assail me very often, and then they mostly came at night.

However, they did appear en masse during that Christmas holiday when Bessie kept her promise and sent a card. I clearly remember that it contained the news that she was well, that Dr Mac had sold his practice to a young doctor with a plain wife and taken himself off to Scotland, and that his daughter was said to have married and settled in Italy. I thanked the Lord for that blessing, and hoped she would stay there. Tom was fine but remained one on his own, though occasionally seen with Frank, and she had not yet decided what to do about the picture. Lucy was melancholy and rarely seen, keeping herself to herself. She had hired the man from East Halsey to run the farm while putting some of the land up for sale—everyone in the village was up in arms about that in case houses were built on it. That was about all. I sent one in return but wrote only a few lines, including, 'Best Wishes to Tom.'

Subsequent cards were in a similar vein and, in time, having married and with you on the way, I hardly glanced at them, unwilling to revive emotions. One, I know, impressed itself on my memory, when it mentioned that Frank and Tom had left school with Frank teaming up with an older boy to write jazzy songs, Frank the words and his friend the music. So Frank was still making use of his talent for rhyming, I remember thinking, hoping, together with Bessie, that the two would have some success. Tom was running the farm himself, not that there was much to do now that so much of the land had been sold and 'those horrid little houses' built.

At least Tom was free to wander in his beloved woods and paint. I intended to write and ask him if he had continued with his painting and sculpture, but Hitler's war began, I went into the Army, and different horrors overlay the other nightmares. We moved house several times and subsequent Christmas cards failed to arrive, so it became easier to stifle any recollection of West Halsey—that is, until nearly three weeks ago when I unexpectedly found myself back there again. This brings me to the reason I started writing this . . . what did I call it? . . . confession.

Turning the pages back to where I began on Day 1, I see that I left myself reminiscing in the half-demolished school, shaken out of my customary complacency, and wondering what had become of those long-dormant figures of yester-year who had arisen from out of nowhere, becoming so alive. Where were they now? Then the demolition men had resumed work and I realised that I should begin to make my way to rejoin the coach party, so bade the school a last farewell and started off. When I came to the church I stood looking in vain for the humpback bridge while deciding that the stream must have been diverted into a culvert, then noticed a movement behind the lychgate. On an impulse I followed, hurrying up the path in the overgrown church-yard between unkempt graves with mossy headstones top-pled over, and came up behind a man as he was unlocking the heavy church door.

'Excuse me,' I said. 'Are you the vicar?' You never know, these days, do you, Paul? Once you could tell them at a glance.

He shook his head. 'No, I'm the sexton—for the time being, anyhow. No congregation, you see, so Vicar's gone and the church closed. Had our last service on Easter Day. I'm just going in to check that all's OK. D'you want to take a look around? My name's Braddon, by the way.' He held the door as I went inside.

'Thank you—I'm Edward Parr. I used to worship here many years ago. Would you be kind enough to tell me what's happened to some of the people I knew?'

'I've only been here a few years, but I'll do my best if you name some names.'

I spoke of the Pipers, Bessie, the Acasters, the Carters, and Wills, but none drew any response. 'Silly of me to think you could help,' I said. 'Most of them must be dead by now.'

His face brightened. 'That's given me an idea. Let's look in the Register of Burials—and there's a telephone direc-tory in the vestry, too.'

We went through, and while I searched for familiar names in the directory and found none, he unlocked an old safe containing a few papers and books. 'Silver's been taken away already,' he informed me, opening the register. 'These will follow it next week. You're lucky.'

I began to search from 1929, finding an entry for George Piper but none for Robbie. The pages were well filled to start with but gradually became less so. My eyes, already weak with age, grew tired, and names had begun running into one another when I reached 1946 and espied: 'Piper, Lucy Margaret, Walnut Tree Farm, b'd January 18th, aged 45 yrs.' So Lucy had not left the district and neither had she remarried. Poor, sad Lucy—had she ever known the truth about her Captain? And what had happened to Methy—and Tom? I was determined to contact him somehow.

I ploughed on, finding entries for James and Grace Carter within a week of each other, but no Bessie Marsham. I mentioned this to my companion, who pointed out that Bessie is a diminutive of Elizabeth, so I searched back and found it there under 1955: 'Marsham, Elizabeth May, W. Halsey Nursing Home, b'd September 28th, aged 67 yrs.' Sadly, she was gone, and all I could think of, foolishly, was that I had never asked her how she got home from choir practice where I had left her that awful night.

So, after studying the directory for other names, with no success, I thanked the man for his trouble and, turning to go, saw an unframed painting standing on a shelf in a dark corner, leaning against the wall. I caught my breath. It was, without a doubt, 'Girl in a Yellow Dress', though the colours were dull with dust. My jaw must have dropped open with surprise. How on earth had it ended up here? Who had last possessed it? Lucy? Tom? Or had Bessie kept it?

'Where did this picture come from, Mr Braddon?'

'I'm afraid I've no idea. People donate things that get forgotten—I doubt there's anything recorded. Can't see it having much value.'

'What's going to happen to it now?'

He shrugged. 'It'll be taken away with the rest and probably burned with the odd bits of furniture. Most things here are riddled with woodworm.'

I felt the original excitement rise in me as I lifted it

down, studying it, begrimed and needing expert cleaning. I began to wipe away the dust with my handkerchief, to find, stuck on the back, what seemed to be two undated newspaper cuttings. The older one was torn, yellowed and hard to read, but a photo showed a face I had never wanted to see again. I managed to make out most of the faded print and, in short, it said, '. . . an Englishwoman, Signora Fiona Vent . . . ini . . .' with much of the next part unreadable until, '. . . is on trial accused of spying for Italy during the war. If found guilty, which is probable due to the weight of evidence already proved against her, she will suffer the death penalty . . .'

Feeling no emotion whatsoever, I supposed that to be a fitting end for a witch, and one that would have effectively prevented any further corruption of young or old. Who had stuck it there? I presumed it to have been Bessie who had died in '55—not Tom. He would never have abandoned this picture if he had possessed it.

The second cutting was folded over. As I opened it, I was hoping to read that the Royal Academy had accepted a painting by Thomas Piper, or something similar. Instead, a headline proclaimed, 'SUCCESS FOR SONGWRITERS' over a story of how Frankie and Ray had been put under contract by an American Music Corporation, had said goodbye to England and flown to New York to live and work. That had to be Frank Acaster with his aptitude for rhyming! I felt inordinately pleased that he had found success.

Then, with my time running out, I decided I must make a quick decision, so said to the waiting sexton, 'Would it be in order for me to buy this, d'you think? I remember it well, and actually knew the girl in the picture. The artist died young, soon after he painted it, without having time to make a reputation, so it can have no great monetary value but has a sentimental one for me. I'm prepared to offer the Church a cheque for . . . What shall we say?'

I named a reasonable figure and he looked amazed. 'That's very generous of you—and I'm sure it will be acceptable.'

'The thing is,' I went on. 'I'm only here for the day, so could I take it with me? You can have my address and a proof of identity . . .'

He studied my face for a long moment, coming to the conclusion that I was an honest man and not some crook that had recognised an Old Master, so the deal was agreed. He wrapped it in a discarded curtain, securing it with the strings that had held the top edge in gathers, and I departed, delighted with my prize.

Conscious of having to make haste, I hurried down the path with my unwieldy parcel but found I needed to read-just the strings to make a more comfortable handle for carrying, so, once in the street, I stood it on the pavement resting against the War Memorial. As I was bent down, I saw that in line with my eyes were the names of those Service people lost in the Second World War, added below those of 1914–18.

The first name I read was that of a boy I had taught in my class and my head swam. Why had I not prepared myself for that possibility? I read down the rest of that pitiful list, recognising others from the school. Then I saw: PIPER. T. DFC. RAFVR. FIGHTER COMMAND. 1942. Tears filled my eyes and pain gripped my aching heart . . .

So his wish had been granted—to feel something of how a bird must feel. I knew how he must have gloried in the joy and freedom of flying, but by my cowardly avoidance of the past I had denied us both the chance to discuss it, for him to tell me how he felt about the experience, sharing the moments with me. I desperately wanted to know what had happened during those lost years, if he and Frank had found things in common to enjoy, had joined the RAF together, become pals or indulged in rivalry to the end—

never knowing will now become a great part of my punishment.

Why had I not kept in touch with them and Bessie and all those others I had regarded as my friends? They must have felt they meant nothing to me—which I swear was never true. Had I cut them out of my life and memory simply to forget Fiona, George, Robbie and all the unpleasant things? But it was not that, was it? It was the easiest way for me to deny my fear that 'The Ballad of Halsey Manor' had ever had a basis in fact, or accept that my brain had used it as an excuse for me to yield to an irresistible temptation. Yet, during the long hours of the night, I am still able to see that ghostly hand over mine with George's leering face above it.

Well, Paul, I seem to have come to the end of this narrative. With it, in the secret drawer, you will have found a plasticine model of a kestrel. Take good care of it. As I regard it now, I see my golden boy moulding it, a boy who dearly wanted to know what it would be like to fly and succeeded in his ambition by earning and wearing his own wings. Swing high, on your way to the stars, sweet bird! Per ardua ad astra.

You will also have received 'Girl in a Yellow Dress', which I am sure you will appreciate as much as I have done— especially now you know her history.

My confession ended, I leave you, my dear son, to consider your verdict, guilty or not guilty? Did I kill or not? God will already have made His own judgement.

With deep love and affection for yourself and the family.

I remain, and ever will be, your very loving Father.

Edward Parr

Tuesday, 28 April 1979

P.S. Do you believe in ghosts?